the
**RACHEL
RILEY**
Diaries

THE
LIFE OF
RILEY

JOANNA NADIN

the RACHEL RILEY

Diaries

THE LIFE OF RILEY

OXFORD
UNIVERSITY PRESS

OXFORD
UNIVERSITY PRESS

Great Clarendon Street, Oxford OX2 6DP

Oxford University Press is a department of the University of Oxford.
It furthers the University's objective of excellence in research, scholarship,
and education by publishing worldwide in

Oxford   New York

Auckland   Cape Town   Dar es Salaam   Hong Kong   Karachi
Kuala Lumpur   Madrid   Melbourne   Mexico City   Nairobi
New Delhi   Shanghai   Taipei   Toronto

With offices in

Argentina   Austria   Brazil   Chile   Czech Republic   France   Greece
Guatemala   Hungary   Italy   Japan   Poland   Portugal   Singapore
South Korea   Switzerland   Thailand   Turkey   Ukraine   Vietnam

Oxford is a registered trade mark of Oxford University Press
in the UK and in certain other countries

British Library Cataloguing in Publication Data
Data available

ISBN: 987-0-19-273388-7

1 3 5 7 9 10 8 6 4 2

Printed in Great Britain

Paper used in the production of this book is a natural,
recyclable product made from wood grown in sustainable forests.
The manufacturing process conforms to the environmental
regulations of the country of origin.

For the Duke gang—
Hels, Boo, Frosties, Jude, Julia,
Stu and Sprog

I'm RACHEL RILEY
- welcome to my so-called life.

January

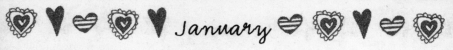

Sunday 1
New Year's Day

Am in agony. And not due to highly anticipated cider and blackcurrant-induced hangover from best friend Scarlet's New Year's Eve party, but to fact that Dad had moved second best friend Sad Ed's ladder and I fell off the drainpipe in my attempt to escape my facially disfigured (i.e. acne-ridden) ex-boyfriend Will, God-bothering cousin Boaz, and uber-chav neighbour Thin Kylie. So, instead of spending the evening looking vintage and dancing to seminal music, had to sit in A & E for three hours with Dad, James, and local madman Barry the Blade, who, it turned out, was fine but had nothing better to do. Then the weary doctor (who looked about sixteen but was in fact twenty-six and a half—James checked) said I had only suffered minor bruising and it was lucky my fall had been broken by the mini-trampoline (disused due to injury risk—how ironic).

So am now on sofa with Baby Jesus (aka my uncle) and the dog watching one of Dad's *Lovejoy* DVDs and sipping Lucozade (me, not Baby Jesus. Or the dog—it is eating leftover green triangle Quality Street instead). Mum has taken James and Boaz to Mole Hall Wildlife Park (total exotic wildlife count now reduced to three otters due to unexplained marmoset death); Grandpa and Treena, parents of Baby Jesus, are at the January sales (i.e. Superdrug); Will never came home from Thin Kylie's;

3

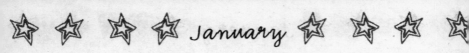

and Dad is fixing the drainpipe under strict orders from Mum who fears that squirrels will get in and devour the electricals.

4 p.m.
Scarlet and Sad Ed have just left. It is all too depressing. I have clearly missed a potentially life-changing experience. Apparently Scarlet's mum, Suzy, drank too much Merlot and did dirty dancing to Christina Aguilera (proto-feminist singer, according to Suzy). My mum would never do that. She only dances to Rod Stewart and it is excruciating to witness. Also, malodorous Year Eleven lesbian Oona Rickets got off with a MAN in the downstairs toilet, then had a panic attack over her sexuality and had to have emergency counselling from Suzy. She has redeclared herself 'bicurious'. What is that meant to mean? It sounds like bivalve. Apparently Scarlet didn't get off with anyone. She is still too traumatized by her illicit liaison with non-goth and possible love of my life Justin Statham. I asked Scarlet if Justin had snogged anyone and she said no he was too busy doing requests on his electric guitar. Sad Ed said why didn't I ask if he had got off with anyone, so I asked him and he said no, so I said point proven.

5 p.m.
Have just got text from Scarlet's brother Jack: Hp u bounce back soon Riley! Ha! X!
Hilarious.

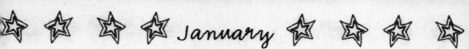

7 p.m.

Will came to say goodbye—his mum Fiona is driving up from Fulham in the morning to collect him. She is too hungover to come today due to the frivolities at the Tory organic beer and Twiglets party in Notting Hill. (Mum says it is more likely down to drugs and weird sex. She thinks all politicians spend their spare time getting drunk and breaking the law, except that ginger Lib Dem, whom she is convinced is going to save Britain from moral turpitude and juvenile delinquency.) Will was with Thin Kylie who had four love-bites (I counted them) on her neck and her hand up Will's shirt. Will did not have love-bites. Not even Thin Kylie would dare go near that amount of sebaceous secretion. I said I was glad that love could conquer their social and mental divide. Thin Kylie said, 'I ain't no mentalist. You're the mental one to chuck him. He's like one of the royals, innit.' Then they went off to do karaoke with Terry and Cherie. It will not last. He is used to caviar while Thin Kylie thinks crisps are a food group.

This is not a good start to the year. I will be fifteen in eight months. I should be at my peak of general brilliantness, not sipping glucose drinks in Mum's terry towelling dressing gown and watching Ian McShane with a mullet with my one-week-old uncle.

New Year Resolutions:

1. Attempt to discontinue friendship with Thin Kylie. We have nothing in common and her Bacardi habit is worsening.

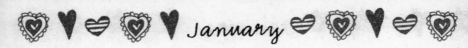

2. Repatriate Suzy's glow-in-the-dark rabbit vibrator asap. James has lent it to Treena to vibrate Jesus to sleep.

3. Concentrate on school—GCSEs now a mere year and a half away and do not want to end up serving doughnuts in Dorrington's like Maria Pearce (aka Pie Shop Pearce) for the rest of my life.

4. Experiment with alcohol or drugs or sex. According to Sad Ed, it is the law to have been sick on Strongbow and have seen several willies (or minkies in his case) by the end of Year Ten. So far have only seen James's (bath-sharing economy drive by Mum), and Grandpa Riley's (horrific bathroom lock failure incident), which do not count, according to Sad Ed.

5. Find THE ONE. Will utterly not snog random Tories with congenital acne but will save myself for long-haired creative type with interest in tragedy and general literariness and with musical potential i.e. Justin. For a minute last year during on-stage *Bugsy Malone* snog thought it might be Jack but he is *a*) Scarlet's brother and *b*) Scarlet's brother.

Monday 2
Bank Holiday

Auntie Joyless is coming from Redruth to collect Boaz at lunchtime. Grandpa and Treena have been sent to DFS for the day with the baby (warm, plenty of seating, crisp

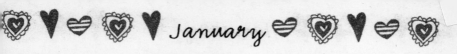
machine). Mum thinks Auntie Joyless may have a nervous breakdown and have to summon emergency Episcopal services if she finds out Grandpa has an illegitimate son called Jesus with someone from Bolton.

4 p.m.
Boaz's return to Cornwall did not go as smoothly as Mum had planned. Dad is driving Auntie Joyless back to Redruth in the Passat now that her new Mini Metro is wedged into Clive and Marjory's Granada saloon in a generally mangled state and Len Viceroy (aka Fat Len) from Viceroy garage can't separate them until next week as he is having surgery on a varicose vein.

Timetable of events:
12.15 p.m.
Auntie Joyless arrives in new Mini Metro, as purchased from Denzel's Crazy Car Warehouse in Camborne, complete with 'I brake for Jesus' sticker on the window and lucky crown of thorns hanging from rear-view mirror.

12.30 p.m.
Boaz apologizes for running away and agrees to attend Reverend Ray's 'Bible Bash' camp for delinquent teenagers in February half-term. James asks if he can attend for research purposes. Request denied by Mum on 'because I say so' grounds.

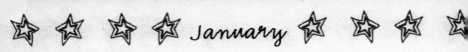

January

1.00 p.m.

Dog eats Delia's vegetarian shepherd's pie (puritanical, but with a Christmas theme, i.e. shepherds) during Auntie Joyless's enforced saying of grace (eyes shut all round).

1.10 p.m.

James and Boaz sent to Mr Patel's to buy emergency lunch.

1.30 p.m.

James and Boaz return with four chicken korma ready meals, a tin of cling peaches and a semi-melted Viennetta (Mr Patel's freezer on blink). Dad says he is secretly glad dog ate vegetarian pie, Delia or no Delia.

1.45 p.m.

Fight breaks out in DFS between Mrs O'Grady and Ying Brewster over last remaining white leatherette corner set. Police and ambulances called and DFS closes until further notice.

2.30 p.m.

Grandpa and Treena arrive on doorstep four hours early. Mum sends James (crucial mistake in retrospect) to hide Baby Jesus in his bedroom.

2.45 p.m.

James appears in dining room and declares an emergency.

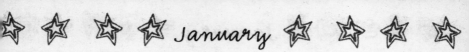

2.50 p.m.

Auntie Joyless says, 'Nothing is beyond the power of our good Lord,' and demands to know nature of said emergency.

2.51 p.m.

James says Baby Jesus has been sick on his Prince William doll, and it is now not singing 'God Save the Queen'.

2.52 p.m.

Auntie Joyless storms upstairs to find 'second coming' lying on *Lord of the Rings* duvet between sick-covered Prince William and giant glow-in-the-dark rabbit vibrator (on).

2.53 p.m.

Auntie Joyless declares the house is inhabited by Satanists and demands Boaz strap himself in the Metro.

2.54 p.m.

Auntie Joyless reverses Metro at full speed into Clive and Marjory's driveway whilst trying to cross herself at same time.

3.30 p.m.

Auntie Joyless and Boaz depart in Passat with Dad and the dog.

3.31 p.m.

Mum demands to know provenance of giant glow-in-the-dark rabbit vibrator. Rachel vows it is more than her life's

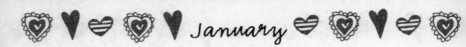
worth to divulge the sex secrets of vague acquaintances. Mum says, 'Was it Suzy?' James says, 'Yes.'

3.45 p.m.
Rabbit vibrator sealed in Jiffy bag with stern letter from Mum requesting that Suzy keep her menacing sex toys to herself.

3.50 p.m.
James and Rachel sent to rooms to reflect on inappropriate use of menacing sex toys in front of evangelistic humourless relations.

Thank God school starts in two days. How am I supposed to be tragic and literary with my ridiculous family? I bet Emily Brontë never had to put up with this sort of hoo-ha.

Update:
3.00 a.m.
Dad and dog arrive back from Cornwall. Dog wakes up entire house in incident involving leftover chicken korma.

Tuesday 3

Mum is in a panic. She says Jeremy Paxman has informed her that there is a plague of sex register pervert teachers in schools. I said I didn't know she had a hotline to Paxo. She said don't try to be funny, it was on the news, and are there

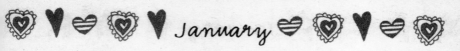
any at John Major High, apart from sex-pest Geography teacher Mr Ingham, who is on permanent sabbatical? Said, 'No.' Did not inform her about Justin's ex-girlfriend Sophie Jacobs's ongoing gropings with student French teacher Mr Vaughan. Or lesbian PE teachers Miss Vicar (stick-thin; no breasts; facial hair) and Miss Beadle (overweight; bulgy eyes like Joey in *Friends* or rabbits with myxomatosis).

Went round Scarlet's to discuss sex pervert crisis. Suzy said it was all blown out of proportion and that most of them were not paedophiles but merely fulfilling the Oedipal desires of sexually charged sixteen year olds. She is thinking of writing to the Prime Minister (Suzy thinks they have some kind of friendship following their brief encounter at the school dinners visit last year, during which she was arrested for possible terrorist activity). I wish my mother were an enlightened sex therapist instead of a former tax clerk with a Cillit Bang obsession.

Also, school starts tomorrow. And, with it, my quest to find THE ONE (as long as THE ONE is not a teacher or other pervert). I predict it will be Justin and we will be snogging by half term.

Wednesday 4
First day of school.

Thin Kylie has already chucked a sickie, due to post traumatic stress disorder (according to poorly spelt note from her mum

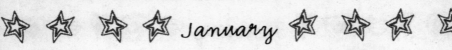
Cherie, given to me to hand in, through a cloud of Marlboro fumes and Impulse). Registration was awash with rumours that she had snogged a royal. (Fat Kylie told trainee Year Eight chavette 'Primark' Donna (little sister of Leanne Jones, free giver of sexual favours), who is easily confused, and who told the entire lower school by first break.) Even Ms Hopwood-White was overexcited. I said that he was not a member of the monarchy, he was an acne-ridden Tory from Fulham. But Fat Kylie said, 'You're just jealous. Because no one's been near your chuff.' Luckily, attention was diverted by news that we are getting a new girl in class tomorrow. And not one of Mrs Duddy's Retards or Criminals this time either. She comes from London and is called Tuesday Weeks and is the product of a totally broken home! According to Mrs Leech, her dad, who is American, ran off with his psychiatrist. Oh my God. She is my ideal me! I bet she sings in a band and spends all weekends getting spotted as a model at the giant Topshop. Or, even better, maybe she is black! Fat Kylie is claiming her for chav corner. She is planning to take her to sightsee the drive-through McDonalds in Harlow so that she doesn't feel homesick. The Kylies are going to be disappointed. Tuesday is bound to be on the Zone diet and will only eat Sushi and raw vegetables. Which could be a problem in Saffron Walden, which is sorely lacking in Japanese cuisine.

1 p.m.
Thin Kylie is back in school, following a miraculous recovery, according to Cherie, or success at procuring morning-after

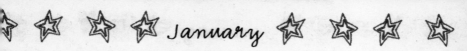

pill from Dr Braithwaite (huge hands; lazy eye; bottle of whisky in desk drawer), according to Thin Kylie. Although Primark Donna told her she should keep the baby as it would be heir to the throne and she could sell her story to *Chat* for £500. Fat Kylie said she would get more from *Pick Me Up*, and she should know, her mum has sold several stories to them, including: 'I married a murderer' (not true) and 'I'm in love with a ghost' (possibly true, although probably under influence of Smirnoff Ice).

Thursday 5

Tuesday is not black. She is a very white EMO, complete with excessive eyeliner and daring attitude. Sad Ed tried to talk to her in French but Ms Hopwood-White caught him and made him conjugate 'manger' on the new electronic whiteboard. Which he got wrong and broke in the process, due to his oversized fingers. So we are back with chalk and felt pens until the new financial year, according to headmaster Mr Wilmott.

At lunch, Tuesday sat at the end of the Alternative Music Club table (i.e. anyone with a guitar or a copy of the *NME*—main members Jack, Justin, and Stan Barret from Year Eight who once saw Paul Weller in John Lewis)—eating peanut butter and jam sandwiches (compulsory American food) with her iPod on. I tried to warn her this was totally against school rules, but I don't think she could hear me. She is clearly uber-cool and wildly dangerous. I absolutely have to

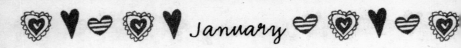

get to know her before the end of the week. Especially if she has access to Justin at lunch.

On the plus side, the Kylies have been unsuccessful in luring Tuesday into their fake-Burberry-clad clutches as well. They are clearly concerned that she may be harder than they are because they locked official school midget Dean 'the dwarf' Denley in a locker in last break just to reinforce their position.

Asked Mum if I could have peanut butter and jam on 'rye' for lunch tomorrow. She said I could jolly well have school dinners or take in a cheese and tomato bap. She is in a mood because it turns out she was wrong about the Lib Dem. According to the six o'clock news, he is a total alcoholic. Granny Clegg rang in triumph—her motto is never trust anyone ginger or with a beard. Plus she voted UKIP.

Friday 6
Epiphany

Ooh. Epiphany would be a good name. Epiphany Riley. I may well ask Mum if I can change my name by deed poll, like Edward Pratt from four doors down, who is now called Edward Edwards.

Tuesday was sent to see Mr Wilmott in registration due to three breaches of school uniform rules (nose piercing, visible Wonderbra, visible thong) and lack of remorse about

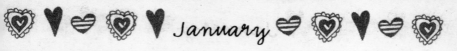

said breaches (she held up three fingers to Ms Hopwood-White and told her to 'read between the lines'. Which is brilliant, even if she did steal it off Jack Black, and Ms Hopwood-White didn't get it.) Scarlet is going to organize an anti-uniform rule rally in sympathy. We are all going to wear visible Wonderbras and pants (even the boys) to school next Monday. She is going to get Jack and Justin to spread the word among Year Eleven. So Justin and I will be reunited in political endeavour, following Jack's (failed) election last year. Hurrah.

4 p.m.

Asked Mum if I could get a Wonderbra (size 32A) in Cambridge tomorrow (Saffron Walden does not stock Wonderbras). Mum said what was wrong with my M&S training bra? I said it was for a political feminist cause and everyone had one, even Marjory next door (I saw it on the washing line once, it must only come out for special occasions). Mum said she didn't care if the Queen had one, I was not going round looking like 'Britney Aguilera' and, besides, she didn't have time to go to Cambridge as she had to regrout the bath. Then James pointed out that the Queen does not need a Wonderbra as she has enormous breasts anyway, so he was sent to his room for thinking about naked royalty.

Will have to find new source for Wonderbra. I do not want to let Tuesday or Justin down. Possible targets are: Oxfam, Treena, and Thin Kylie.

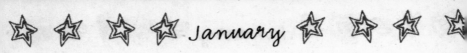

Saturday 7

Offered to take Baby Jesus for a walk into town in his pram, but was overruled by Mum on grounds that one of her Conversational French friends might think I was a 'gymslip mum'. I said that no one knows what a gymslip is, plus I am notoriously sexually inexperienced. But Mum just made her lips go super-thin so I took the dog instead. He is feeling left out now Grandpa is giving all his attention to Jesus. He is still in charge of bottle feeding, nappy changing, and reading all the manuals. Treena is in charge of wardrobe.

No Wonderbras in Oxfam. Mrs Simpson (aka hygienically-compromised lady tramp) must have bought them all. So went to lurk outside Goddard's to watch Justin do something revolting with a bit of a pig. At least that was the plan but the dog very much wanted to be inside and overpowered me, knocking a display of mince all over Justin in his blood frenzy (I blame Mum for banning beef and chicken-based dog food on the grounds that it might contain bird flu or mad cow disease, and the dog is mad enough as it is).

Had to pay for the mince spillage at a cost of £11.97 (most of my Christmas money). Mum is right. The dog is a liability. Justin looked excellent in his butcher's coat, though. Like a blood-spattered Kurt Cobain. I just need to prove that I am his Courtney Love. Without the looks, or clothes, or position as lead singer in a girl band.

Asked Treena if I could borrow a Wonderbra. She said yes, but the proffered item was suspiciously grey and stained and

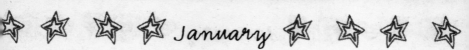

January

should clearly, under no circumstances, be visible to the human eye, rally or no rally. Options now reduced to Thin Kylie.

Sunday 8

Went round to Thin Kylie's (against New Year resolution to distance myself from chav neighbours, but ruled acceptable due to nature of Wonderbra emergency) but she was round Fat Kylie's helping her pierce baby Whitney's ears (again), according to Cherie. Asked Cherie if she or Kylie had a Wonderbra, size 32A. Cherie said don't be daft, her 'la-las' were 34FF (she has had two breast enlargements and is fast-approaching Katie-Price-esque proportions) and Kylie's were all in the wash now that Mark Lambert is back on the scene. (It turns out he did not get some 'gyppo' from the fair pregnant, after all. It was Candy Floss Ken.)

Am going to have to wear visible white cotton M&S bra instead, which is totally non-political and probably within school rules.

Monday 9

8 a.m.
The day of the anti-uniform rally dawns, and with it will dawn my friendship with iPod-wearing, rule-breaking, half-American Tuesday Weeks. And possibly my love affair with

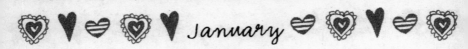

THE ONE i.e. Justin. Am wearing M&S bra and will pull pants into visible range once I am out of Mum's jurisdiction (i.e. within school grounds). It is a shame the pants are white with a cat motif though, and not black, or a thong, like Tuesday's (thongs are on Mum's banned list on grounds of hygiene).

9.30 a.m.
Anti-uniform rally over due to disappointing turnout of masses and general unsluttish nature of underwear. But, luckily, Scarlet and Jack had gone all out in Suzy's Agent Provocateur tasselled and crotchless numbers, so they were sent straight to Mr Wilmott, along with Tuesday, who was inexplicably wearing a sequinned bowler hat. I said what about me, but Ms Hopwood-White said there was nothing wrong with nice cotton underwear, it let everything breathe. This is typical. But Scarlet has promised to befriend Tuesday for both of us during detention, and mention my general tragicness and literary leanings. I told her to remember all the stuff about liking Sylvia Plath, and she said she would try, but she also had to get in some stories about her and Axe, the juggler from Brighton that she snogged at Glastonbury last year, so there might not be time. (School counsellor 'Doddy' Doddington is doing detention today and he lets everyone off after fifteen minutes so he can get home in time for *Deal or No Deal*.)

6 p.m.
Called Scarlet for update on Project Tuesday, but Suzy answered and said she was in her bedroom listening to

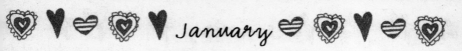

Eighties punk music with a 'fascinating American' and why wasn't I there? And, while I was at it, did I think my mother was orgasmically repressed (following repatriation of glow-in-the-dark rabbit vibrator) and would she benefit from some group therapy? Hung up. This is absolutely typical. Scarlet is obviously going to be eating grits or clam chowder with Tuesday and the rest of her glamorous family within a week, while I am stuck at home eating fishfingers with an eight year old in a mermaid outfit (no idea). Texted Sad Ed but he was busy watching *Star Trek* and told me not to disturb him for at least four hours.

Tuesday 10

Tuesday gets more exciting by the minute. Her mum is a drink-addled former Eighties model called Edie and her dad is now living in Malibu with his BOYFRIEND, which is why Tuesday has moved. Apparently Edie went to school here! So there is hope for us all yet. In twenty years' time, Scarlet and I could be alcoholic former models with gay ex-husbands and tattooed teenage daughters. Brilliant! I asked Scarlet if she had managed to mention my literary leanings and hidden dark side but she said Tuesday kept banging on about some seminal writer called Hunter S. Thompson and she couldn't get a word in.

Am immediately going to read something by Hunter S. Thompson to impress Tuesday. Will go and see hairy school librarian Mr Knox during 'reading time' (aka texting and

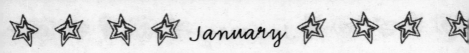

flicking through *Heat* in the lower hall, due to woeful lack of functioning classrooms).

Wednesday 11

Everyone has gone perverts-in-schools mad. Fat Kylie forgot her gym skirt so Miss Vicar made her play hockey in her giant PE knickers. Fat Kylie called her a sex case for wanting to look at her bikini line. So Miss Vicar said she would be amazed if anyone wanted to look at Fat Kylie's bikini line (which is true—it is potentially horrendous, if the rest of her is anything to go by and, anyway, it is school rules). But Fat Kylie is going to report her anyway for 'paedoism'. Scarlet said that wasn't a word. But Fat Kylie threatened to do something painful with her hockey stick so Scarlet shut up.

Tuesday didn't do games. She has a note from her psychiatrist (seriously!) excusing her on the grounds that she is exceptionally sensitive and the competitive nature of school sports might induce instant anorexia. Miss Beadle has asked her for a full medical report by next week proving her condition, otherwise she will be dribbling a hockey ball on the sheep field with the rest of us.

7 p.m.
Amendment to New Year Resolutions:

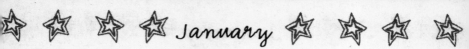

6. Get psychiatrist. Everyone has one these days. They will uncover my deep and troubled life and blame it all on my mother for banning Ribena and *EastEnders*.

Thursday 12

Went to see Mr Knox to get book by Hunter S. Thompson, but he said the only copy of *Fear and Loathing* had been lent out to Sad Ed last year and had had to be scrapped due to an entire mini Mars bar being stuck on page 57. He offered me a *Sweet Valley High* or the new John Grisham instead. I may well write to the Prime Minister to complain. What hope is there for the literary future of the country when school libraries are so poorly stocked?

Also, Mum is learning to drive. Apparently it is one of her New Year resolutions, along with unblocking the downstairs loo and growing her own beetroot. She is going to be taught by Michael Majors (41; highlights; reputation as middle-aged lothario type) in one of his fleet of Ford Fiestas. Dad did not look happy. But he cannot complain as it was his idea on the grounds that he is sick of being the only one having to ferry her 'inbred relatives' up and down the A303. Her first lesson is tomorrow (i.e. Friday the 13th). I said that this did not bode well, date-wise. But James said that statistically there are fewer accidents due to everyone being super-cautious or staying in to watch horror films.

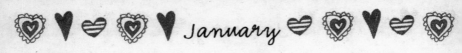

Friday 13

Mum is jubilant. She says Mike (!) says he has never seen anyone stick so rigidly to the ten-to-two position in all his fourteen years as a fully-qualified motoring skills adviser (i.e. driving instructor). Apparently he also heaped praise on her staying at least ten miles under the speed limit and her almost maniacal mirror-signal-manoeuvre checking. Dad said he bet 'Mike' had never got behind the wheel of a man's car in his life (Dad's greatest regret is not becoming a Formula One driver, due to Grandpa Riley's lack of finances and there being no car tracks in North Essex), but Mum said, on the contrary, he once sat in a Subaru Impreza with Jeremy Clarkson at the Birmingham Motor Show. So Dad humphed off to check the oil on the Passat.

Saturday 14

Went into town with James to get Hunter S. Thompson book from WHSmith but Mrs Noakes (no chin; bad perm; calls trousers 'slacks'; habit of ringing parents to inform them you are buying potentially corrupting literature) was on the till so had to dither for an hour in the magazine section until she was on her tea break. Bought *Fear and Loathing in Las Vegas*. James bought a *Lord of the Rings* calendar, discounted due to March being missing.

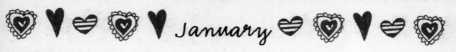

8 p.m.

Am reading *Fear and Loathing*. It is a modern masterpiece and is absolutely full of swearing and sex and drugs I have never heard of. Am going to have to hide it from Mum. It will be banned for sure.

Sunday 15

Went round Scarlet's. Bob answered the door in his underpants and said everyone was in the den, before running back upstairs to shrieks from Suzy and another, unidentified female voice. But when I got to the 'den' (i.e. the sitting room in any normal, British house) Tuesday was sprawled provocatively on a black leather bean-bag and was watching some film with subtitles and ugly people in it with Scarlet, Jack, and Justin. I asked if they were thinking of turning over to E4 but Scarlet said if I wanted to watch children's telly I could go to Sad Ed's and watch *CBeebies*. Tuesday laughed and stretched her scarily long legs out even more so that her toes (purple nail varnish) touched Justin's leg (blue Levi's). He moved it. So point one to me. Ha! Said I had to get back to babysit Baby Jesus. Scarlet said 'Whatever.' Tuesday said, 'Oh, my God, is she a happy clapper?'

9 p.m.

I cannot believe I have been 'whatevered' by Scarlet. What is going on? Also, why does Tuesday not like me? I am

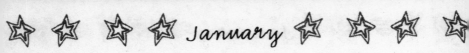

totally literary and would be an excellent listener to all her hilarious stories about getting drunk with many and various rock stars. Texted Sad Ed and he agrees it is an outrage. We are going to boycott all things Tuesday and be a rival camp of tragedy and tortured youth. Then she will absolutely want to know us. It is reverse psychology. James is trying it on the dog. He is encouraging it to eat random objects in the hope it will stick to dog food. Although early signs are not promising—it ate a pot of Vaseline this morning.

Monday 16

Tried to get Scarlet to sit with me at lunch but Tuesday headed her off at chips and beans and they went to sit with Jack and Justin on the Alternative Music Club table, so had to make do with Sad Ed and the Maths Club geeks instead.

Tuesday is still trying to lure Justin into her clutches. I saw her offer him an iPod earphone and an Alphabite. She cannot have him.

Tuesday 17

Oh my God. Justin thinks he has found THE ONE! He told Jack who told Scarlet who told me. Maybe Justin told Jack

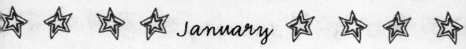

to tell Scarlet to tell me. Because it is me! I am totally his type—I like guitars and wear vintage clothing.

7 p.m.
Or possibly Tuesday. Oh, God, please don't let it be Tuesday.

Wednesday 18

Jesus was up eight times last night. Dad has taken to sleeping with Radio 2 being piped down his headphones. He says he would rather listen to The Corrs all night than Jesus screaming. Mum is not happy as she says she now has to put up with Jesus, tinny headphone guitar, and Dad murmuring 'Andrea' in his sleep. She is going to ring Mr Lemon at the council again to press the urgency of Grandpa and Treena's housing needs.

Tuesday did not do gym again. She had brought Miss Vicar a letter from her psychiatrist (Dr Rubenstein). Miss Vicar said psychiatry was about as real as aromatherapy or ghosts and what was the point of 'finding yourself' if you were so fat by the time you did that you couldn't see your own toes. Then Miss Beadle added that a good dose of netball never did anyone any harm. Tuesday said, 'Whatever,' and went off in the direction of the bike sheds (aka sex corner).

Miss Beadle is wrong anyway. Netball is life-threatening and horrible, especially now that Fat Kylie has been made

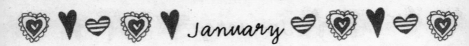
Wing Defence on account of her gargantuan weight advantage.

4 p.m.

Mr Lemon has agreed, under severe pressure from Mum, to move Grandpa and Treena up the housing list (Mum is good at persuasion (i.e. open threats). She should be employed as a CIA interrogator.) Only Mr Whippy (aka Dave Tennick, who sleeps in the ice cream van) and several O'Gradys are above them now. Mr Lemon has estimated their moving date as April next year. Mum has vowed to take her fight to the local paper, the reactionary and ineffective *Walden Chronicle*.

Thursday 19

I fear Mum may have competition in the form of perverts in schools. The front page of today's *Walden Chronicle* (only two weeks behind the *Guardian*) is headlined 'Who's teaching your kids?—How to spot the school sex pest' emblazoned above a picture of a possible sex pest (i.e. moustache and staring eyes).

Friday 20

Mum had another driving lesson after school today, but was thirty-seven minutes late coming home (James timed

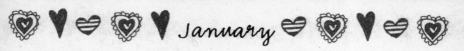

her and told Dad at dinner). Mum said Mike was spot testing her on the Highway Code and they lost track of time (she got an unprecedented 100 per cent), but Dad did not look thrilled at this and has decided he is going to take over and give her some lessons in the Passat instead.

Saturday 21

2 p.m.

Dad is no longer Mum's driving instructor. Mum says she sacked him for excess sucking of air through his teeth every time she tried to change gear. Dad says he sacked her as he needs the car to commute and the transmission will fall out with her hamfisted attempts at reversing around Waitrose car park. Mum said she would be glad to be back in the hands of someone who actually knew what they were talking about (i.e. Mike) and Dad said if that man's hands ever came near her he would personally crash test the Passat against his fleet of Fiestas. Then Mum said violence never solved anything. And James said what about in *Ninja Turtles*, and at that point everyone stormed out. This is worrying. Mum and Dad never argue. Except over things like whether own brand cornflakes taste the same as Kellogg's. Ooh maybe I am going to be the child of a broken home after all. They will battle over who gets custody of me and James

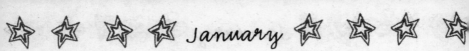
(and the dog) in court. I will definitely live with Dad. He is far more lax when it comes to potential spillages and watching ITV.

8 p.m.
Although Dad can only cook boil-in-the-bag Bird's Eye things and doesn't know where the Hoover is.

9 p.m.
What if neither of them want me? I could end up in care like Tracey Beaker. Which, according to CBBC, is kind of like boarding school for poor children and life is full of midnight feasts and hilarious incidents with vacuum cleaners and you get to call everyone by their first names without having TV banned for a fortnight.

9.30 p.m.
Although Thin Kylie went into care when her mum's breast implant burst and she says she had to live with a 'fat God-botherer' called Merryl who had no telly. Maybe I will concentrate on staying on Mum's and Dad's good sides for the moment so they both want me.

Sunday 22

Made Mum and Dad tea in bed. Mum sat bolt upright and said, 'What have you done? Are you pregnant?' I said I was

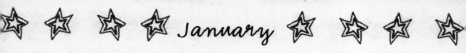

merely fulfilling my duties as a loving daughter and that no, I was not with child. So she said, 'Did you squeeze the teabag properly otherwise it drips on the lino on the way to the bin?' I don't know why I bother. Even making tea is fraught with potential stain-making activity.

Texted Scarlet to see if she wanted to come over but got no reply. She is probably becoming American with Tuesday, i.e. drinking root beer and listening to grunge. Texted Jack but he said SORRY CRUCIAL DRUM JAM, LTRS. Tried Sad Ed but he said he was in a shopping precinct in Ipswich waiting for Aled Jones to cut the ribbon to Discount Deals. So broke resolution and went round to Thin Kylie's but Mark Lambert answered the door in a pair of Get It Here boxer shorts so I left rapidly as I do not want to get anything from Mark Lambert. And James was busy making wholegrain low fat muffins with Mumtaz, so ended up watching *Lovejoy* again. Laughed enthusiastically to show Dad how we share a love of Nineties comedy drama i.e. why he will want to keep me, but Dad just said, 'What is wrong with you, Rachel? Now I will never know whether Tinker's codpiece is genuine.' Which is not true—he has seen this episode at least seventeen times. It is fake.

9 p.m.

Am ploughing on with Hunter S. Thompson. It is excellent. Apparently it is called 'New' Journalism and involves drinking too much and gambling and driving dangerously whilst writing. It is certainly not like anything I have read in

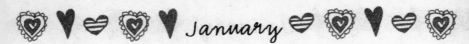

the *Walden Chronicle*. Though the O'Gradys would make excellent subject matter.

Monday 23

Sad Ed has switched to the dark side i.e. the Alternative Music Club lunch table, now officially renamed 'Tuesday's table'. He said Tuesday is a 'breath of fresh air in this God-forsaken backwater' (he is still trying to be poetic in everyday situations) and that he can't understand why I am boycotting her, she is literary and tragic and has nine different pairs of Converse, including limited edition pirate ones. I said there was more to being tragic than having yellow plimsolls and a psychiatrist and he said, 'Well, you hardly qualify to comment.' This is rich coming from someone whose parents have a shrine to Aled Jones in the spare room and still buy his Christmas presents from Toys 'R' Us.

Although he does have a point. Why, oh why, isn't Edie my real mother? Then I would be guaranteed some tragedy.

8 p.m.
Maybe Edie is my mother and Tuesday and I are actually identical twins like in *Parent Trap*, only without looking anything like each other, obviously.

8.30 p.m.
Although I definitely have Granny Clegg's knees. And,

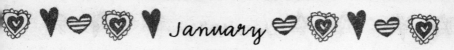

anyway, I don't think uber-cool alcoholic Edie would have slept with my dad. He is called Colin and has been known to wear thermal vests.

Tuesday 24

Sad Ed is on a diet. He opted for Mrs Brain's 'country salad' at lunch today (tinned coleslaw and a pickled onion). He is so transparent. It is all clearly a bid to impress Tuesday. Anyway, it will not last. He only managed two days of the cabbage soup diet in Year Eight before he was back on chocolate digestives.

I am the only one who appears immune to Tuesday's 'charms'. I will remain steadfast on the Maths Club table. Even though I had to sit next to Paul Banner at lunch today and he brings soup in a flask and makes funny noises after each mouthful.

Wednesday 25

Lunch with the maths geeks is not as easy as I thought. They have composed a loud and totally crap rap about logarithms. I had to hide behind my sandwich. Luckily it was a large granary bloomer so I may have got away with it.

But I will not give up in my one-woman anti-Tuesday protest. I will not be moved.

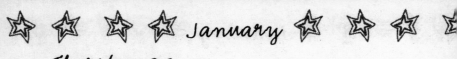

Thursday 26

Have given up lunch protest. Paul Banner asked me if I wanted to go shopping with him on Saturday to look at hard drives. It was all too much. Am now an official Tuesday's table member (had to trip Stan Barret up at the jelly queue in order to secure a seat). Tuesday was telling everyone about the time Pete Doherty gave her a lift on his moped. But unfortunately Ms Hopwood-White heard her and told her she was breaking school rules on incitement to drink, take drugs, or ride motor vehicles underage. So Tuesday called her a 'fugly cow' (this is London speak for not very attractive person) and got sent to Mr Wilmott. She is so rebellious.

Sad Ed has lost a kilo in two days. He says it is down to a rigorous exercise regime and his new salad lunch (cold pasta today—full marks to Mrs Brain for recycling yesterday's 'spaghetti surprise') but it may also be due to the fact that the vending machine has been out of Mars bars since Monday. A petition has been handed in and Mr Wilmott has promised to restock at Mr Patel's if next week's delivery does not include best-selling snack items.

Friday 27
Holocaust Memorial Day

Not celebrated, due to ongoing ban on 'made-up' religious days, following excess requests from Fat Kylie on grounds of

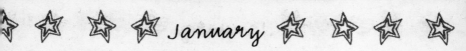
her Catholicism (she asked for days off for Saint Clare—patron saint of television and conjunctivitis; Saint Cornelius—patron saint of earache and cows; and Saint Ambrose—patron saint of schoolchildren and wax-melters. She should have gone for Hilary—patron saint of morons). Mr Wilmott says he is only 'doing' Christmas, Pancake Day, and Easter this year. Tuesday (who is half-Jewish, on her gay dad's side) claims Mr Wilmott is in denial of the holocaust and posted his name on the 'most wanted' section of an anti-fascist website during IT. I suggested she might have been a bit hasty; after all, Mr Wilmott has always been extremely welcoming to Ali Hassan (admittedly C of E but of definite brown hue) but then she accused me of being an anti-semite so I shut up for fear of alienating Scarlet and Sad Ed again, who were all for the fascist outing. I am with the French. Schools should ban all mention of religion, it is a hotbed of potential *faux pas*.

Saturday 28

Have received invite to Thin Kylie's birthday party next Saturday (her birthday is actually on Friday but Cherie says Mr Hosepipe, the fireman strippergram (aka Mark Lambert's dad, Darren) was booked for a ninetieth at the Conservative Club so he could only do Saturday. Am going to have to get her a present now. What do you give the chav who has everything?

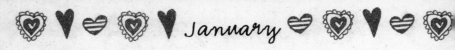

Sunday 29

11 a.m.
The dog has eaten Baby Jesus's talking Tigger. Every time it walks past it boings or says 'Let's bounce faster!' It is getting quite annoying. Even for the dog. It is confused as to where the voice is coming from and is barking at its own stomach. Mum says we will have to wait until it comes out one end or the batteries die. Grandpa said, 'What if the dog dies first?' Mum said, 'God willing,' but Grandpa couldn't hear as the dog did a particularly loud 'boing' at that point.

3 p.m.
James is taking bets on which end the Tigger will appear. I have £1 on mouth.

7 p.m.
I have won £3.20 and a Ninja Turtle figurine (Donatello—who apparently 'does machines'). The dog has sicked up Tigger along with one of Dad's socks that went missing before Christmas. They are both in the wash. Mum said, 'Waste not, want not.'

Monday 30

9.15 a.m.
School has been evacuated due to a terrorist bomb threat! According to Tracey Hughes, whose mum answers the

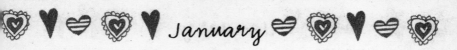

phones at the police station, Mrs Leech, the school secretary (bad hair; too much face powder; biscuit habit) opened a letter addressed to Mr Wilmott claiming there was an explosive device somewhere on C Corridor. She has been taken to hospital for trauma (she was eating a HobNob at the time and breathed an oat in the wrong way). We are huddled on the sheep field until further notice, much to Miss Beadle's annoyance as Fat Kylie's stilettos are sinking into the hockey pitch under her weight.

10 a.m.
The police force (by which I mean two men and an Alsatian) have arrived and are dithering outside. Apparently the bomb disposal unit is on an awayday at Chessington World of Adventure so they have decided to call the fire brigade instead.

10.30 a.m.
Fire brigade arrives. Female teachers (with notable exceptions of PE staff) flock to catch glimpse of Mr Hosepipe (aka Mr Lambert).

11 a.m.
Anglia TV crew arrives and asks for intelligent students to interview on crisis. Mark Lambert is heard telling reporters that it is most likely the 'lezzer PE teachers' or Mrs Cruz the lab assistant, who 'looks a bit terrorist' (she is Spanish).

Rachel Riley (i.e. me) rings the *Walden Chronicle* to warn them of this front-page story on their doorstep but their

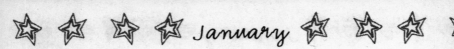

reporting team (i.e. one reporter) is otherwise occupied covering the St Regina's newt pond so Rachel Riley offers to catalogue events for them in new bid to become literary journalist Hunter S. Thompson type.

12 noon
Entire school queues at Mr Patel's Pot Noodle stop, due to Mrs Brain's canteen being cordoned off, bill to be funded by Education Authority. Tuesday takes photo of mass Pot Noodle eating to send to Jamie Oliver.

12.15 p.m.
Mr Whippy parks up at school gates to cash in on crowd's lust for junk food and Fat Kylie's lust for Mr Whippy.

1 p.m.
Miss Beadle organizes mass game of dodgeball in bid to keep warm.

1.15 p.m.
Dodgeball cancelled due to use of Dean 'the dwarf' Denley as ball. Ambulance called.

1.45 p.m.
Firemen locate suspicious device in cupboard of Mrs Duddy's Retards and Criminals room. School declared shut until further notice and everyone sent home (except the Kylies and Mark Lambert who left an hour ago in Mr Whippy's van).

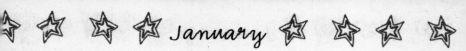

3.15 p.m.
Suspicious device turns out to be Retards and Criminals attempts at Meccano and school declared safe for lessons tomorrow.

4.00 p.m.
Ambulance arrives for Dean Denley.

Tuesday 31

9 a.m.
School open.

10 a.m.
School shut following arrival of letter claiming to have infected school sheep with anthrax and blaming Mr Wilmott for his rabid hatred of Vanessa Feltz and various other celebrity Jewish people.

10.30 a.m.
Police arrive with Mr Mercer the vet.

10.45 a.m.
School sheep declared anthrax-free and school reopened. Mr Wilmott questioned in makeshift interrogation room (i.e. the language lab) under race hate laws.

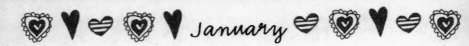

January

11.00 a.m.
Tuesday Weeks called out of double Science (burning peanuts) to explain appearance of Mr Wilmott's name on anti-fascist website.

11.15 a.m.
Mr Wilmott officially declared non-racist by police and reinstated as Head of School.

11.18 a.m.
Tuesday Weeks given a week's detention for abuse of IT facilities (investigation also revealed she had downloaded seventy-nine songs off iTunes using Mr Wilmott's credit card).

11.19 a.m.
Tuesday Weeks tells Mr Wilmott to 'Keep your hair on, Rog.'

11.20 a.m.
Tuesday's detention increased to two weeks. (She will be excluded by mocks if she keeps this up. She is totally out of control.)

11.21 a.m.
How does Tuesday know Mr Wilmott's first name?

I'm RACHEL RILEY
– welcome to my so-called life.

February

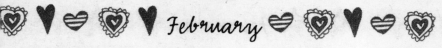

Wednesday 1

9 a.m.
School open.

11 a.m.
School shut again. One of the Criminals and Retards 'accidentally' blocked the lower school toilets with a chicken. Students forced to leave via staff room window due to flow of raw sewage down C Corridor.

3 p.m.
The *Walden Chronicle* has rejected my Hunter S. Thompson-style report on the bomb scare. They claim none of the sentences were in the right order and some of the words weren't in the spellchecker. I said it was called New Journalism and was very popular in London and America and the woman on the phone said Leann Rimes is popular in America but it doesn't make her good. I had no answer to that so I hung up.

My journalistic career will just have to wait until I can find a more forward-thinking publication than the *Walden Chronicle*, which is too focused on sheep sales and whether or not Saffron Walden needs new traffic lights at the notoriously congested Waitrose junction (answer—yes).

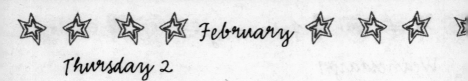

Thursday 2

School definitely open, though smelling slightly of drains. Mark Lambert said it was like being in Africa, but without the 'people with the big stomachs'. Then he saw Sad Ed and was about to say something else but Ms Hopwood-White quickly intervened and sent him to (officially non-racist) Mr Wilmott.

Friday 3

Thin Kylie has got a dog for her birthday. It is called 'Fiddy' (as in Cent) and is a pedigree miniature Pinscher (aka a small but potentially threatening yappy thing). She brought it into class in her fake Moschino bag where it remained undetected until first break when it made a mad dash for Fat Kylie's Peperami Hot and was confiscated by Ms Hopwood-White. Cherie was forced to switch off ITV and come and collect it from the school caretaker Lou, formerly of Criminals and Retards. It is lucky she got there when she did—Lou once ate the school rabbit.

I asked Kylie if I could bring Scarlet, Sad Ed, and Tuesday (so we could mingle ironically with the chavs) to her party but she said there was a strict 'no lezzers or fat poofs' door policy. So now I am going to have to mingle with Fat Kylie and Primark Donna on my own. Which is not really ironic, just sad. Plus I still haven't got her a birthday present.

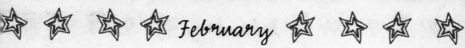

Saturday 4

Am giving Kylie a bottle of Bacardi Breezer and a pirate Vin Diesel DVD. Treena got them both cheap off Ducatti Mick in the White Horse last night. (I admire the way she is refusing to let Baby Jesus prevent her from continuing her social life.) But am now in a dilemma over what to wear. Do I remain true to myself and go vintage, thus risking being compared to Marjory by Cherie again, or do I do chav chic (i.e. mini skirt and bra top) and risk being compared to Cherie by Mum.

6 p.m.
Am going to wear jeans and gold halterneck (formerly Cherie's). I will look like am edgy hipster at a Hoxton art gathering. Will sip 'virgin' cocktails (i.e. non-alcoholic) and do karaoke in ironic manner before retiring early to read more enlightening Hunter S. Thompson.

1 a.m.
Feel sick.

1.15 a.m.
Have done purple sick three times.

1.17 a.m.
Oh, more sick coming.

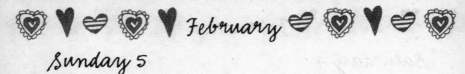
Sunday 5

8 a.m.

Feel awful. Woke up on bathroom floor with purple sick in hair, dog licking sick, and James taking photos of ensemble with his camera. Cannot remember how got here. Am going to bed.

9 a.m.

Can hear Mum cleaning bathroom in fury. Even the spray of Cillit Bang hurts my ears. Will try to eat Shreddies to revive self.

9.15 a.m.

More sick. Some Shreddies actually came back up square. Mum Cillit Banging again. Will go to bed and sleep it all off.

2 p.m.

Oh my God. Have remembered something. Oh God, oh God, oh God. Need to talk to Thin Kylie urgently.

3 p.m.

Oh God, oh God, oh God. Thin Kylie has confirmed the worst. Have snogged an O'Grady. Not Fat Kylie (would have to kill myself) but her brother Kyle, who is only twelve and is already high up in the Criminal and Retard rankings. Cannot possibly go to school. Will have to fake serious illness like meningitis or Lyme disease.

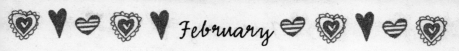
5 p.m.
Have been grounded by Mum for a week (for underage drinking, coming in late, and excess vomit on pedestal mat).

7 p.m.
Oh God. Have had message from Kyle—TXT ME FOTO OF TITS X. Declined.

Monday 6

Mum says James's purple felt tip does not look at all like septicaemia (apparently Grandpa has already tried this to avoid a prostate check) and I am jolly well going to school. Oh God. My reputation as a tragic and literary eccentric lies in ruins. This was not supposed to happen. Was supposed to wait for THE ONE. Justin can never know. It is like Courtney Love snogging someone in bad boyband. Kurt would never have forgiven her.

9 a.m.
As I feared. Kyle was waiting at the school gates. He offered to take me up the bike sheds in first break (not sure if this is a euphemism) but told him I was far too busy what with being in Year Ten and having a boyfriend already. He said, 'You ain't got no boyfriend, I checked and anyway, Fat Kylie is always up the bike sheds.' I said Fat

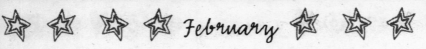

Kylie's sexual preferences were of no concern to me and that I had double French and to please leave me alone. At least Scarlet will sympathize. She actually licked Carex anti-bacterial soap after snogging Justin due to his non-gothness. I, on the other hand, would never wash if I got to snog Justin.

3 p.m.

Overestimated Scarlet's capacity to sympathize. She just said she hoped I had taken precautions as the O'Gradys have been isolated as the source of the infamous Saffron Walden chlamydia scare. I said I had not been near any potential chlamydia-infected areas but she said after six Pernod and Strongbows, I could have given him a blow job and not know about it. (I definitely didn't—I checked with Thin Kylie; besides I don't know how to do it—do you actually blow?)

Tuesday says she doesn't know what all the fuss is about. She once snogged a twenty-five year old after too much Stella (beer not McCartney). Sad Ed seemed distant. I said at least it was one down, one to go on the sex and alcohol experimentation front, but he said binge drinking with a rat boy is hardly Kafkaesque. Jack didn't say anything. He and Justin have a gig next week (Certain Death are supporting Kilgore Trout) so he was probably just nervous about his drum solo. Thank God Justin had a dentist appointment so he is none the wiser. It is the first time I have been grateful to sadistic Mrs Wong.

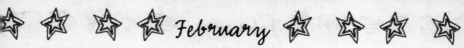

February

Tuesday 7

Kyle is not giving up. In first break he sent Primark Donna to find me (hiding with Scarlet in upper school toilets) to give me a Yu-Gi-Oh pen and a packet of Monster Munch (pickled onion flavour). I told her to take them back—I did not want any tokens of affection from a twelve year old with a criminal record. At lunch he hovered outside the upper school canteen with his Dairylea Dunkables before being removed by Mr Wilmott for breaking the rules that prevent Criminals and Retards eating in public except under strict supervision (following Lou's school rabbit incident).

Am going to claim a food allergy so that I have to spend every break in the sealed language lab with Emily Reeve who lives in fear of being within three metres of a peanut butter sandwich.

Justin still off school with Mrs Wong-inflicted injury.

Wednesday 8

Mum has refused to back my alleged food allergy—despite me relaying the horror of last year's incident with the Snickers bar and Mr Patel's sticky lino. So am at mercy of Kyle and his pre-pubescent longings.

10 a.m.
Kyle has texted me a photo of his bottom. If he thinks it will

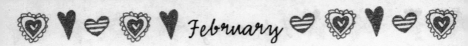

win me over he is sorely mistaken. It is spookily like Fat Kylie's (glimpsed during last year's illicit liaison with Mark Lambert in the Paris Travotel while Thin Kylie was being sick in le bidet).

2 p.m.
Kyle has just sung 'You Raise Me Up' to me outside the mobile science labs. Is there no end to his obsession?

Thursday 9

Apparently there is. It turns out that Primark Donna has fancied him for ages and she will do anything for a packet of NikNaks. I am a stalkee no more.

Justin finally back, though lisping slightly. Mrs Wong gave him six injections and they, and the pain, have only just worn off.

Friday 10

The dog has disappeared. Last confirmed sighting (James) was approximately 5.15 p.m. yesterday when it was chewing the back door. Mum does not seem to be sufficiently distraught. I said he could have been stolen by pet torturers or mangled outside the notoriously dangerous George Street turning. She said at least she will not have to cordon off the Sunday roast again.

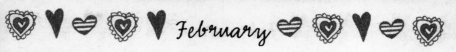
9 p.m.

Fiddy is making a racket over the road. Mum has catalogued it in her anti-social behaviour book. She says at least the dog didn't bark excessively, which is about the only thing she can find in its favour. Grandpa said, 'That dog was a saint, Janet. What did it ever do to you?' She said 'Where shall I start?' So Grandpa went off to search Marjory's herbaceous borders with a pink toy torch.

Saturday 11

9 a.m.

The dog is still missing. Grandpa has called the police. Tracy Hughes's mum answered. She said the only dog in the pound is Fat Kylie's poodle Tupac, who was involved in a fracas at the White Horse last night. She suggested he try Abrakebabra, who are apparently under investigation for suspicious meat provenance, although it is a secret so she will be in trouble yet again.

4 p.m.

The dog has been found! He was not lost or turned into a kebab at all but has been hiding in Thin Kylie's garage in an attempt to be closer to Fiddy. He is in love. James suggested we let them mate, as an experiment (he is hooked on David Attenborough). Cherie looked horrified—she said it would be like 'letting Barry the Blade have a go at Zara Phillips'.

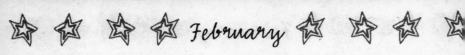

That is a bit harsh. The dog is hairy but he does not live in an Austin Allegro. Plus Fiddy is hardly royalty—she came from the Whiteshot Estate.

7 p.m.
The dog is missing again.

8 p.m.
The dog is back. Terry brought it over. He says Cherie is going to inform the police if we don't keep it locked up. Mum is beside herself with potential anti-social behaviour tit for tat. She says she will turn in the Britchers for having a provocative dog (Fiddy wears a pink jewelled coat).

Sunday 12

11 a.m.
The dog is going bonkers. It is not allowed out of the dining room for fear it will make a dash for the Britchers'. Mum will have to give in soon though. It has already chewed two chair legs.

4 p.m.
The dog is out. Mum could take no more after it started digging up the carpet. Grandpa had to agree to conditions to secure its release though. It has to be kept on a lead at all times and is being booked in for 'the snip'. Grandpa complained

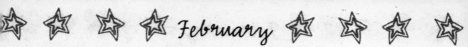

and said no man should be forced to give up their masculinity and what if it went all funny (i.e. gay). But Mum said Dad hadn't shown any signs of losing his masculinity and maybe Grandpa should have given it some thought before foisting his overeager loins on us all (she is annoyed because Jesus woke up seventeen times in the night).

Although Dad does like Jeremy Clarkson a bit obsessively. Maybe this is down to the 'snip' after all.

Monday 13
Half term

It is Valentine's Day tomorrow. Feel sick with anticipation. Potentially I could get a card from Justin. Am still keeping up campaign to prove I am his ONE. And we are definitely getting closer. Last week he actually smiled and said, 'Thankth, Riley,' (Mrs Wong-induced lisp still slightly present) when I told him he was totally better at guitar than Danny Wheatley in Year Thirteen.

Called Scarlet to discuss Justin situation but she was at the vet's with Gordon and Tony who have been fighting again. Jack answered. He asked me if I had sent any cards. I said, 'Of course not; as well you know, Valentine's Day is a made-up non-event perpetuated by evil card manufacturers.' (The Stones are totally anti-Valentine's Day.) Jack said, 'Oh, right,' and hung up. I think he was stunned into silence by my excellent political monologue.

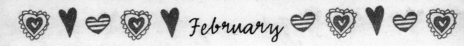
Tuesday 14
Valentine's Day

9 a.m.
No cards. This is typical. Am going to text Scarlet to confirm my support for her ongoing anti-Valentine's Day stance.

10 a.m.
Scarlet has ended her anti-Valentine rally. She got a card from Brighton i.e. from unhygienic tent-dwelling juggler Axe. She is in love again and is trying to persuade Suzy to drive her to his bivouac tomorrow. Jack and Tuesday are going to go with her. I have asked if I can go too. Brighton is the UK centre of teen tragedy and general edginess. According to Julie Burchill there is lesbian snogging and drugs on every street corner.

Wednesday 15

8 a.m.
Suzy has agreed to take us to Brighton. She is totally forward thinking when it comes to teenage sexual urges. (Unlike Mum. Thank God she has not read *Sugar Rush*.)

I wonder what Axe will be like. Scarlet claims he looks like a young Brad Pitt but I suspect he is more like a younger Barry the Blade.

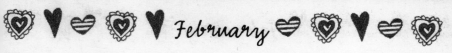

9 p.m.

Not the day of gritty multicultural urbanity I had hoped for. For a start we had to go in the Mini Cooper (Bob has taken the under-seat-heated Volvo to an annual gynaecologists conference—it is entitled 'Light at the end of the tunnel'). Then Sad Ed decided to come (to escape a day of lurking outside Radio 2 studios to get Aled to sign his mum's polo-neck) and insisted on playing a CD of some man called Leonard Cohen, who is as utterly cheerless as Sad Ed. Then Suzy went round the M25 the wrong way (she was trying to talk to Bob about penis dysfunction on her non-hands-free mobile and said it was easier to turn left than right) and we didn't get to Brighton until two o'clock. We then spent four hours looking for Axe's bivouac (there are a surprisingly large number of hairy men living in tents in Brighton) only to find that he had gone to his mum's barn conversion in Malvern for the week. Scarlet sat in silence all the way home. Suzy says it is because she has been betrayed. (He told her he was from an estate in the Midlands. She had pictured a crime-ridden council high-rise in Birmingham.)

Plus Tuesday was being weirdly nice to Sad Ed. She kept giggling mentally at his crap jokes and then she asked him to go to Jack and Justin's gig on Saturday with her. She did not invite me or Scarlet (although we will be there anyway so her snub is pointless). Maybe his diet is paying off after all. Although having spent four hours wedged in his armpit I estimate he still has twelve kilos to go to hit his target. Not aided by the fact that we have eaten seven bags of Doritos,

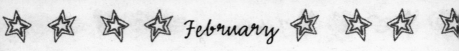
two jumbo bars of Bournville, eight Ginster's Cheese and Onion pasties (not pasties according to Mum and the long-running subject of her 'real pasty' campaign) and a three pack of Jaffa cakes (also the subject of one of Mum's 'misnamed food' campaigns—apparently it is down to whether they get soggy or dry if left out). All purchased from the Mecca that is the Junction 8 services. As opposed to eating fish and chips on Brighton beach with gay people, which is what we should have been doing. It is all utterly depressing.

When we got back to Saffron Walden, Tuesday refused to let Suzy drop her off at home. She made her drop her outside Mr Patel's claiming she needed to buy a Turkish Delight before her blood sugar levels dipped too low and she got violent. This is a lie as she ate most of the Jaffa cakes. It is because she doesn't want us to see where she lives. It is totally like that bit in *Pretty in Pink* when Andie won't let Blane know where she lives because he is a rich prep boy and she is a poor but beautiful eccentric from the wrong side of town (although she does own a car, which goes to show that being poor in America is actually better than being me in Essex). It is so unfair. She is probably living knee-deep in rats and gin bottles in elegant squalor, while I am living in citrus fresh Summerdale Road.

Thursday 16

Scarlet and I are both in utter shock. It turns out that her Valentine card was not from Axe at all. It was from Justin.

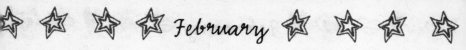
Justin was at his Aunt Renee's bungalow in Hove for the weekend and posted it from there. According to Jack, Aunt Renee lives with a woman called Leslie. She is a stand-up comic and has a shaven head. Even Justin has interesting and Julie Burchillesque relatives. I want him even more now. Why, oh why, does he like Scarlet and not me? Actually I know why. It is because she has permissive parents and knows the exact location of the G spot. He is wasting his time though. She has taken a vow never to snog anyone who has highlights again.

Friday 17

Took Treena's copy of *Heat* round to Scarlet's to comfort her out of post-Axe trauma (it has pictures of Marilyn Manson without make-up) to find her and Suzy eating authentic peasant lunch of Waitrose olives and hummus and debating whether kissing should be banned in school plays on hygiene grounds (did not pass on Mum's opinion on this as she is renowned for wanting to ban most things on hygiene grounds). Suzy said Bob had once fondled her breasts during a production of *Joseph and his Technicolour Dreamcoat* when they were at school. So Bob said that was nothing to do with the plot that was because the lights went out. But then Jack said, 'It's not like it means anything anyway. It's just tongues. No one really enjoys it.' At which point I choked on an olive stone and had

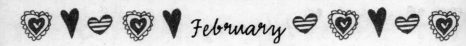

to go and cough it up in the loo. Why did he say that? Maybe he is trying to hide his true feelings. After all, our *Bugsy Malone* clinch was fairly heated. Oh God, maybe he fancies me. Maybe he is THE ONE and I have been mistaken all along!

7 p.m.

Or what if he is telling the truth and he didn't enjoy it? He is an excellent actor after all—as testified to by *Walden Chronicle* drama critic (and editor) Deirdre Roberts. That is it. Of course he doesn't fancy me. I am practically a medical midget and my hair is mental. Plus I have hopelessly untragic relatives and a dog who eats furniture. Am going to give up on men. So far my record is: Brian Drain on a Year Seven trip to Peterborough Roller Rink (I was momentarily distracted by Thin Kylie trying to beat up the bus driver); acne-ridden fascist Will; Kyle O'Grady under severe influence of purple alcohol; and Jack, who was only doing it in the name of art. I will be like Kirsten Dunst in that weird film and die a virgin and everyone will say what a waste of beauty and literary genius it all is.

Saturday 18

11 a.m.

It is Jack and Justin's gig at the Air Training Corps hut tonight (youth group for the criminally weapons-obsessed).

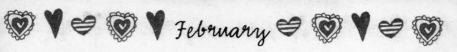

Scarlet and I are going to show our support for him.
And obviously monitor Tuesday and Sad Ed. We have
vowed not to snog anyone (not hard in my case—I am
unlovable). We are going to concentrate on being brilliant
literary types and writing genius first novels before we
leave school.

11 p.m.
Oh my God. Sad Ed snogged Tuesday. Or rather, she snogged
him—he seemed to be in shock and stood there with a
Coke in one hand and a Milky Way bar in the other while
she mauled him with her purple fingernails during Certain
Death's ironic cover version of 'Ugly' by the Sugababes.
No one has ever snogged Sad Ed before. Unless you count
his cousin Julia, which we have agreed we don't. Maybe
Sad Ed is actually the sort of person everyone in London
goes for. Which would mean I have been living practically
next door to Saffron Walden's answer to Johnny Depp for
years.

Plus Scarlet snogged head goth Trevor Pledger (he has
black hair and a pet rat, so he passes all her strict criteria).
So now I am alone in my adolescent torture.

Although Sad Ed and Tuesday will never get together. It
will definitely be a one-night stand. I will go round there
tomorrow and we will laugh about it and watch a *Buffy*
DVD and everything will be normal again with Ed being
fat and hopeless and me being tragic but potentially more
likely to snog someone.

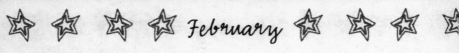
Sunday 19

It is not a one-night stand. She is coming round to his after lunch to snog again and watch French films. I said didn't she mind about his upper arm issues and the fact that his mum is obsessed with a Welsh Evangelist and he said, according to Tuesday, he is a tortured soul trapped in a suburban nightmare, and inside him a drug-addled East London rock star is straining to get out, which is totally Tim Burton, and anyway Aled Jones is Methodist.

Monday 20

Back to school.

Sad Ed and Tuesday were all over each other in first break. Well, she was all over him. He is as unenergetic in his snogging as he is in PE. She let him share her iPod headphones so they could listen to New Wave French Electropop together. But Ms Hopwood-White saw them and confiscated it. Sad Ed is clearly blinded by lust because he actually told Ms Hopwood-White to 'chill'. He got sent to Mr Wilmott immediately and has detention after school with scarily strict Head of English Mrs Butfield (aka Buttface). He says it is worth it as he acted in the name of love. Although it means he will miss *Neighbours* so I bet he doesn't try it again.

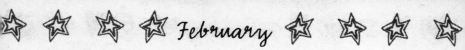

Tuesday 21

The dog has had the snip. Mum dropped it off at Mr Mercer's before school. It was all excited until it saw Rosemary, the severe veterinary assistant. I think she brought back bad memories of when it got a torch wedged in its windpipe.

When it got home it lay whimpering with its head on Grandpa's lap. Grandpa tried to console it with a packet of chocolate digestives but it was sick all over Grandpa's trousers half an hour later so Grandpa's theory that the dog would suffer an immediate personality change has proved unfounded.

Wednesday 22

Tuesday says Sad Ed is a repressed love-god. She has given Scarlet and me detailed descriptions of their sexual activity (no genitals yet but she did let him stroke the waistband of her ironic Calvin Klein boxer shorts). She has compared him to a young Bob Geldof. She is mistaken. He looks more like a young Chris Moyles. I asked her if she loved him. She said she is just using him sexually.

All evidence points to Sad Ed actually being my ideal man, i.e. THE ONE. How can this be? Although I suppose he does look quite good in his Morrisey T-shirt.

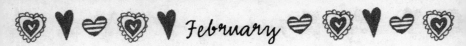

Ugh. Have just done involuntary shudder at thought of thinking about Sad Ed that way. No he cannot be THE ONE. He is like Buttons in the pantomime and Justin is Prince Charming.

Thursday 23

Mum had another driving lesson today. She says, according to Mike, she could benefit from extra tuition on her clutch technique. Dad is refusing to discuss it. He is convinced Mike is going to seduce her with his rugged good looks and three-point-turn ability and that she will fling herself across the Fiesta at him in abandonment. I said this was unlikely as Mum has more self-control than the Puritans, plus the seatbelt arrangement wouldn't allow it, but Dad is still unconvinced. He says he has seen that look in men before. I said in who and he gave Grandpa a withering look.

Friday 24

Have decided to start my genius first novel tomorrow. Will purchase leather-bound notebook and supply of pens from WHSmith plus candles for added inspiration and general atmosphere of torture.

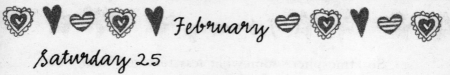

2 p.m.

Have bought pens (ten blue Bics—£1.99) and notebook (Slightly uninspirational (and prohibited) cover with whimsical kitten as it was on discount and WHSmith doesn't stock leather due to lack of demand. I said surely the McGann or Marlon off *Emmerdale* (Saffron Walden's entire celebrity population) must ask for them to pen their diaries and other actorly things, but Mrs Noakes said the last time Marlon came in he bought a copy of *Woman's Own* and a NOW CD.) Have also lit several candles and drawn curtains. Am going to write about a homeless teenage prostitute in King's Cross (notorious inner-London drug den) who is also a hidden literary marvel and goes on to be the darling of the London arts world before dying tragically of syphilis on the eve of publication of her memoirs.

2.15 p.m.

Have opened curtains slightly. Cannot see pages of whimsical notebook in gloom. How on earth did Jane Austen cope?

3 p.m.

Progress not brilliant due to arrival of Mum to investigate smell of wax. She has ordered me to put out candles due to potential fire hazard of M&S curtains and duvet

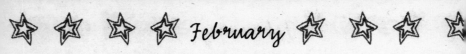

set. So atmosphere somewhat less tortured than I had hoped.

4 p.m.
Will just have some biscuits. According to James the brain needs a teaspoon of sugar an hour to function. (He regularly just eats a teaspoon of demerara to ensure he is in tip-top condition brain-wise. Mum has not seen this or she would ban it for sure.)

5 p.m.
Ooh. *X Factor* is on. All writers need a break from deep and meaningful thoughts and reality TV is ideal. Will write after I find out who gets to the sing-off.

8 p.m.
Will just watch *Casualty*. It will be useful for medical information.

10 p.m.
Too tired to write. Will start in morning.

Sunday 26

9 a.m.
Am in utterly literary mood. Have eaten brain-stimulating toast and marmalade and drunk obligatory cup of coffee

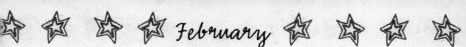

(Nescafé decaffeinated). Think I will focus on descriptions of urban degradation and squalor.

10 a.m.
Have realized know nothing about King's Cross. Will change location to Cambridge railway station instead. I have been there several times and the toilets are vile so it is fairly gritty.

11 a.m.
Also know nothing about drugs. Maybe will give her Benson and Hedges habit instead.

12 noon
Think have writer's block.

1 p.m.
Will just eat lunch.

2 p.m.
And maybe watch *Maisy* DVD with Baby Jesus.

3 p.m.
Will definitely go back to novel once have found out where Maisy is taking her train today.

4 p.m.
Got text from Scarlet demanding my presence to discuss Trevor Pledger situation. (He has failed to demand sex. Not

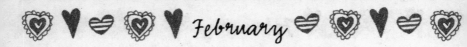

that Scarlet wants to do it with him. She just wants to show how feminist and forthright she is in respecting her minky etc.) Will write when I get back. True poets always work at night anyway. It is a well known fact.

10 p.m.
Very tired due to endless discussion of whether Trevor Pledger is actually gay. Conclusion—not, but with possible religious issues. (Scarlet found a WWJD bracelet in the pocket of his vegetarian leather goth coat. Apparently it stands for What Would Jesus Do? She is going to confront him next week.)

Will lie on bed thinking literary thoughts. And will close eyes to block out uninspiring view of *Mr Men* height chart (still three cms off the top).

Monday 27

7 a.m.
Oh God. Fell asleep. Woke up with dog retching in ear. It had eaten a candle and the wax was sticking to its tongue. Will have to do novel after school.

5.35 p.m.
After *Neighbours*

6 p.m.
And tea

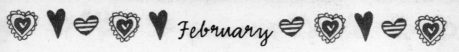

February

8 p.m.

Oops. Forgot have French homework. Have to write 200 words on one of our parents in French. Am doing Mum as have no idea what Dad does. Will use excellent internet translator tool discovered by James. Novel will have to wait. I am not worried. I do not leave school for at least two and a half years (A levels being compulsory in this house) so have plenty of time to reveal precocious talents.

Tuesday 28
Shrove Tuesday

Dad's birthday. Luckily Mum had got him a present from all of us (a day with Saffron Walden golf professional (and closet homosexual) Russell Rayner) because I had totally forgotten what with all the novel writing. BUT more importantly Dad got himself a present—it is Sky TV! We have joined the modern age. Mum did not look happy. Satellite is on her banned list due to excess sports and porn. She is making Dad set parental guidance controls to block E4 (to prevent Grandpa and Treena watching back to back *Hollyoaks*), BBC3 (to prevent me watching tortured teenage drama involving drugs and lesbians) and Bid-Up (to prevent James buying cooking equipment and gold-plate jewellery). We are allowed to watch the other channels when we get home from school.

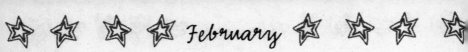
8 p.m.

Sky TV is not all it is cracked up to be. With our limited subscription package and parental controls, the choice was: news, *Lovejoy*, or a programme about monkeys. We watched *Lovejoy*. Dad is beside himself with the prospect of Ian McShane on every night. I do not know why. He has most episodes on DVD anyway. Luckily the dog made up for lack of entertainment by eating twelve pancakes and an entire Jif Lemon.

I'm RACHEL RILEY
— welcome to my so-called life.

March

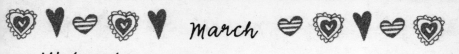

Wednesday 1

St David's Day/Ash Wednesday

Got French homework back. An E-. Am not using internet translator tool again. It translated 'obsessed with Cillit Bang' as 'obsessed with silly sex'. And it spelt stain remover wrong.

Thursday 2

Sad Ed came round after school. I asked him if Tuesday is THE ONE. He said one what. He does not read *Cosmopolitan*. I said, 'You know, like Cathy and Heathcliff, or Bridget and Mark Darcy. Or Richard and Judy.' He said that Tuesday did not believe in Mr Right. She says it is all about Mr Right Now. Clearly Tuesday does read *Cosmopolitan*. Then he asked if I knew who my ONE was. I said I thought there had been two potentially but one thinks Scarlet is the ONE and the other one has made it clear he definitely does not want to be the ONE. Sad Ed said my ONE is probably right under my nose I just don't know it yet. Maybe he is right. Maybe it is someone I sit next to at school. Oh God. I sit next to Mark Lambert in Citizenship. It cannot be him.

Friday 3

And have been moved next to Fat Kylie in Maths. There is no way she is my ONE. I am definitely not a lesbian.

Saturday 4

Trevor is not a closet God-botherer. Scarlet confronted him with the WWJD thing last night but it turns out the J stands for Jez, who is some goth singer who once sacrificed a chicken on stage. And then he stuck his hand up her bra so she got to shout at him for taking advantage and is now over the moon. Asked her if she wanted to come over tonight to lounge around wearing black and generally agree about how crap Saturday nights in Saffron Walden are, but she is going to Trevor's so she can spurn his sexual advances some more. Texted Sad Ed but he was waiting for Tuesday to come over so he could do the opposite. He still hasn't been to her house though. What is she trying to hide? If I had an ex-drunk mother I would be getting everyone over to watch her struggle with the cooking sherry.

Sunday 5

This is why I need to find the ONE. Because otherwise my weekends will be spent watching wrinkly celebrities

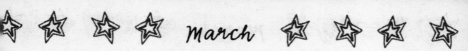

talking about God and going for family walks around garden centres. Because all my so-called friends are too busy snogging.

Monday 6

Ms Hopwood-White reminded us it is work experience week next week. We are supposed to have arranged to go into a local business to see what the real world is like. Except I totally forgot about it. Scarlet is going to sit in on her mum's sex counselling sessions. Sad Ed and Tuesday are both going to work in Roadshow Records. They are beside themselves as they get to choose what music they want all day (i.e. foreign and depressing). Ms Hopwood-White asked what I was going to do. I said some last minute details still had to be finalized. Did not tell her all the first minute ones were sketchy as well.

Tuesday 7

Have had stroke of genius. Will offer literary skills to *Walden Chronicle* and revive prematurely abandoned journalistic career.

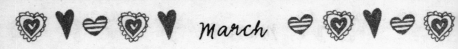

Wednesday 8

Have secured work experience on condition that I use real words and do not try to 'sex up' any stories. I start Monday morning. I cannot wait. This is how Julie Burchill began her star-spangled career. Admittedly it was on the *NME* and she lived in gritty London not Saffron Walden but this is a definite step in the right direction none the less.

Thursday 9

Today is the second anniversary of the death of Fat Kylie's dad Les. He choked to death on a Findus Crispy Pancake (chicken and sweetcorn variety). The O'Gradys are all off school to mark the occasion. They are probably weeping at his oversized grave. It is utterly tragic.

Friday 10

Fat Kylie has detention for a week. It turns out the O'Gradys did not spend yesterday weeping at Les's headstone but went to TK Maxx in Harlow instead. Kylie made the fatal mistake of bringing her haul of discount chavwear to school. She told Ms Hopwood-White it is what her dad would have wanted. Which is probably true.

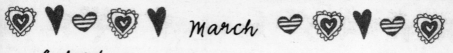

Saturday 11

Yet another Saturday night with no friends. Scarlet is round at Trevor's trying to buy bats off the internet and Sad Ed and Tuesday are experimenting sexually and watching films with subtitles. Not even Mum and Dad want to stay in with me. They are going for casserole at Clive and Marjory's. And Treena is going down the White Horse. So will end up watching censored Sky with Baby Jesus, James, and Grandpa.

11 p.m.
I wrote too soon! James had, by a process of elimination, deduced Mum's Sky pin number and removed all parental controls (it is '0915'—the use-by date on her women's vitamins). Grandpa made a half-hearted attempt to stop him but then he remembered that *LA Rocks* was on so he just said James had to reprogramme the set-top box afterwards.

Sunday 12

Dad is thinking of sending the Sky back as it is now refusing to let him watch *Pie in the Sky*. Mum said it is showing good sense.

4 p.m.
Sad Ed has just been over for emergency counselling. He and Tuesday are having sexual problems i.e. she wants to

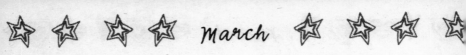

do 'It' but he is not so sure because of *a*) upper arm fat, *b*) penis size, and *c*) fears of statutory rape charges being brought by litigious gay American father and ending up on front of *Walden Chronicle*. I said I was not the right person to speak to but he said he can't talk to his mum because she refuses to even say the word penis (or vagina—she still calls them weewees and front bottoms) and Scarlet is too intimidating with her encyclopaedic knowledge of all things penis-related. So I told him *a*) he should keep a long-sleeve top on and claim he has that disease whereby extremities get cold and go numb (Grandpa Clegg gets it), *b*) gross, and *c*) his mum is more likely to file charges against Tuesday. Then, for some reason, I got all funny about the thought of him and Tuesday doing 'It', and remembered that *Clueless* thing he kept spouting at me last year and said, 'It's like Alicia Silverstone says—to thine own self be true.' But he just said, 'That was Polonius, you moron. God, you are so unliterary,' and went off to do 'It'.

9 p.m.

Sad Ed has not done 'It'. He says he had a panic attack and visions of his mother looming above him shrieking, 'If Aled can wait, so can you!' Plus he says he didn't feel very aroused due to appearance of his dad to offer them Jammie Dodgers. He is going to stick to foreplay until he is at least sixteen (i.e. in seven months). Plus he says he hasn't even worked out how to undo her bra strap so it would be like trying to sit Maths AS without doing Key Stage 2.

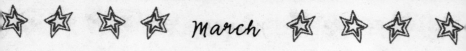

Am relieved. Not that I want Sad Ed for myself. That is too weird. Ooh, got that shudder thing again. But he is too good for her. Anyway, Sad Ed says if he is Tuesday's Mr Right Now she will wait for him. Did not mention the using him sexually thing.

Work experience week starts tomorrow. Hurrah. Have converted my genius first novel whimsical kitten notebook into my new journalistic career notebook. When I am famous and interviewing world leaders on *Breakfast News* I can sell it on eBay for thousands of pounds. I cannot wait to get started. I am going to focus on investigative journalism (i.e. uncovering fraud and crime at the heart of Saffron Walden high society (i.e. the golf club)).

Monday 13

Not the glittering start to my career that I had imagined. I had to sit with the receptionist, Mrs Connolly, who answers the phones (i.e. reads *Woman's Realm* all day). Deirdre, the editor, said it would give me an overview of the bustle of a hectic newsroom. There were three phone calls. One from a kitchen company offering to install shaker-style units and a microwave, one from Deirdre's husband asking her if she had seen his nine-iron and one from Mum to check if I had my lunch money. Anyone with an urgent news story would have a job getting through anyway, as Mrs Connolly spent most of the day on the phone to her sister who apparently

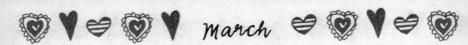

has problems 'down there'. On the plus side, they are going to let me open the post tomorrow.

8 p.m.
Spoke to Scarlet who has been listening to sexual revelations with Suzy all day. Apparently Ying Brewster has got inverted nipples.

Tuesday 14

Nine letters: one bill, one invite to the Young Farmers Annual Barn Dance (i.e. a load of straw-chewing inbreds in checked shirts listening to Shania Twain), and seven letters to the 'Why, Oh Why' letters page (there is a lot of moaning to be done in Saffron Walden). For example:

Why, oh why has the library filed Thaxted-raised science fiction writer Diana Wynne Jones under J for Jones. I spent literally ten minutes floundering in the Ws before realizing their mistake.

And:

Why, oh why is Saffron Walden in Essex? We would benefit enormously tourist-wise if we could move it five miles over the border into Cambridgeshire, which enjoys a better class of visitor all round.

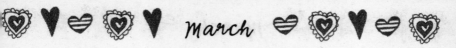

Mum had sent two of them, complaining about: *a*) Waitrose moving the yoghurts without prior warning; and *b*) graffiti on the Bernard Evans Youth Centre (not so much the graffiti per se as the fact that it is grammatically incorrect, i.e. 'Leanne Jones have huge tits').

I put them in the bin. I do not want anyone thinking I am doing her any nepotistic favours.

Asked Deirdre if I could do anything resembling actual reporting tomorrow. She said I could do the office cake run to Dorrington's and stock the photocopier. This is so unfair. I bet no one makes John Pilger go and buy Viennese fingers off Pie Shop Pearce. Am going to take a stand and demand to put my excellent journalism skills to better use.

8 p.m.
Scarlet has been banned from sitting in on Suzy's counselling. It is because she broke the official sex counselling secrets act with the inverted nipples thing. She is going to watch Bob the abortionist at work from tomorrow instead. She says it will be less distressing anyway.

Wednesday 15

10 a.m.
My stand has paid off (or possibly fact that got five doughnuts and a jam slice free from Dorrington's due to presence of Thin and Fat Kylies on pie shop work experience). Deirdre

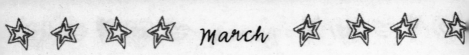

March

has agreed to let me go out this afternoon with ace reporter (i.e. only reporter) Glen Davies. We are going to cover the ongoing affordable housing crisis (Suzy is for it, rest of Saffron Walden is against it), including an interview with Hugo Thorndyke, evil MP for Saffron Walden and environs, at his Tudor manor in Seward's End! It will be totally Jeremy Paxman with me and Glen asking awkward questions and Hugo looking shifty in his lap of luxury.

5 p.m.

Our in-depth interview turned out to be tea and macaroons (home-made by red-faced Mrs Thorndyke) and Glen saying, 'Anything for the record, Hugo?' and then Hugo just banging on about militant Labourites into a dictaphone. I tried to ask a question about needy refugee families but my mouth was sticky with macaroon and I just ended up coughing macaroon dust onto the Axminster. I am very disappointed at the *Walden Chronicle*'s interview technique. I hope the *Guardian* does not operate on this basis.

8 p.m.

Sad Ed called. He and Tuesday have been sacked from Roadshow Records for refusing to let Cherie buy a Daniel O'Donnell CD on grounds of taste. Sad Ed says he is glad. Tuesday was showing an unhealthy interest in Dave, the part-time sales assistant and one time pop star (he played third synthesizer on an Erasure single once). Ed is considering amending his no-sex rule in a bid to keep Tuesday. I told

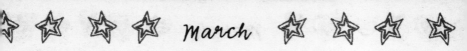

him to be strong and fight for his dignity. But he said there was nothing dignified about being ditched for a middle-aged Saturday boy with a mullet.

Thursday 16
Publication day.

The *Walden Chronicle* front page is headlined 'Not in My Back Yard' and has a picture of a beaming Hugo Thorndyke with Mrs Thorndyke hovering in the background with her macaroon plate. It is all about how enormous blocks of affordable flats will block out views of the church, cause mass riots, and send crime in sleepy Saffron Walden soaring. It has a quote from Hugo saying, 'It's not that I don't want these people to have homes, I'm just saying there is an alternative to blots on our landscape, and it's called Haverhill.' Haverhill is not an alternative to anything. Except possibly Loughton.

Mum asked why neither of her 'Why Oh Why' letters made the paper. I said there were a lot of tough hard-nosed news decisions to be taken. So she said why is there a letter from Emily Reeve's mum demanding that Nestlé develop a non-sticky fruit Polo (a sweet that has never made it into our house as they are not real Polos because all Polos should, by law, be mint flavoured). I said it is because Mrs Reeve knows Mrs Connolly's sister with the downstairs problems. Mum is outraged. She is going to complain about

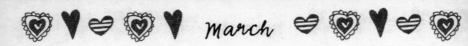

the complaints page to higher beings (i.e. Deirdre's boss, East Anglian media tycoon Jethro Pledger, owner of the *Stowmarket Reporter*, the *Ipswich News* and *Fens Fortnightly*). She will get nowhere. He is married to Mrs Connolly's sister with the downstairs problems.

Friday 17
St Patrick's Day

Went to *Walden Chronicle* for final day of somewhat disappointing journalistic work experience but office was shut. Saw Glen outside the Co-Op and asked him if there had been a bomb scare or other breaking all-hands-on-deck type story but he said they have a 'casual' Friday rule i.e. no one shows up at all due to general lack of news and Deirdre having a three-hour drive to her holiday home in Cromer. I said what if terrorists took over the town hall and he said chance would be a fine thing. So came home and watched *This Morning* with Grandpa, the dog, and Baby Jesus. Mum was out with Mr Wandering Hands. Which was a good thing as one of the items was about a team of synchronized labradors who could leap over metre-high fences and Grandpa got excited and tried to get the dog to jump over the coffee table but it missed and knocked over Grandpa's carton of illicit Ribena. I got out the Cillit Bang. I am well versed in stain removal.

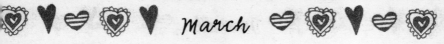
Saturday 18

Mum and Dad are going to dinner with Dad's boss Mr Wainwright tonight. This is excellent news, TV-wise. James is already lining up *Wife Swap* repeats. We should nominate Mum for that programme. Maybe we would get a spill-happy TV-loving crisp fiend for a week!

5 p.m.
In addition to Treena that is.

Sunday 19

Mum has changed her Sky pin. She found Grandpa and Baby Jesus watching *Pimp my Ride* at 2 in the morning.
    Saw Thin Kylie walking Fiddy (i.e. letting her poo on Marjory's gravel). She and Fat Kylie got sacked from Dorrington's for a catalogue of misdemeanours including doughnut theft and making comedy penis shapes in the celebration range icing. Fiddy is getting fat already. I expect it is her unwholesome diet of Microchips and Kraft Cheese Slices.

Monday 20

Work experience week has been declared a success. There were only seventeen sackings this year—a new

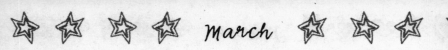
low (the Kylies, Sad Ed and Tuesday, and some Retards and Criminals who seemingly find it impossible not to let off fire alarms at every available opportunity). Plus Mark Lambert has been offered a job at Brenda's Hairdressing when he leaves school (which could be fairly soon if Ms Hopwood-White has her way). Apparently he shows remarkable promise shaving Union Jack designs into the heads of rat boys.

Also Mr Wilmott has installed a new 'Cooler' at school. It is a room for delinquents (i.e. the disused needlework mobile) where they are deprived of all privileges and just have to read calming poetry. Apparently he got the idea off the TV and is going to supervise the delinquents himself. I predict Mark Lambert and the Kylies will be in there before the term is over.

Tuesday 21

The cooler has been temporarily closed due to overcrowding. Mr Wilmott is having to revise his referrals policy—currently Mrs Leech is in charge and in her enthusiasm is just sending anyone who is lurking outside Mr Wilmott's office, including three Year Sevens with suspected nits. From now on, you can only get in if you have verbally or physically abused a member of staff or fellow student.

Wednesday 22

Twenty-three people got referred to the cooler today including:

- Fat Kylie—calling Thin Kylie a 'lezzer';
- Thin Kylie—calling Fat Kylie a 'lezzer';
- Mark Lambert—asking Kylies to demonstrate 'lezzer sex';
- Tuesday and Scarlet—actually demonstrating 'lezzer sex';
- Lou the caretaker—adjusting the Coke and crisp machine so that you can get NikNaks for 1p. (Personally I think this shows a good grasp of physics, maths, and metalwork, and should be rewarded.);
- Most of Criminals and Retards—too numerous to list— it is like a badge of honour to get referred for them.

Mrs Duddy has complained to Mr Wilmott. She says the cooler is disrupting the Retards and Criminals curriculum. Mr Wilmott mentioned the calming Shakespeare but she said most of them are still struggling with *Olga da Polga*.

Thursday 23

10.30 a.m.
Apparently Justin has been referred to the cooler for likening hairy librarian Mr Knox to a yeti. Am going to get myself referred immediately so I can bond with him over our delinquency. Will call Tuesday a 'lezzer' within Ms Hopwood-White's earshot. Tuesday will know I am being ironic.

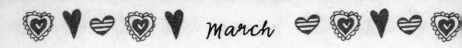

March

11.30 a.m.

Have black eye (Fat Kylie thought I was referring to her and is not so understanding of irony and Ms Hopwood-White distracted by Mark Lambert trying to undo Thin Kylie's bra one-handed for a can of Coke and a Picnic off Fat Jim Warner). Am not in cooler but in Mrs Leech's office eating reviving bourbons.

1 p.m.

The cooler has been closed until further notice so now will never get to show Justin how we are both misunderstood by conventional society. Apparently a fight broke out between the Year Eight Retards and the Year Nine ones and Mr Wilmott is now in Addenbrookes with a compass wound. He is going to leave the delinquents to Mrs Duddy from now on.

Friday 24

James's birthday. Got him some stickers for his *Lord of the Rings* album (stickers being recently unquarantined but still under strict review pending any incidents of rogue stickers being found on furniture). He is not having his official party until tomorrow. He and Mumtaz are having a joint celebration at the Lord Butler Leisure Centre. Mum is not happy but Mrs Patel has organized it. It involves twenty nine-year-olds rollerskating, swimming, eating vast quantities of chips and neopolitan ice cream, and a disco (i.e. a Tweenies

CD on repeat). Mum says it will end in tears and/or vomit.
She is taking a box of Kleenex and a squeegee.

Saturday 25

Went into town with Sad Ed for annual ritual of finding
Mother's Day cards and presents. He says Tuesday is getting
impatient with his True Love Waits attitude towards sex. She
is going to a seance with Scarlet and the goths tonight and has
not invited him. I said I wasn't invited either but he pointed
out that I don't own enough black clothing. Got Mum a non-
whimsical card with daffodils on and a bar of Green and Blacks.

5 p.m.
James is back from his birthday party with broken fingers
('Mad Harry' rollerskated over them). Apparently it is not
the only injury. There were two concussions (trampolining)
and a near drowning (neapolitan ice cream). Mum says she
is sticking to educational museum visits next year.

Sunday 26
Mother's Day

10 a.m.
Mum has threatened to consign the satellite dish to the bin.
James got her a five-piece copper-bottomed Anthony Worral

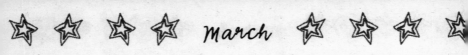
Thompson saucepan set for Mother's Day (£5.99 off Bid-Up via Grandpa's credit card). She asked how anyone could have worked out her new pin. James said it was easy—it is the last four digits of the Vanish Oxy-Action barcode. Dad is fighting back over the Sky TV. He says he will only give it up if she agrees to give up driving lessons with Mike the Molester. Mum says she would rather walk to Cornwall than learn with rival instructor Carl Kent (of Kent's Kar Klasses). His failure rate is second to none in North Essex; he deliberately misspells for alliterative effect; plus he has Micras instead of Fiestas and Mum has never trusted the Japanese.

Monday 27

I fear Sad Ed may have overanticipated Tuesday's willingness to wait for true love. I saw her smoking behind the ATC hut with Dave from Roadshow Records after school. But I cannot tell Sad Ed. It may break his heart. He is notoriously sensitive.

4 p.m.
Have told Sad Ed. He is going to confront her immediately (or at least after *Charmed*).

9 p.m.
Sad Ed has not confronted Tuesday yet due to fact that she let him borrow her copy of *The Catcher in the Rye* and

touch her left nipple. I said wasn't he concerned about being two-timed with a sexually experienced former rock god. He said he couldn't afford to be choosy. I said that is not the attitude but he said I was in no position to comment. Which is true. No one wants to snog me. Maybe it is because I am rubbish at snogging. That is it—that is why Justin has rejected me. Jack must have told him about my crap snogging. Oh my God. I need to learn to snog properly. And fast. It is the end of term disco on Friday and the air will be thick with adolescent hormones (and Lynx). Plus Justin will be there.

Tuesday 28

Have asked Scarlet for snogging advice. She said it is not really a matter of technique, it is about chemistry, but that Sean Woodley in Year Eleven will snog you for 50p and taught Leanne Jones everything she knows. Am going to his 'office' at lunch tomorrow (aka the upper school toilets).

Wednesday 29

Went to Sean Woodley's 'office' but it was being 'manned' by his Neanderthal sidekick Vincent Miller. Apparently

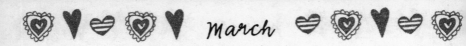

March

Sean has mumps and is off for a fortnight. And there is no way I am snogging Vincent. He only has one eyebrow. So yet another school disco will be spent eating crisps and watching the Kylies get felt up.

Thursday 30

Oh my God. Tuesday and Sad Ed have broken up. She says she chucked him because she is sick of boyfriends getting all 'possessive' on her. Sad Ed says HE chucked HER for adultery. I pointed out that they were neither married nor adults but it seemed to fall on deaf ears. He is refusing to go to the disco tomorrow due to heartbreak. And the fact that *Buffy the Movie* is on.

Friday 31

8 a.m.

It is the school disco and I still haven't found anyone to teach me how to snog. Plus I will have to stand on my own in goth corner—a vintage rose in a sea of black bat people (Scarlet is going to let me in—being the girlfriend of head goth Trevor Pledger bestows you with immediate 'door' privileges). Am going to force Sad Ed to go. Will tell him Tuesday is showing interest in rekindling their romance.

12 midnight

OH MY GOD. I have to stop doing this. Have snogged someone else totally non-tragic, although this time not an O'Grady and above the age of twelve. It is Sad Ed. Oh God. Feel sick. Am going to bed before I bring up the four bags of Quavers and two apple Tangos I had from the 'bar'.

I'm RACHEL RILEY
– welcome to my so-called life.

April

Saturday 1
April Fool's Day

Oh God. So this is what happened. Sad Ed and I were busy being depressed (him) and vintage (me) in goth corner, watching Fat Kylie pretending to be Beyoncé by gyrating her giant behind, when I said it was very likely no one would ever snog me again. So, for some reason I have not yet fathomed, Sad Ed said he would snog me. And for some reason, possibly because Tuesday says he has excellent tongue technique, and because I was desperate, I agreed. And so we snogged, which I have to admit, technically wasn't horrible (apart from the fact that Fat Kylie was still dancing at the time and I could see her buttocks banging together out of the corner of my eye). Then Tuesday saw us and stormed over and shrieked, 'I can't believe you've dumped me for that pubic-headed loser.' (So it is true, Sad Ed did chuck her!) I said it meant nothing and was just practice so I could snog Justin without him being so revolted he decided to become gay or celibate. But Tuesday said talk to the hand, but accidentally smacked Fat Kylie when she thrust her bejewelled fingers at me, and Mark Lambert saw this and thought it was a free-for-all against the goths and then a mini riot broke out and Mr Wilmott had to use a fire extinguisher to separate some of the Retards and Criminals who had improvised weapons with giant Tizer bottles.

So all in all it was a total disaster. I have snogged Sad Ed, who is not the ONE and is practically my brother, and

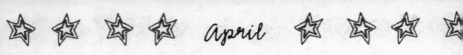

alienated my only lifeline to tragedy (i.e. Tuesday) and now neither of them are speaking to me. And Scarlet was not too happy either due to the closure of goth corner— it was full of foam. They had to relocate to maths geek corner (the maths geeks agreed to combine forces with the farm club people). Worst of all, Jack and Justin saw the whole thing, including the actual Sad Ed snog and the bit about me actually wanting to snog Justin. Jack just said, 'Another triumph, Riley.' But he did not smile this time. Why is he still being mean to me? It is his fault I am having to practise snogging in the first place. Thank God it is the holidays. I predict everyone will have forgotten the hoo-ha by next term. Will go round Sad Ed's later and ensure he knows it meant nothing to me. Then maybe he and Tuesday can patch it up.

4 p.m.

Sad Ed is in mourning. I told him that I was sorry and that I would never snog him again, however desperate I was. And he said, 'Well, I feel so much better,' then went back to listening to the Smiths in the dark and eating Minstrels. I will give him some more time. He will soon be back to normal and we can get back to being tragic and single together.

Plus it is Grandpa Riley's birthday but no one remembered. Not even Treena. He thought it was just an April Fool at first but by four o'clock no one had given him any socks or miniature whiskies so he locked himself in the shed with the dog. He says it is the only true friend he has ever had. He will be out by 8. It is cold outside and *Casualty* is on.

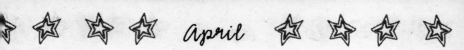

8.05 p.m.

Grandpa is out and on the sofa. Treena bought him a Pavarotti CD and some Liquorice Allsorts to say sorry. Plus the dog was going bonkers through sensory deprivation. It started to chew its own leg.

Sunday 2
Passion Sunday

Oh, the irony. The only passion in my life is Grandpa and Treena's audible conjugating over the sound of a dead opera singer.

Monday 3

No school. Called Scarlet but Suzy said she was consoling a devastated Tuesday. And Sad Ed is still off limits. According to Mrs Thomas he hasn't come out of his room since tea last night, not even for *Songs of Praise*. She says he has taken the entire biscuit cupboard in with him. I do not know why he is being so weird. After all, Tuesday was definitely flirting with Mullet Dave, and like Jack says— it's just tongues.

Watched *News 24* on Sky with James for five hours (Mum in Cambridge making potentially life-changing purchase of new Hoover). Ate tea (fishfingers and beans). Admired new

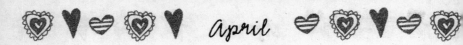

dog-hair eliminating Hoover with five turbo attachments. Watched *Lovejoy*. Went to bed.

Tuesday 4

Took dog for a walk. Ate tea (toad-in-the-hole). Went to bed.

Wednesday 5

Called Sad Ed. Mrs Thomas says he is improving. He has switched from the Smiths to the Killers and has been out of his room twice. Once for more KitKats and once for a poo. She is hoping he might have a shower tomorrow. Then she started on about how clean Aled always looks so I said I could smell burning and hung up.

Called Scarlet. She was down the Mocha with Trevor and Tuesday drinking coffee and being generally alienated from society.

Thursday 6

12.30 p.m.
Watched *CBeebies* with Baby Jesus for three hours. James says I need to get out more. He has invited me to test out the new 'slide of death' in the park on the common with him

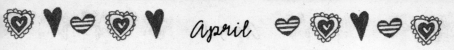

and Mumtaz this afternoon. I actually cried at his kindness. I may well go. It is my only source of social life.

4 p.m.
Slide now on Mum's banned list. James has broken another finger after shooting off end of 'perilously steep' helter-skelter thing and landing on top of Mad Harry.

Friday 7

A cow has fallen off the edge of a cliff in Scotland and helicopter crews are battling to rescue it. *Sky News* are beside themselves with potential time-filling television. So far they have interviewed a policeman, a man from the newsagent's down the road, and some woman who likes cows. Mum is glued to Sky. She has finally found a use for it.

10.50 p.m.
The cow is alive. Mum can finally go to bed in peace.

Saturday 8

Went round Sad Ed's to see if he has showered. He hasn't. Told him to pull himself together but he said I wouldn't understand, having never been in love. I said, on the contrary, I was deeply in love with potential rock guitarist/mince

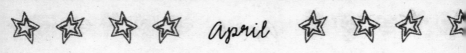

april

machine operator Justin Statham, but Sad Ed just said, 'Oh, spare me,' and shut the door. At least he is out of bed though. That is a good sign. Once he stayed under the covers for two days when he watched *American Pie* and realized that Willow had for ever tarnished her image as netherworld lesbian.

Sunday 9
Palm Sunday

Granny Clegg rang to say 'Happy Birthday' to James. James answered and pointed out she was over two weeks late. Dad said, 'Bloody Cornish still think it is 1985.' At which point Mum commandeered the phone. When she got off she looked pale and panicky. It turns out that Granny and Grandpa Clegg are planning an Easter visit i.e. in five days. Mum warned them there was no room, what with the dog and Baby Jesus, but Granny says they will be happy to 'bed down' with one of the neighbours (this is the sort of weird thing they do in Cornwall). Only Clive and Marjory don't like the Cleggs after Grandpa accused Clive of being 'a poof' two years ago, for wearing a pink Pringle jumper, plus we are in their bad books due to fact that their Granada is still on blocks at Viceroy's, awaiting demangling, and they are having to use Marjory's Fiat Uno, which has a 'tricky' biting point. And Granny Clegg doesn't like Aled Jones because his voice isn't high

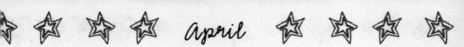

any more, which rules out Sad Ed's. So that leaves Terry and Cherie!

Monday 10

Mum is refusing to ask Terry and Cherie if the Cleggs can stay there. She is going to book them into the Chestnuts B&B on the Ashdon Road (aka a 1930s semi with a view of a conker tree four doors down). I fear the worst. It is run by Les Brewster and his wife Ying (erstwhile proprietors of the Siam Smile, formerly the Dog and Bucket) and Grandpa Clegg is notoriously racist.

Tuesday 11

Sad Ed has showered. Mrs Thomas rang to announce the news. I am going round tomorrow to see him. Obviously he is back to being just normally depressed as opposed to suicidal.

Wednesday 12

Went to see Sad Ed. He says he is committing his life to being a misunderstood and celibate genius poet like Morrissey. He is writing a song about it all. It is called 'Hope She Dies Before I Get Old'. (It must be about Tuesday.)

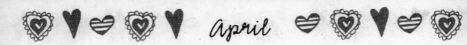

April

Thursday 13
Maundy Thursday

Fat Kylie is over the road with baby Whitney who is pushing Fiddy around in her Barbie pram. Fiddy is huge. She can barely walk so it is probably a relief to have someone wheel you about. Also it is good practice for Whitney. She will be pushing a pram for real by the age of sixteen if Mrs O'Grady is anything to go by.

Friday 14
Good Friday

10 a.m.
Dad left at five to pick up the Cleggs from St Slaughter (Auntie Joyless is refusing to have any contact with the 'heathen' wing of the family). He has taken Mum with him so she can memorize the route. He says the only good thing that will come out of her 'relationship' with Mike is that she will have to queue behind all the wretched caravans for three hours on the A303 come August. Grandpa has put *Hollyoaks* on. He says we should enjoy our last hours of freedom before the Clampetts arrive.

7 p.m.
Mum and Dad are back. Granny and Grandpa Clegg have been deposited at Chestnuts with their Spar bags. Mum

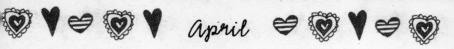
is nervous. She says Grandpa Clegg had a definite look of menace about him when he met Ying.

10 p.m.
Granny Clegg just rang. She says conditions at Chestnuts are intolerable and has sent for Dad to collect them. Dad said they cannot be worse than in Cornwall, which is practically the third world, but Mum sent him out with one of her evil glares.

10.30 p.m.
Granny and Grandpa Clegg are here. Grandpa Clegg says he will not share a bathroom with anyone who owns a bikini-line trimmer (Ying's, I assume, not Les's). Granny Clegg is backing him all the way. She says she would rather be under the same roof as a dirty old man and an illegitimate messiah than a foreign prostitute.

So I am in with James and the dog again. Mum is going to call Cherie in the morning.

Saturday 15

Woke up with James, a Prince William doll, the giant David Beckham, and the dog in my camp bed. James said he had a bad dream involving a *Blue Peter* badge and needed to bring his 'friends' with him. Plus Grandpa Clegg and Grandpa Riley are still refusing to be in the same room at the same time until they can agree on whether or not Terry Wogan is

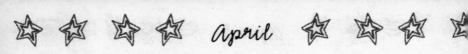

the greatest living broadcaster or an annoying Irish twit so there is a ridiculous hoo-ha every time one of them needs to move around the house. The sooner Mum calls Cherie the better.

11 a.m.

Cherie has agreed to let the Cleggs sleep in their spare room. She is moving the abdominizer and the sunbed into the garage. Granny and Grandpa are going to get a shock. I have seen the spare bed and it has black satin sheets and a vibration setting. They are going over in an hour to inspect the facilities but Granny Clegg has warned Mum they will be straight back if there are any signs of deviancy. I don't know if Channel 5 is included in this list. I hope not.

1 p.m.

Granny and Grandpa Clegg have moved over the road. Her fridge check revealed a Fray Bentos pie and some Kraft cheese slices. She thinks she has found her soulmate. Plus Fiddy has taken a liking to her. It is her vast bosoms. Animals like to sit on them. We are all going over for 'nibbles' later.

5 p.m.

Granny Clegg is in heaven. She is eating processed cheese with Cherie and discussing Buckingham Palace (they are in agreement it is not 'castley' enough). Grandpa Clegg is happy too. Terry is just as racist as he is and they are singing

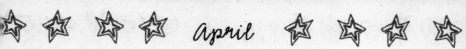

april

'Light My Fire' in comedy Indian accents. It is pitiful. Thin Kylie is not happy though. She said, 'Oh. My. God. Your relatives are, like, idiots. They wash their pants in the sink. It is minging.' For once I had to agree with her.

Sunday 16
Easter Day

10 a.m.
Five eggs. Am going to hide them in my wardrobe to avoid repeat of last year's shameful binge.

11 a.m.
Oh my God. Fiddy has given birth on Granny Clegg's cardigan. She was not fat after all but pregnant. All fingers are pointing at the dog. The puppies have the same wiry hair and perpetual look of idiocy. Granny Clegg is going to have one of them.

Cherie is in shock. It is the thought of Fiddy and the dog doing 'It'. It must have been on his walk that time when he went missing for five minutes when James found 20p glued into the tarmac and tried to get it out. The dog is clearly a fast mover. Fiddy must have stood on a chair or something though—there is nearly a metre height difference. Grandpa Riley is taking the dog over to meet his offspring later. He says he will instinctively know they are his—it is how he felt when he first saw Jesus.

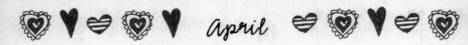
6 p.m.

The dog did not take too well to the puppies. Apparently it went into a barking frenzy and Grandpa had to stop it trying to chew one of them.

8 p.m.

The dog has found all the Easter eggs. There is a pile of foil-studded sick outside my bedroom door. Only the generic Trago Mills one is left. I wonder what is wrong with it? Will just try a little bit.

1 a.m.

Have been sick. Granny Clegg has poisoned me with out-of-date confectionery. Even the dog had better sense than to eat it, and it seemingly enjoys being sick.

Monday 17
Easter Monday

Granny and Grandpa Clegg are going home today. The Spar bags are already in the car but Granny Clegg is spending her last few minutes with 'Bruce' (as in Forsyth)—the puppy who has been singled out for her affections, and a lifetime of boredom and pasties in Cornwall. She has asked Dad to bring him down as soon as he has had his injections. Grandpa Riley said he would need typhoid and malaria to cross the border. Luckily

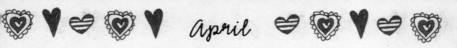
Bruce had his tongue in Granny Clegg's waxy ear so she didn't hear him.

School starts tomorrow. Hopefully the end of term snogging fiasco will be consigned to history: Justin will have suffered amnesia about the confession, Tuesday will forgive me as an act of sisterhood, and she and Sad Ed will ignore each other like grown-ups. Excellent.

Tuesday 18

Snogging utterly not consigned to history but luckily it is outdone by a shock revelation—Tuesday is not living in elegant squalor at all. She is living in a mock-Tudor four-bed on Pleasant Valley with Mr Wilmott. It turns out she is his niece! The news unfolds as follows:

9.10 a.m.
Sad Ed tells Tuesday he never loved her, she was his rebound girlfriend. (Who from? His cousin Julia?)

9.11 a.m.
Tuesday punches Sad Ed in stomach causing partial regurgitation of Wheat Crunchie (Worcester Sauce flavour).

9.12 a.m.
Mark Lambert offers to set up a bout with her and Fat Kylie, uncontested school fighting champion.

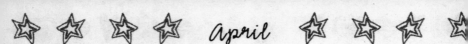

9.13 a.m.

Fat Kylie punches Mark Lambert to prove her fighting skills.

9.14 a.m.

Ms Hopwood-White sends for Mr Wilmott.

9.15 a.m.

Mr Wilmott says he is sick of Tuesday taking advantage of her relationship to him to get away with murder.

9.16 a.m.

Mark Lambert says, 'Oh my God, she's shagging Mr Wilmott.' Mr Wilmott says, 'Relationship to, not relationship with, you moron,' and that he is not shagging her, she is his niece and is staying at his house on a temporary basis.

9.17 a.m.

Tuesday storms out in an 'oh my God you are so embarrassing' fit.

9.18 a.m.

Order is restored and class goes back to discussion of whether Lennie in *Of Mice and Men* was autistic or seriously mental.

Wednesday 19

Tuesday is leaving school. She says Dr Rubenstein says her mental health is at risk in the comprehensive system.

But she was mental before she got here. She is going to the Quaker school instead. I would think that is far more damaging. They have to wear green. Mr Wilmott is relieved. So is Fat Kylie. No one has ever threatened her position as fighting champion of John Major High before, not even Fat Jim who is eighty-nine kilos and in the Air Training Corps.

Thursday 20

Tuesday has gone. Scarlet, Sad Ed, and I have agreed we will never be blinded by pseudo-tragedy again. Although Sad Ed says he will die a virgin now. This is probably true.

Friday 21

Grandpa and Treena have set a date for the wedding. It is December 30th. Jesus is chief page boy. They are going to see if they can get a contraption so the dog can carry him down the aisle. I am a bridesmaid. I asked Treena if Des has signed her mental cruelty divorce papers but she was too busy showing Mum a picture of Katie Price in a pink meringue dress. This does not bode well for my bridesmaid's outfit.

Saturday 22

Scarlet came over with a book of witchcraft symbols. Apparently she and Trevor are planning tattoos to demonstrate their commitment to each other and to general gothness. James said she is not old enough and besides, she will look undignified in her old age but Scarlet said she is planning to die young anyway. We chose a pentangle. Trevor is getting a bleeding skull. They are going to Maudsley Mick's in Harlow tomorrow. Apparently he will do underage jobs for a bottle of Tesco whisky.

Sunday 23
St George's Day

Not marked in this house following last year's fracas with the dog, Marlon, and Hugo Thorndyke. Mum is hovering near her anti-social behaviour catalogue. It is because the Britchers have painted a red cross on the garage door (and not of the biblical variety). Mum says it is encouraging jingoism not to mention graffiti.

5 p.m.
Went round Scarlet's to admire her tattoo. She was reluctant to show me at first so I had to sneakily pull down her skirt when she walked upstairs (thank God for elasticated goth clothing). I said I couldn't see anything so she pointed out a

blue dot on her upper thigh. Apparently she fainted when the blood started seeping. Trevor did not even make it that far. He passed out when he saw Maudsley Mick's array of needles. How they expect to drink blood like Dracula I do not know.

Monday 24

Called for Scarlet on the way to school but she has an infection in her thigh and is going to see Dr Braithwaite. So had to walk with Jack instead (Suzy's idea). Jack asked how my relationship with Sad Ed was. I said I did not have a 'relationship' with Sad Ed unless you count listening to dirge-like music and anyway, what did he care? Jack said he didn't. Then we walked in silence until we got to Mr Patel's where I pretended to need to talk to Thin Kylie about something (she was outside menacing some Year Sevens). What is going on? Jack and I used to be friends. It is because we crossed an uncrossable line and kissed. I have learnt my lesson. I will never snog a friend again. You either end up heartbroken or in a fire extinguisher fight.

I didn't mean heartbroken. Obviously. Jack did not break my heart.

Tuesday 25

Scarlet was back in school. Her tattoo is seeping though, so she has a note to get off games tomorrow. I asked if Suzy had

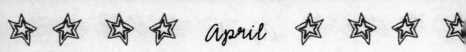
grounded her but she said no, Suzy said self-mutilation was a rite of passage. She has an Egyptian fertility symbol tattooed on her left buttock and Bob has a ring on his unmentionables.

Also £1.50 has gone missing from Mum's purse. She suspects Grandpa. He came home with a four-pack of brown ale. She asked him where he got the money and he said Dad had lent him £5 yesterday. Mum is not convinced but has given Dad a verbal warning anyway.

Wednesday 26

A national scandal has occurred. One of the gigantic, balding Labour politicans has been having an illicit affair with his secretary. James said that the secretary must have gone on top due to the MP's vastness so Mum sent him to his room. How does he know so much about sex? At his age I thought babies came from John Lewis. I feel sorry for the cheated wife. She looked very sad on telly, under her enormous hairdo and thick make-up. She must have thought she was safe with someone that revolting. How wrong she was. Granny Clegg is right—all politicians are sex cases.

Thursday 27

Mum's purse has been raided again. And for £1.50 again. How does she know the exact amount? She has a tighter

grip on finances than the chancellor. Mum has called an emergency family meeting at 6.30 (after tea and before David Attenborough) to identify the culprit.

6.45 p.m.

The culprit is James! He is being bullied for money with menaces by Mad Harry (second toughest in the juniors, according to James, after Stephen 'Maggot' Mason, who eats mud). He has to pay him £1.50 a day or Mad Harry is threatening to beat up Mumtaz. James said it was a matter of love and honour. I'm not sure what Mum is more angry about—the money or the religious divide relationship. She is going into school tomorrow to talk to Reverend Begley about the bullying policy at St Regina's.

Friday 28

Mad Harry's mother has been called into school next week for a meeting with Mum. Reverend Begley is going to mediate. I do not rate Mrs Mad Harry's chances. Or Reverend Begley's. Mum is terrifying in a heated debate.

Saturday 29

Something utterly exciting is happening to Saffron Walden. Suzy is going to be on TV! She has been given her own

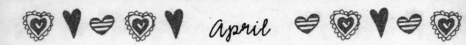

sex show on Channel 5. It is going to be on at 2 a.m. on Fridays. She got spotted by one of the producers when she helped him with his perverted sexual problems. So now we will have three celebrities. Although the McGann has not been spotted for several weeks and there are fears he may have moved to Sawbridgeworth, which has a Pizza Express. Mum will ban it for sure. I do not care. I will watch it at Scarlet's. They are going to record every episode so they can send it to Granny Stone in St Helier. Apparently she is very sexually progressive as well. She was the first woman in Jersey to get a delivery from Ann Summers.

Sunday 30

9 a.m.
Something is wrong with the dog. It has refused to eat its breakfast and is just pacing up and down.

9.30 a.m.
The Sky TV remote control is missing. Yet the channel keeps mysteriously changing of its own accord. Which is annoying enough except the dog is still pacing up and down and so I can't see what is going on anyway.

9.45 a.m.
Two mysteries solved. Dog belched and suddenly forbidden E4 came on. It has swallowed the remote. Dad is outraged.

He is going to miss the Open unless Mr Mercer can do an emergency operation this afternoon and retrieve the controller. Grandpa is rubbing the dog's tummy to calm it. Which has stopped the pacing but the channel is now flicking furiously.

11.00 a.m.
Mr Mercer can do the operation but not until 3 p.m. as he is watching the golf. Dad is livid.

11.15 a.m.
James has had a genius suggestion. He is rubbing the dog's tummy until the golf comes on then he is going to take the dog out of range of the telly (i.e the shed) until it goes to the vet's. It will mean we have to watch Eurosport all day but Dad says it is a small price to pay to ensure he can study Tiger Woods's vice-like grip on his three iron.

2 p.m.
Dad happily watching golf. Treena is going to drive the dog to the vet's in the Passat.

2.15 p.m.
Dad not happily watching golf any more. The dog made a run for it when Treena let it out of the shed and it raced through the sitting room to get to Grandpa who was asleep with Baby Jesus and turned the telly to E4 on the eighteenth hole. And James can't get it to switch back. He fears the

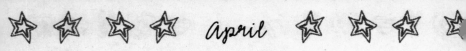
batteries may be flat. So now Dad is taking the dog to the vet anyway.

4 p.m.
Dog is back. It has a shaven patch on its side again. It seems happier though. The remote has been forensically cleansed by Mum and appears to be functioning normally. Which is a miracle given the other contents of the dog's stomach (a Bic biro, two buttons, and a sweetcorn holder, according to Mr Mercer).

I'm RACHEL RILEY
– welcome to my so-called life.

May

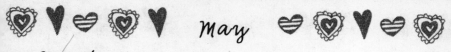

Monday 1

May Day Holiday

Went round Sad Ed's. He is totally over Tuesday now. Apparently he got a text from someone called Lisa in Year Nine yesterday asking if she could test out his legendary snogging powers. His reputation will overtake Sean Woodley at this rate. He will be able to oust him from the upper school toilets. I reminded him of his pledge to be celibate and misunderstood. He said I had misunderstood him, so he was already halfway there. Ha ha.

Tuesday 2

Mrs Mad Harry has taken full blame for the bullying incident. Apparently he was also extorting money from Douglas Pole, who has diabetes, and Archie Knox, son of hairy librarian Mr Knox, who has premature shaving issues. She has suggested the two boys 'get to know each other better' to quash their differences. Mum is not entirely happy but has agreed. She says James needs more contact with normal boys (as opposed to Mumtaz).

Wednesday 3

Have dentist appointment with sadistic Mrs Wong tomorrow.

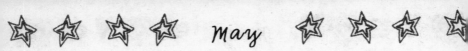

May

Am going to dose up on Nurofen in anticipation. James is coming too. He is not scared. Mrs Wong says he has the teeth of a Great White. Which is totally unfair, given his demerara habit. Although he is vigorous bordering on the obsessive with his brushing routine.

Thursday 4

Yet another filling. I will have no teeth left by the time I am sixteen. Mrs Wong said she blames the parents for letting children overdose on Coca-Cola and Haribo. I said chance would be a fine thing. Or at least I would have had my mouth not been filled with blood and gritty filling bits.

Friday 5

The road sign to Saffron Walden from the A11 has gone missing. Mum has rung up the council to complain. She says it could lose the town literally hundreds of pounds in tourist revenue. She says Mike is backing her campaign (the missing sign was spotted during her dual carriageway lesson this afternoon). They are going to the press (i.e. the *Walden Chronicle*) if the council doesn't act within the week. Dad says she will be the talk of the town if she joins forces with Mr Wandering Hands. Mum says she doesn't care, they have taken Saffron Walden off the map and it is a matter

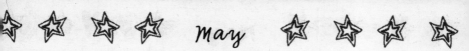
of principle. (Actually this once really happened—Saffron Walden wasn't on a WHSmith Road Map. I have never seen Mum so militaristic. WHSmith had to do a national recall and reprint the whole thing. Apparently Plymouth and Milton Keynes were missing as well. I am not surprised. It is because they are totally pants places and no one would want to visit them anyway.)

Saturday 6

Mad Harry came over for tea. It was not the bonding experience Mrs Mad Harry had hoped for. First he encouraged James to feed jigsaw puzzle pieces (Windsor Castle) to the dog, then he climbed on the shed roof and refused to come down until he got a packet of Hula Hoops. Mum had to call Mrs Mad Harry to collect him early. James begged Mum not to send Harry away though. So her plan to oust Mumtaz has backfired. She has acquired Satan in nine-year-old form instead.

Mum is right to be concerned. At one point Mad Harry tried to look up my vintage skirt. He is a menace.

Sunday 7

Barry the Blade has been kidnapped. Treena says he got bundled into a car outside the White Horse last night. I

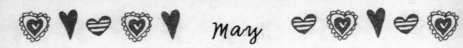
asked Treena whether she had called the police and she said they were singing 'Chirpy Chirpy Cheep Cheep' on the karaoke in the saloon bar at the time so she didn't bother. Have made her call them now. Her description of the car was disappointing however—she said it was blue with a 'thingy' on the bonnet.

Monday 8

Mr Wilmott reminded us we all have mock exams in two weeks. He says we should not be misled by the word 'mock', they are totally important and real and should be treated as such. He is lying. He is just trying to avoid a repeat of last year when only ten people passed maths and no one turned up at all for mock Rural Studies. Am going to revise though. Have decided my best route to tragedy is to get into Cambridge or Oxford and study classic literature. I will be totally like Sylvia Plath and that one off *Mission Impossible 3* and will meet all sorts of future politicians and philosophers and be inspired by the ancient architecture and traditions. Unlike at Stoke on Trent University (formerly Derbyshire Adult Education Centre), whose alumni include Justin's cousin Bez. According to him, the only traditions are the annual Angel Delight eating competition. He got a 2.2 in media studies and is now working in a TV shop. So he is in a related profession at least.

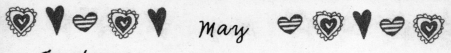

Tuesday 9

The police rang for Treena. Barry the Blade has been found alive and well. Apparently he was a willing participant initially as Stacey O'Grady had promised him a 'bunk-up' with Mrs Simpson if he got in the boot of his Toyota. Only then he and Darryl Stamp drove Barry to Haverhill and left him on the B1054 with no trousers.

Wednesday 10

Communal showers have been banned after PE due to the ongoing water shortages. This is excellent news so now we will not have to witness the vastness of Fat Kylie's bottom and I will not have to be subjected to 'hilarious' jokes about my 32A chest. Not that anyone actually showered anyway—we just got our feet wet and ran round the changing room in case Miss Vicar came in for inspection. On the downside it means that Oona Rickets will have to be quarantined.

Thursday 11

Barry the Blade's kidnap is the cover story of the *Walden Chronicle*. It says:

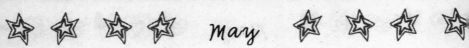

WALDEN JOINS ASBO WARS AS POLICE PULL THE PLUG ON O'GRADY SHOW

Clean-living Saffron Walden is set to hand out its first-ever ASBO to habitual nuisances Stacey O'Grady and Darryl Stamp, the criminal minds behind last year's heist at Mr Patel's. It follows their kidnapping of Barry Hooton (also known as Barry the Blade, or Mental Barry) and attempts to 'pimp' out local madwoman 'Lilo' Lil Simpson. The police say crucial evidence came from community-minded Treena Nichols, twenty-nine-year-old mother of baby Jesus, who witnessd the events from her bar stool at the White Horse.

Treena is worried the O'Gradys are going to stalk and possibly grievous bodily harm her. She is going to call the police and demand witness protection for her, Grandpa, and Baby Jesus. Grandpa said it would mean they would never be able to walk the streets of Walden again, but Treena said they would get a new house and the dog could come—they could dye its hair. Mum is hoping they do have to change their identities. She is getting sick of the endless smell of

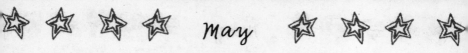
toxic nappies and dribble on the M&S sofa. Plus now she has been out-manoeuvred on the anti-anti-social behaviour front by Treena, which has called her entire existence into question.

Friday 12

Mum is putting in for an early driving test. She has scored a hundred per cent on all her Highway Code quizzes including the notoriously tricky flying motorbike sign. Dad said the sooner she was out of Mike's wandering hand range the better. But Mum said she was thinking of doing the advanced driver course immediately so Dad stormed off to polish his golf clubs. Anyone would think Mike Majors was some kind of irresistible George Clooney type. I have seen him, he looks like Eamonn Holmes with a moustache.

Also, the police have refused to put Treena and Grandpa under witness protection. They say they are under financial pressure and struggling with the Alsatian budget as it is—they are on own-brand Netto instead of high quality Pedigree Chum. Treena is disappointed. So is Mum. She was planning to re-woodchip their room (Grandpa and James have picked out all the chips in the current wallpaper). Luckily Fat Kylie is not speaking to Stacey at the moment after he ran over Tupac's foot in his Toyota. So she is on our side.

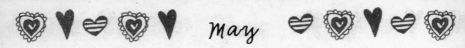

May

Saturday 13

James has gone round Mad Harry's for the day. Mumtaz called for him so I lied and said he was at the library. But she said she had already checked there and I should be ashamed of myself. I said I was and confessed the truth. Mumtaz did not sound happy. She said Mad Harry is a bad influence and is heading for a life of crime.

Told James Mumtaz had called. He said he was 'laying off the "ho"s for a while' so Mum sent him to his room to reflect on his sexist attitude. Grandpa said it was good James was building up his defences against the never-ending demands of the opposite sex so young so Mum sent him to his room as well.

Sunday 14

Terry has got a black eye. Grandpa and James saw him when they were walking the dog round the block and Terry was letting Fiddy and the puppies poo on Marjory's gravel. Grandpa asked him if he had been mugged. Terry said he was the victim of domestic violence. James said it goes to show Mad Harry is right. All women are mentalists. Terry said, 'Too right, son.' Then the dog tried for a repeat performance with Fiddy so they all came home.

Grandpa is jubilant. He says not even the snip can keep a Riley down.

May

Monday 15

The A11 roadsign is back. It says 'Saffron Wallden—twinned with Bad Wildungen and Chichicastenango.' Mum has already rung the council. She says she would rather have no sign than a misspelt one.

On the plus side, I did not know we were twinned with Chichicastenango. Have looked it up on Google. It is a deprived village in Guatemala. Excellent. I am going to suggest a cultural school exchange to Ms Hopwood-White. It will be far more mind-expanding than the usual French one, which just involves wandering around Carrefour and dancing to crap Euro-pop. We will be able to live in stone huts with indigenous peoples and grind coffee beans. It is utterly romantic.

Tuesday 16

Ms Hopwood-White did not seem too keen on cultural Guatemalan exchange programme. She says she went to Nicaragua after her finals and spent two weeks in hospital after drinking a shamanic asthma remedy. Plus Mr Wilmott is still wavering on rubber-stamping foreign field trips following last year's Paris disaster. Will get Mum to write a letter. She is good at the art of persuasion.

5 p.m.
Mum says I am going to Guatemala over her dead body.

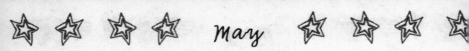

It is riddled with revolutionaries and I will be killed or infected with dysentery within five minutes of landing. I should have got Scarlet to talk to Suzy instead. She is always going on protests to back South American freedom fighter types.

Wednesday 17

Saw Tuesday after school in her new uniform. She was in Mr Patel's, which is totally out of bounds to Quaker school students, according to unwritten John Major High rules. She is lucky Fat Kylie wasn't there to enforce them. Tuesday evil-eyed me over the Pot Noodle machine so I evil-eyed her back. So she said 'bothered' and went back to reading *NME* with Daisy Truelove Jones. They are suited to each other. Daisy is a pseudo-tragic type as well. She claimed that her dad works in films but it turned out that he owns BJ Video (aka Blow Job Video, actually Bob Jones Video).

Thursday 18

Oh God, just remembered have mocks on Monday. Will start gruelling revision schedule after school in bid to escape middle-class clutches of Saffron Walden and get into Oxford.

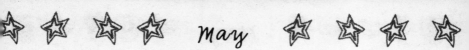

7 p.m.

Why, oh why did I opt for geography? I cannot remember where the Isle of Man is let alone the rest of the world.

Called Sad Ed for advice and possible joint revision session but he was doing text sex with some Year Nines. He has reinvented himself as a sort of love guru. He says the celibacy thing just seems to make them keener.

Friday 19

Have had emergency pep talk from Mr Wilmott about mocks. He says our lives depend on them (he is constantly in fear of being inspected). Am totally going to revise all weekend. Scarlet is coming over tomorrow so we can do cosines and remember whose side Stalin was on.

Saturday 20

Strict revision schedule not going according to plan due to interruptions from: *a*) The dog (trying to get at our brain-stimulating chocolate); *b*) Mad Harry (offering Scarlet fifty pence for a look at her bra); *c*) Baby Jesus (inexplicable hatred of Grand Prix coverage).

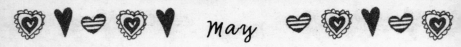

May

Sunday 21

Went round Scarlet's. Suzy says the secret of passing exams is not to worry too much. Plus to write stuff on your legs and surreptitiously look up your skirt if you get stuck. This is how she got As in all her O Levels.

Suzy was rehearsing for her TV series. She starts filming in three weeks in the old *Family Fortunes* studio. The show is called *Sex with Suzy* and she is going to delve into celebrities' sex lives and give them useful tips on the way. Her first guest is Jeffrey Archer. I said I was surprised he had a sex life. She said she is going to talk to him about prisons and masturbation.

Monday 22

9 a.m.
Feeling totally prepared. Have followed Suzy's advice and have large sections of *The Crucible* on thighs in blue Bic.

3 p.m.
Was not drama. That is tomorrow. It was maths. Am going to fail it.

Tuesday 23

Am also going to fail drama.

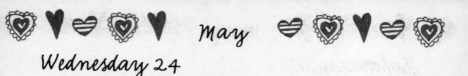

May

Wednesday 24

And French.

Thursday 25

And Rural Studies. Jack was lying about it being a cinch. There were all sorts of revolting questions about goat gestation periods and mastitis.

Friday 26

8 a.m.
At least will pass English. Literature is my life so will breeze it easily even though have only read three pages of *The Tempest*.

3 p.m.
Who is Ariel? Must be comedy laundrywoman or something. That will be where name comes from.

5 p.m.
Oh God, have just checked. Am going to fail English as well. Have written 200 words on importance of mad magical laundrywoman in Shakespearean tragedy.

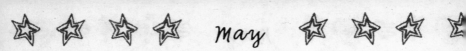

May

Saturday 27

10 a.m.
Something is going on over the road. A suitcase has just flown out of Cherie and Terry's bedroom window.

10.05 a.m.
Followed by several vests and other undergarments.

10.15 a.m.
Terry is now on the front 'lawn' (scorched brown patch) piling alarmingly small pants into the suitcase while Cherie and Thin Kylie throw socks and shoes out of the window. Am not sure what is going on. Mum is hovering by the phone—the situation is fraught with anti-social behaviour potential.

10.20 a.m.
Marjory has arrived to peer through our double glazing (the view is better as we have no obscuring hydrangeas in the way (outlawed for being unnaturally blue)). She says Clive saw him coming out of the Saffron Hotel with Lorna Green, who works on the Waitrose checkouts, so he has possibly been having an affair! That would explain the black eye as well.

10.45 a.m.
Terry has loaded his Cherokee with the suitcase, the abdominizer, and two of the puppies and has driven off. I hope one of them wasn't Bruce. Granny Clegg is expecting

delivery any day soon. Although frankly they all look the same—hairy and mental. Cherie is now playing Take That at full volume. Am going over the road to offer sympathy to Thin Kylie at this tragic time.

11.15 a.m.

May have worsened situation. I said I was sorry to hear about Terry and Lorna from Waitrose. Cherie said, 'Who? I thought he was just doing that girl from the bookies. The lying bastard!' Then she turned up the volume on Gary Barlow. Thin Kylie is gutted. She says Terry was supposed to be taking her, Cherie, and Fat Kylie to Faliraki for half term and now she'll have to go to Butlins with the O'Gradys. I asked her if it was this bad when her real dad left. She said, 'Are you, like, mental? My real dad only took me to Clacton. God, you are so f**king stupid.' So I left her to her grief. Will go back tomorrow when she is ready to share her feelings.

Sunday 28

Went to console Thin Kylie but she was out at an illegal minibike race with Mark Lambert and Mr Hosepipe. Cherie looked terrible. She was in her pink dressing gown eating cherry liqueur chocolates and watching MTV with Fiddy and the puppies. I asked her if she needed anything and she said, 'A packet of Benson and Hedges and a vibrator.' I said I would have to pass on the cigarettes as Mr Patel knows I am

underage but that she should call Suzy about the vibrator. She is always willing to help in that department.

James says the lottery is to blame. Statistically lottery winners are thirty-seven per cent more likely to be adulterous than non-winners. He googled it.

Monday 29
Bank Holiday
Half term.

Called Scarlet to see if she wanted to go and lurk outside Goddard's later (Justin is working all half term—he has been promoted to the till temporarily because Mr Goddard is at his sister's in Weston-Super-Mare) but there was no answer. Then remembered they have all gone to Jersey to see Granny Stone. Why do we never go away on holiday? Asked Mum if we could go to Cornwall (even St Slaughter would be more interesting than Saffron Walden). But Mum says there is no way we can all fit into Bellevue unless I want to share a single bed with James (not) or a room with Granny and Grandpa Clegg (double not) plus Auntie Joyless has vowed never to let a Riley darken her doorstep again. I said this was exactly why my Guatemalan exchange was a good idea otherwise how would I ever get to learn about other cultures. So Mum said she would take me to Cambridge to look at the Aztec pipe players busking outside Gap. This is typical. It is because Mum

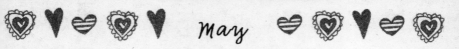
did not leave a ten-mile radius of Redruth until she was eighteen.

Went round Sad Ed's to commiserate. We have decided to make the most of our lot and culturally explore Saffron Walden for the next five days. We are going to start with the cemetery tomorrow. Sad Ed says someone famous and poetic is bound to be buried there.

Tuesday 30

There is no one famous buried in the cemetery unless you count Niall O'Grady, notorious uncle of Fat Kylie etc. O'Grady, who accidentally blew himself up with a can of hairspray in 1989. We are going to go to the museum instead tomorrow to immerse ourselves in Saffron Walden's grim medieval past.

Wednesday 31

Have given up on cultural Saffron Walden experience. Since when are stuffed ducks historical? Plus Mr Cremin, who dusts the exhibits, got annoyed with Sad Ed's text sex beeping and asked us to leave as we were disturbing the other three visitors.

I'm RACHEL RILEY

– welcome to my so-called life.

June

Thursday 1

Cherie came over to ask if Dad could pop round later and help her undo some jars. She said she would ask Clive but he looks like he has weak wrists and Dad's look much more manly. Mum did not seem too thrilled but said she would send him over after his casserole. Cherie looked a lot better. Her make-up was in the right place and she didn't smell of Bacardi. Plus she was wearing a Wonderbra so she is definitely back on form.

7 p.m.
Dad has gone to unscrew Cherie's jam or whatever it is.

8 p.m.
Dad is not back. Mum says nothing takes that long to undo, not even Granny Clegg's rhubarb and potato chutney (1985 vintage).

8.30 p.m.
Dad still not back. Mum is going to send James over if he is not home by 9. Grandpa asked why she wasn't sending him but she said James is more authoritative.

8.55 p.m.
Dad is back but has drunk four daiquiris and a Harvey Wallbanger and has been sent to bed. It was not jam. It was maraschino cherries and peaches in brandy.

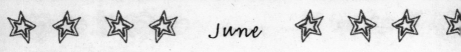
Friday 2

8.30 a.m.
Dad is too hungover to go to work. Mum has phoned in sick claiming he has food poisoning—not a total lie, it could have been a rogue maraschino cherry that put him over the edge. I asked why she never did that for me and she said Dad would wish he was in work by the time she had finished with him. She is not happy about him lingering at Cherie's with his manly wrists.

10 a.m.
Dad has gone to work. Mum's Spanish Inquisition style questioning was too much for him. He insists that nothing untoward occurred and that Cherie just had a lot of cocktail-related jars that needed undoing but Mum is unconvinced. Then Dad said Mum was in no position to talk, seeing as she was about to spend forty-five minutes within a few centimetres of Mike Major's molesting fingers so Mum said, 'That man is a saint whereas Cherie Britcher has sin written all over her too-tight trousers,' (actual, not metaphorical) so Dad got the Passat keys and his briefcase and left. He is still wearing his M&S moccasin slippers. I do not know how he is going to explain that to Mr Wainwright. All this arguing is very disturbing. I am definitely going to be in care by the end of term at this rate. Maybe Suzy and Bob will take me in. Then I could become totally interesting and sexually advanced. And vegetarian.

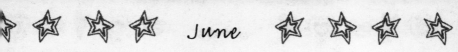
Saturday 3

Mum and Dad have made up. Mum says it is tension due to general overcrowding and the constant demands on her array of cleaning products. Dad has promised to tackle the situation head on. He is taking Grandpa to see an estate agent about renting a flat for them this afternoon.

3 p.m.
The rental situation is not promising. Grandpa turned down all three flats on the books of Mullock, Mullock, and Cheffin. One because it was painted yellow, the second because it had the 'wrong sort of electricity', and the last because it is above Abrakebabra and Treena doesn't like looking at the elephant leg in the window (though she will happily eat it). Dad said beggars can't be choosers but Grandpa said he wasn't begging. He is quite happy in Summerdale Road. Mum is going to pester Mr Lemon again. Dad offered but she said he had already proven his ineffectiveness.

Sunday 4
Whit Sunday

Granny Clegg rang to check up on Bruce. James answered and said that he had seen him eating gravel the day before

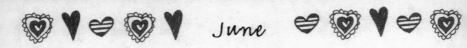
and that he is living in a broken home now that racist Terry has run off with Lisa from Tony's Turf Accountants. Granny Clegg demanded to speak to Dad and has instructed him to remove Bruce from the Britchers' forthwith and bring him down to Cornwall so she can put him in the St Slaughter fete 'most lovable pet' competition. There is no chance he will win. He has bad breath. Plus, if he takes after his father he will be sick during the ceremony. Dad is going to pick him up later and then drive him down next Saturday. Mum is not happy. She says Granny Clegg will not know if we leave Bruce there an extra week but Dad said that Granny Clegg had threatened to get on the bus and collect him herself tomorrow and we all know what happened last time she tried to use public transport.

4 p.m.
Dad has gone to fetch Bruce. Mum has sent James with him to make sure he doesn't lurk at the Britchers' too long, plus she has made Dad wear gloves to cover up his manly wrists.

5 p.m.
Bruce has arrived. Mum has cordoned him off in the kitchen using Jesus's playpen (Jesus is in a makeshift arrangement of clothes airers, but as he seems to take after Treena in the not moving and watching telly stakes, it is fairly safe). The dog is going mental and throwing itself at the kitchen door. Grandpa keeps telling him that Bruce is his own flesh

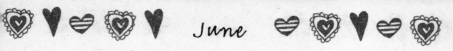
and blood but the dog does not seem moved by this at all. It has already broken one hinge and is fast loosening the second.

6 p.m.

The dog has knocked itself out on the kitchen door and is being revived with brandy. To make matters worse, Bruce squeezed through the playpen bars and got into the cereal cupboard. The kitchen is a sea of Shreddies. He has now been moved to safer quarters i.e. Marjory's cat carrier. Mum has suggested Dad takes the day off work tomorrow to drive Bruce to his new home. Dad says there is no way he can cancel Jeremy from Head Office to chauffeur a puppy to the Cleggs'.

Monday 5

8 a.m.

Dad is driving to the Cleggs'. Overnight, Bruce ate the cat carrier door, a box of apricot muesli, and two tea towels. Plus the dog, who was locked in the shed for safety reasons, bit the lid off a tin of creosote and is now highly flammable.

11 p.m.

Dad is back. He says that is positively the last time he is traipsing down to the back of beyond to do favours for a Clegg. Apparently Bruce ate the tuning knob off the radio.

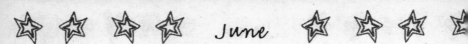

So Dad had to listen to Kiss FM for a total of twelve hours. He says he may well need counselling.

Tuesday 6

We are going on a school trip to the ballet in three weeks! It is to see former Retard and Criminal Davey MacDonald in his debut performance in *Swan Lake*. He is in the corps de ballet so he is probably a tree or something. Mark Lambert has forbidden Thin Kylie to go. He is worried she will fall for his penis-revealing special needs again and dump him. Thin Kylie said, 'Don't be a twat, he's, like, a poof now, innit, like that Billy Elliott.' So Ms Hopwood-White sent them both to Mr Wilmott before it got out of hand. She says she is resorting to preventative punishment in order to keep the peace. Maybe Davey MacDonald is gay now though. That would be excellent. Then I would know a genuine homosexual. As opposed to Oona Rickets who is swinging all ways.

Wednesday 7

Suzy has gone to London to start filming for Channel 5 today. Scarlet says she did not sleep at all last night and has taken two valium to calm her nerves. Luckily they sent a car to pick her up or she would never have got there. Bob had to carry her and strap her in as it was. I asked if

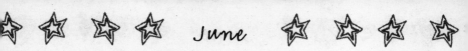

it was a stretch limousine with a uniformed chauffeur but apparently it was a dented Granada driven by a fat man called Steve. We are going to Scarlet's on Friday to watch it being broadcast. It is at 2 a.m. so we are sleeping over. I said I hoped Jack had invited Justin. Scarlet said she hoped he hadn't as Trevor was going to be there and she didn't want them to brawl over her in her goth pyjamas. I said this was unlikely as Trevor would definitely lose given his gothic pallor and weedy forearms. Then Scarlet got all shirty. I don't know why—I am just pointing out the facts.

Thursday 8

Cherie came over after school to ask if Dad could change the fuse on her hair straighteners. Mum said he was out all evening at the Round Table voting on who will be Carnival Chairman, now that Graham Ferris is moving to Sudbury, and that she should try Mr Atkinson at number 18. This is a lie. He is due back at 9. Mum is clearly not taking any risks with Dad and his manly charms. Since when did Dad become a sex god? It is very disturbing.

It is Suzy's sex programme sleepover tomorrow. Have told Mum we are going to bed straight after the *News at Ten*. This is not a total lie. But have not mentioned that Jack is under strict instructions to wake us up at 1.30 a.m. Oh please let Justin be there. I am going to wear my Topshop-style boxer short pyjama things especially (note the word style, rather

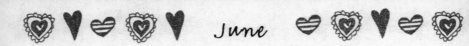
than actual. In fact a pair of Dad's old boxer shorts and a vest top—Mum has refused to let me go to Cambridge to buy 'draughty nightwear' just because I have seen it on TV).

Friday 9

10.30 p.m.
Justin is not here. Apparently he is grounded on Fridays until GCSEs are over. What an unenlightened mother he has. Something else we have in common.

Plans to actually go to sleep have been abandoned. We are all going to watch DVDs in the den. Scarlet and Trevor are hovering in the seventies loveswing thing like a pair of giant bats, Sad Ed is on a pouffe with a box of Green and Black organic pralines, which leaves me and Jack on the sofabed. Am determined not to feel any untoward urges to touch his hair or anything weird like that so have wedged a pillow between us. Jack has wedged several cushions. Not that he has any untoward urges obviously. He has made that clear. It is to ward me off.

Saturday 10

8 a.m.
Oh God. Have just woken up with head on Jack's shoulder and drool making a wet patch on his vintage Stone Roses

T-shirt. Thank God he is still asleep. Must have climbed over pillow and cushion barrier in sleepwalking-style incident. Plus have totally missed *Sex with Suzy*. Why did no one wake me up? Would ask Sad Ed but he is asleep under pile of chocolate wrappers with remote control welded to his hand. Scarlet and Trevor are still hovering menacingly. It is not normal.

9 a.m.
Apparently no one managed to stay awake. Except Sad Ed, who switched over to a *Babylon 5* marathon on Bravo and forgot to switch back. So we have just watched it on the recording. Suzy was brilliant. She got Jeffrey Archer to discuss deep thrusts. We are all going into town for 'brunch' (aka toast and mini pots of marmalade at Eaden Lilleys—I don't think Saffron Walden does eggs overeasy yet) to celebrate.

1 p.m.
Suzy is an overnight star. Barry the Blade, Mr Whippy, and (weirdly) Mrs Noakes have all commented on her performance. Even the least famous McGann (not in Sawbridgeworth after all, but apparently filming an episode of *Holby City*) gave her a funny look. He is worried his superstar status is going to be usurped. Got home to find Mad Harry and James trying on my underwear. James is going to be heading the way of Kyle O'Grady if this carries on. Am going to have to rekindle his interest in Mumtaz. She would never walk round with an M&S training bra over her ears.

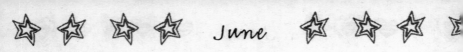
Sunday 11

Granny Clegg rang. Bruce did not win the most lovable pet competition. One of Hester's chickens that looks like it is doing the macarena triumphed. Granny Clegg is outraged. She cannot understand how the judges could have overlooked Bruce's charms for a dancing hen. Although possibly the fact that he ate the microphone and a kilo of Maureen Penrice's heavy duty flapjack had something to do with it.

Monday 12

Scarlet and Jack are enjoying new-found fame at school now that they are the offspring of a TV sex guru. Jack has been invited to the Upper Sixth Cheese and Wine anti-war night—unheard of in John Major history. And Mr Wilmott asked Scarlet if her mother might like to take over from Miss Vicar for this year's sex education lesson. I predict he will regret this decision though. It is fraught with potential perverts-in-schools issues. At least he did not ask my mother. Her version would involve plenty of moist wipes and a bucket.

Tuesday 13

Mum is jubilant. Mr Whippy has been rehoused. He is moving out of his ice-cream van and into a three-bed semi

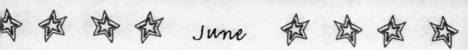

behind Homebase. Now there are only two O'Gradys to go. Mum is thinking of suggesting they all move in with Mr Whippy considering the spacious accommodation he has been given, but James pointed out that that would be like a mini criminal lair and would only encourage anti-social behaviour as they swapped tips on burgling.

Wednesday 14

Granny Clegg rang to update us on Bruce's progress. Apparently Grandpa Clegg is training him to fetch his socks for him. I do not envy Bruce. I have seen Grandpa Clegg's feet and I would not want anything that touched them near my mouth.

Thursday 15

Granny Clegg rang again. Today Bruce has only weed on the telly four times. Mum says Granny Clegg does not need to ring every day—a weekly update will be fine.

Friday 16

Granny Clegg rang again. But it was not about Bruce. It is because St Slaughter has a new dentist and he is black! He

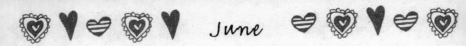
is called Mr Nuamah and has moved from Cardiff. Grandpa Clegg is going bonkers. He says he would not have written to his MP to complain about the lack of dental provision if this was what was going to happen. I pointed out that this was racist but Grandpa Clegg says he is not being racist, he is being practical. He would rather his teeth fall out than have them put under a voodoo spell. I said the Welsh were not renowned for their practising of dark magic but Grandpa Clegg says he once knew a woman from Abergavenny who could turn herself into a goat. There is no answer to that.

Suzy is doing snooker legend Steve Davis tonight. Thank God Mum has not noticed this addition to the TV schedules yet. It is because she snips the Channel 5 column out of the *Radio Times* so that no one is tempted to watch *Trisha* or *Columbo*.

Saturday 17

Went into town with James to buy Father's Day cards and presents (chocolate golf balls—me, a *Dr Who* poster—James). Bumped into Thin Kylie in the *Hello* magazine section of WHSmith. I said it must be awful not knowing where to send a Father's Day card. She said she knows exactly where he is—in the Chestnuts B&B with Les and Ying because Lisa from Tony's has thrown him out. He has been secretly ringing Kylie to get her to persuade Cherie to take him back, but apparently Cherie says she has moved

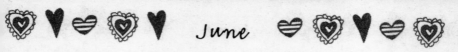
on and is pursuing more sophisticated men who do not have tattoos of Pamela Anderson on their bum. I hope she does not mean Dad. She will never wrest him from Mum's vice-like grip anyway.

Sunday 18
Father's Day

Dad is delighted with his presents. He has already eaten the chocolate golf balls (Mum was out taking Jesus for a walk, or they would have been rationed). He says he will take the poster to work though. Mum will never let him put it up in the house—not because of the subject matter but due to her ban on Blu-Tack and drawing pins. However, he has been outdone in the present stakes by Grandpa who got three (Dad, Jesus, and the dog. Uncle Jim did not send anything. He is still too busy finding himself up a mountain in Tibet with his wife Marigold (not her real name—she changed it from Felicity)).

Monday 19

It is Jack's first GCSE today. Bob and Suzy are very philosophical and have told him that if he fails he can always go to Braintree College and do a foundation course in Rock Music (avec Justin), but apparently Jack is determined to stay

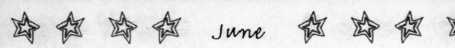
on for sixth form because you can't do politics at Braintree (ousted from the timetable in favour of hairdressing, and bricklaying for beginners). He is hoping to become the first ever person to simultaneously win the Mercury Prize and become Foreign Secretary.

Tuesday 20

Oh God, it is parents' evening tomorrow. Mr Wilmott gave a talk in assembly about how it is nothing to worry about and is all about constructive criticism and making sure everyone reaches their potential, however thick. (He didn't say thick, he said challenged. He means thick.) He is wrong. It is totally something to worry about. What if Mum finds out about the E in French and the internet translator? I am doomed. At least mock results have been delayed until next term. Mr Wilmott says there has been an administrative error but I bet Mrs Leech has mislaid them under a packet of Custard Creams again.

Wednesday 21

6 p.m.
Mum and Dad (his first ever) have gone to parents' evening. Oh, please let something miraculous happen so that Mum forgets to see Ms Hopwood-White.

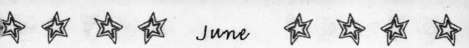

June

8 p.m.

My prayers were answered! Mum and Dad are back from parents' evening already, but are not speaking to each other. Dad has a black eye and Mum is lying down in the dark and no one will tell me what has happened. Will have to phone Scarlet. Suzy will know everything and has no inhibitions about blabbing.

9 p.m.

According to Suzy, Terry showed up to assert his parental responsibility for Thin Kylie (this is a joke—he is utterly irresponsible, he once let her ride around on the roof of the Cherokee with no restraints) so Cherie decided to assert her maternal responsibility and smacked him with her faux Chanel handbag. So Dad tried to calm them both down but Cherie said, 'See, that's what a real man does, Terry, he fights with his brains,' so Terry said, 'Well—can his brains outwit this?' and then thumped Dad (answer—no), so then Cherie got out her Clairol and hairsprayed Terry and Dad at which point Mr Wilmott arrived with Miss Vicar who wrestled both men to the floor at once. Mrs Leech had to be called to administer hot tea and Optrex to several bystanders who got caught in the giant cloud of Clairol. No wonder Mum is not speaking to Dad. It is totally Jeremy Kyle.

10 p.m.

Mum has just demanded to know why Suzy was signing autographs at parents' evening. I said it is because of

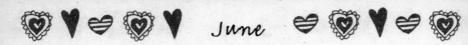
her attempts to overthrow evil Conservative MP Hugo Thorndyke. Mum said she doubted it. One of them was for Miss Vicar and she votes Socialist Worker. I do not want her to find out about *Sex with Suzy*. She may ban me from seeing Scarlet who is my only source of advice, black clothing, and croissants.

Thursday 22

Too late. Suzy is on the front page of the *Walden Chronicle*. It is under the headline 'Sex-crazed and Stoned—is Suzy giving Saffron Walden a bad name?'

The article says:

> Former lesbian and drug addict

(this is following Suzy's on-screen confession to a snog with her flatmate Carol in 1989 under the influence of three bottles of Mateus Rosé and her election confession to inhaling marijuana)

> is causing a stir in sedate Saffron Walden with her X-rated TV show in which celebrities literally bare all

(Suzy managed to get some man off *EastEnders* to reveal his unusual penis in last week's show.)

The paper has been inundated with literally nine complaints about the sordid series. Hugo Thorndyke MP says it is nothing less than he expected from his political adversary. 'This is typical of the Labour Party and just goes to show how right the electorate were to reject Mrs Stone and her manifesto for a sexual free-for-all.'

(Not strictly true—her manifesto was mostly about tax credits and free fruit in schools.)

Mrs Sylvia Thorndyke, chief of the Uttlesford Women's Institute and 4th (Baptist Church) Troop Brown Owl agrees. 'It is her children I feel sorry for. What hope for them turning out normal?' (Turn to page 14 for Sylvia's delicious recipe for macaroons.)

Scarlet says Suzy is not bothered. The *Guardian* has called her Channel 5's answer to Nigella with her 'heaving bosom and come hither eyes'. Suzy is doing Nigella later in the series so it will be an overdose of heaving bosoms and come hithering. Grandpa Riley will not be able to contain himself.

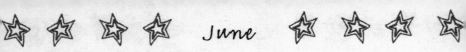
Friday 23

Mum is still annoyed about the Suzy thing. She is getting Dad to record tonight's episode (Lorraine Kelly) so that she can inspect it and decide whether to fire off complaint letters. James said the programme was actually quite informative so Mum asked how he had seen it and Grandpa Riley went very quiet. They are now shampooing the dog as punishment.

5.30 p.m.
Shampooing the dog has been banned. There is foam in every kitchen cranny. From now on he has to go to Dog About Town in Stansted.

Saturday 24

Dad accidentally recorded *News 24*. Mum is going to complain about that instead. They missed out an apostrophe from 'its' in the breaking news scrollbar.

Sunday 25

There is a black-dentist-related emergency in St Slaughter. Granny Clegg has a gippy wisdom tooth and says Hester's traditional remedy (gin) is not working. Mum has told her she has to make an appointment with

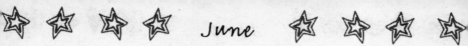

Mr Nuamah tomorrow morning. Granny Clegg says she will blame Mum if she comes back dead. Mum said she was willing to take that risk. Dad said we can only pray.

Monday 26

Granny Clegg has an appointment with Mr Nuamah at 10 tomorrow. Grandpa Clegg is going with her to protect her from hexes.

Tuesday 27

Granny Clegg has rung. Apparently Mr Nuamah has hands 'like the good Lord himself' and has 'miraculously' cured the gippy wisdom tooth (i.e given her a filling). Also he gave Bruce a sugar-free lollipop. She is a complete convert. Grandpa Clegg is livid.

It is the school ballet trip tomorrow. It is totally exciting as it is in London and we are allowed to go early and sightsee (i.e. go to the giant Topshop). I am going to buy a prom dress and fluorescent eyeshadow as seen on Lily Allen who I am absolutely like. Except that she has modelled for Chanel and has a renowned psychotic actor for a dad. Why, oh why, can't Keith Allen be my dad. The whole parents' evening/ Cherie fight would have had a very different outcome then. I bet Tuesday knows Lily. God, it is so unfair.

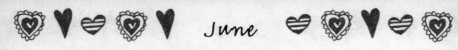

June

Wednesday 28

No prom dress or fluorescent eyeshadow. Ballet trip as follows:

3 p.m.
Bus driver 'Fat' Len Viceroy arrives at school in ancient coach, complete with utter lack of in-flight entertainment and overwhelming smell of sick.

3.05 p.m.
Year Ten boards coach.

3.10 p.m.
Year Ten unboards coach after sick discovered on back seat.

3.15 p.m.
Year Ten reboards coach.

3.20 p.m.
Year Ten unboards coach because there are twenty people too many.

3.25 p.m.
Ms Hopwood-White weeds out the Retards and Criminals trying to catch a lift to Harlow and Year Ten reboards coach.

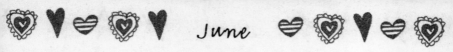

3.30 p.m.
Coach finally departs for London.

4.00 p.m.
Coach stops at services with suspicious rattle coming from luggage area. Mechanic called. Year Ten allowed to access motorway services.

5 p.m.
Mechanic arrives. Suspicious rattle identified as Dean 'the dwarf' Denley who has been stowed away against his will by Fat Kylie. Mrs Denley called to collect him.

5.15 p.m.
Mrs Denley arrives (surprisingly tall) and coach given the all-clear to proceed to London.

5.16 p.m.
Thin Kylie and Mark Lambert reported missing, last seen heading towards the Travelodge. Fat Kylie reported missing, last seen in arcade eating a Double Whopper and playing 'Resident Evil'.

5.40 p.m.
Thin Kylie and Mark Lambert located in Travelodge bedroom. Ms Hopwood-White agrees to pay for 'soiled sheets'. Fat Kylie located in Dunkin Donuts queue.

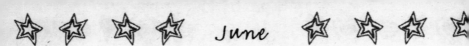

5.45 p.m.
Coach proceeds to London.

6.45 p.m.
Ms Hopwood-White points out to Len Viceroy that, as far as she remembers, St Albans is not a suburb of London.

7 p.m.
Curtain goes up on *Swan Lake*.

8.45 p.m.
Coach arrives at Sadler's Wells. Year Ten enters auditorium to general shushing and tutting noises.

9 p.m.
Davey MacDonald appears on stage in a tutu and swan helmet-type thing. Year Ten braces itself for Mark Lambert's reaction.

9.01 p.m.
Mark Lambert lives up to reputation and shouts, 'Oi, MacDonald, you bender, guess who's knobbing Thin Kylie now?'

9.02 p.m.
Davey MacDonald departs stage and storms up auditorium still in swan helmet and tutu.

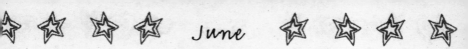
9.04 p.m.
Mark Lambert declared victor having knocked Davey MacDonald out with a pair of opera glasses.

9.15 p.m.
Year Ten told to leave auditorium and reboard coach.

9.20 p.m.
Coach departs Sadler's Wells for Saffron Walden.

12 midnight
Coach arrives in Saffron Walden following detours to Potters Bar and Royston.

12.05 a.m.
Len Viceroy treated for shock by Mrs Leech with her preferred method of Custard Creams.

Thursday 29

Mr Wilmott has given Year Ten a stern talking to. All future mind-expanding trips are under review, including Year Seven's annual Peterborough ice disco. Also Mark Lambert has been moved out of 10 Hopwood-White. He is going to Retards and Criminals next term to do macramé and times tables. It is a wonder he was not in there in the first place. Thin Kylie is devastated. She says she can't last the hour and

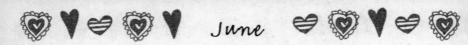

ten minutes between official breaks without groping him several times.

Friday 30

The A11 road sign has been replaced again. It now reads Historic Saffron Walden Twinned with Bad Wildungen, Chichicastenango and Hull. Mum is outraged. Not at the grammar, which even she has to admit is faultless, but that we have been twinned without her knowledge, and to somewhere renowned only for fish and John Prescott. She is ringing the council to complain.

I'm RACHEL RILEY
– welcome to my so-called life.

July

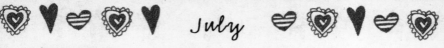

Saturday 1

England are out of the World Cup. James is jubilant. He bet Grandpa £3.10 and a Curly Wurly that this would happen. Grandpa has offered him double or quits on a Brit winning Wimbledon. He has no sporting sense. As Dad pointed out, there is more chance of Mum lifting the ban on Vimto. So Grandpa put £5 on that as well.

Sunday 2

Grandpa is another £5 down.

Monday 3

James came home from school with a Light Sabre. Mum asked him where he got it and he said he swapped it with Mad Harry for his Prince William doll. Mum is not amused. She says it will get out of hand. I do not know what the fuss is about. James got the better deal. Prince William can't sing any more, is naked, and only has one eye.

Tuesday 4

James has swapped his Lego hospital for a doll that wets itself and cries. It is called Baby Wants a WeeWee and

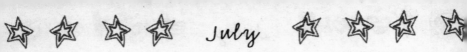

is utterly disturbing. I do not know why he needs a doll anyway—Baby Jesus performs all those functions and more.

Wednesday 5

All the British players are out of Wimbledon. As predicted. The fickle tabloids have turned on them already. When I am a journalist I will stand by my convictions and not be swayed by mob rule. James has offered Grandpa odds on Saffron Walden FC making it through to the third round of the FA Cup next year (no chance—their striker is Fat Len Viceroy) but Grandpa says he can't afford it. He has a long-standing bet on Baby Jesus's first word being 'Daddy'. Another guaranteed loser. It will be 'Fetch the J-cloth, Colin'—the most commonly heard phrase in this household.

Thursday 6

James has swapped Dad's *Swing Like Tiger* golf DVD for a pair of Barbie shoes (size 8). Mum is right. It is getting out of hand. Am going to ask for a lock on my bedroom door to protect my underwear and collection of tragic literature (i.e. *The Bell Jar* and *Fear and Loathing*).

5 p.m.
Mum has said she is not putting a lock on any door in the house as it encourages drug use and underage sex. I said

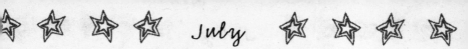
she was making a huge leap of imagination but she said, 'Look at Uncle Jim; Grandpa gave him a lock and now look where he is, up a mountain with someone who thinks fairies actually exist.' She has a point.

7 p.m.
Dad has asked where his *Swing Like Tiger* DVD is. He has a crucial game with Mr Wainwright on Saturday. Luckily for James the dog belched at that point, and Dad is now under the assumption that the dog has eaten it. I feel sorry for the dog. It has been sent to the shed under false pretences.

Friday 7

James has swapped his Barbie shoes for three tins of tomatoes (Sainsbury's peeled plum). I said he was underselling himself and what on earth did he want tomatoes for. He says it is striking the deal that is the reward itself. He needs help.

Also, Suzy is doing a Conservative Party MP (the short, shouty one) on her sex show tonight. Apparently his aides think it will improve his ratings as the housewives' choice. Or the perverts'. Suzy is fast becoming the most famous person in Saffron Walden. She is on *The One Show* next week. Marlon and the least famous McGann will be forced to move to Broxbourne if they want to retain their status.

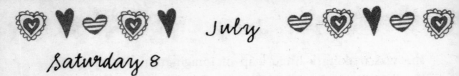
Saturday 8

The dog is missing. James took it for a walk round the block and claims it made a dash for a passing Renault Clio. This is not beyond the realms of imagination. The dog has an inexplicable hatred of French cars.

11 a.m.
The dog did not run away. James swapped it for a packet of Rolos. Mum found him binge eating caramel and made him confess all. Mum says it is a swap too far and has banned all future swapping. He has been despatched with Dad to Mad Harry's to retrieve the dog, via Mr Patel's (for Rolos).

1.15 p.m.
Dad, James, and the dog are back. Mrs Mad Harry could not get the dog out of the house fast enough. Dad said he bets Mum is regretting being so discipline-mad. She is desperate to get rid of the dog and a swap is an ideal solution. Then everyone went swapping mad. Grandpa Riley said he wished he could swap his cup of tea for a pint of stout. Mum said she would happily swap Grandpa Riley for a cup of tea. And Dad said there were times when he wished he could swap Mum for the newsreader from *BBC Breakfast*. Then Mum's lips went thin and she said she was going to practise her gear changes. Dad went a bit pale. I think he is worried she might swap him for Mike 'Wandering Hands' Majors.

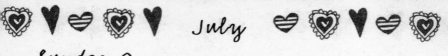

July

Sunday 9

Grandpa Clegg rang to report the outrage that Mr Nuamah has joined the Redruth Freemasons. Grandpa says he is trying to infiltrate normal society and then brainwash them with his weird ways. Dad answered and said there was nothing normal about a bunch of halfwitted Cornishmen sitting in darkened pub rooms doing tricksy handshakes and they should welcome someone who is *a*) educated to more than the 11-plus and *b*) does not think 'arr, it be' is an answer to anything. So Grandpa Clegg hung up. He does not like Dad because he does not come from 'the old country'.

Monday 10

Mark Lambert has been sent for an induction week with the Retards and Criminals. (They can't take him permanently yet due to overcrowding—it is all the O'Gradys). He says he prefers it down there. There is plasticine and Disney DVDs. I pointed out that this was not academically stretching and he should be thinking about his GCSEs which are only a year away, so he said he didn't need GCSEs to shave heads, and why didn't Aladdin have nipples when Tarzan does? I said I had no idea. But it is weird. Why doesn't he have nipples? I will ask James. He is bound to know.

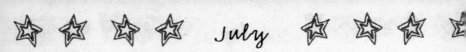

6 p.m.

Suzy has just used the word clitoris live on *The One Show*. Even the dog seemed shocked.

9 p.m.

James is still stumped on the nipple question. Google has failed to come up with the goods. He is writing to Disney.

Tuesday 11

Suzy is in the *Daily Mail* following her *The One Show* appearance but according to Scarlet all publicity is good publicity because Channel 5 have rung and are moving her show to prime time in the autumn, twice a week. She is thrilled. Although apparently Bob is not best pleased—he says Suzy's household management skills have gone out of the window now that she is a star (they were sketchy in the first place—I have witnessed her use a pair of pants to rinse round the bath—Mum would have spasms).

Wednesday 12

It is Mum's birthday tomorrow. Went into town with Scarlet, Trevor, and Sad Ed at lunchtime to get her a present. Got her *How Clean is Your House?* (answer—forensically clean). Then we went to Roadshow Records so that Scarlet and Trevor

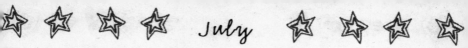
could browse tuneless goth music but Tuesday was in there talking to Dave. When she saw Sad Ed she grabbed Dave and snogged him energetically. So Sad Ed threw me against a giant cut out of Justin Timberlake and tried to snog me but luckily Justin fell over and dislodged the discount bucket and I managed to escape Sad Ed's clutches. What was he thinking of? And since when does he act on impulse? It takes him an hour to choose between black combats or other black combats. Actually I know what he was thinking and that was to win Tuesday back by apparent lack of interest. But I do not see why he has to involve me. Scarlet and Trevor did not see anything. They had headphones on and their eyes shut and were swaying gothlike to something called 'Death Monkey'. When they saw the scene of devastation before them they just said, 'Cool.' Year Ten is fraught with sexual tension and potential broken limbs. Unless you are a goth, clearly.

Thursday 13
Mum's birthday.

Mum says the book is the best present she has ever received. She has already found two new methods of getting red wine stains out of pale shagpile. Dad is annoyed. His M&S voucher and box of Black Magic have paled into insignificance. Even James's Badedas bath foam is looking shoddy and ill-thought-out by comparison. (And rightly so, he swapped it with Mad Harry for a jigsaw of Anne Boleyn, several pieces known to be inside dog.)

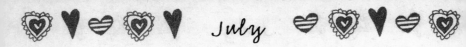

Sad Ed has apologized for the attempted snog. He says he was overcome with rage at confirmation of Tuesday's adulterous nature. I said that was no excuse for foisting himself on me. He said, 'Sorry I revolt you so much. Would you prefer it if I dyed my hair blond and minced some sheep for you.' I said yes. Although he has no chance of emulating Justin. You either have panther-like magnetism or you don't. Sad Ed does not.

Friday 14

It is sports day—annual ritual of humiliation for all concerned. Particularly Mr Wilmott last year when the Retards and Criminals stole the javelins and used them to try to spear the school sheep. Plus it is 100 degrees outside. It is utterly unfair to make us run around and perform sporting feats in heat like this. I bet even Paula Radcliffe is taking it easy with a bottle of diet Coke and *Hello!* Mentioned this to Miss Vicar and Miss Beadle but they said she can afford to lounge around with her bilaterals, whereas we look like the before bit on *Fat Camp.*

3 p.m.
As predicted, sports day was a total disaster. There were forty-seven casualties—forty heat exhaustion (including Scarlet and Trevor who insisted on doing the three-legged

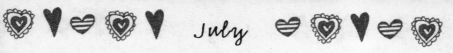

race in full gothwear), six shot-put-related concussions, and a Cox's Pippin lodged in the windpipe (apple bobbing for Mrs Duddy's lot). On the plus side I won the hurdles—all but one of the other competitors were busy being revived by Mrs Leech and her coolbox of Fanta at the time so I only had to beat Sarah Eccles, who has one leg shorter than the other.

Saturday 15
St Swithin's Day

Have prayed for rain to end this heatwave. Even the dog is refusing to go for a walk and is lying lethargically behind the shed with a strawberry Mivvi (panic purchased in bulk from Mr Patel by Treena). Am regretting resolution not to remain friends with Thin Kylie, i.e. the only person in Saffron Walden to own a swimming pool, apart from Lord Butler and his Leisure Centre.

    Mum has got her driving test date. It is on the 24th. She has been on the phone to Mike for half an hour. Dad is hovering near the door trying to listen in. I do not know what he thinks he will hear. They are only discussing emergency stops.

11.59 p.m.
No rain. So we are stuck with third-world-like conditions for forty days. Joy.

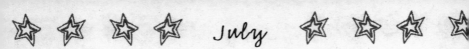

Sunday 16

11 a.m.
Can see Thin Kylie and Cherie lounging by the pool, eating Doritos. Asked Mum if we could get out James's paddling pool but she says it is out of use after she used it to get the creosote off the dog before he spontaneously combusted.

11.30 a.m.
Now Fat Kylie has arrived over the road and has commandeered the Doritos while Thin Kylie floats around on the giant inflatable breasts. Maybe Suzy will have a swimming pool installed now she is famous. It is a totally celebrity thing to do.

11.45 a.m.
Scarlet says Suzy has rejected the swimming pool idea on the grounds it would mess up her anti-nuclear weapon peace garden (i.e. some windchimes and a Buddha statue).

12 noon
Cannot take this torture any more. Am going over to Thin Kylie's in my Speedo on pretext of borrowing her maths homework (far-fetched, I know, but needs must) and hopefully Cherie will take pity on me and force me to take a refreshing swim.

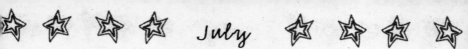
5 p.m.

Cherie did take pity on me but not as anticipated. She said, 'Jesus, look at the state of you, you look like Whitey Wilson.' (i.e. town albino.) 'Fetch the St Tropez, Kylie, it's an emergency.' And then before I could protest she had sprayed me with fake tan and was drying me off with her Nicky Clarke diffuser. And you can't come into contact with water for twenty-four hours so I couldn't swim, or even waft my foot under the garden sprinklers for fear of streaking. I just had to stand on the crazy paving with my arms out while the Kylies read out bits from *Chat*. On the plus side, I will be sporting a natural sunkissed shade of caramel tomorrow, according to the label on the bottle.

Monday 17

Oh God. Am not caramel. Am hideous unnatural shade of Dairy Milk, verging on the Bournville. Have scrubbed myself with a pumice but it has just added a reddish tinge. Dad is in hysterics. He asked me which shade of Cuprinol I had gone for—Dark Oak or Black Ash. Mum is less amused. Have begged her to keep me off school on grounds I may go down with some kind of allergic reaction to all the tanning chemicals but she has refused. James is backing her. He says it will teach me a lesson on the perils of vanity.

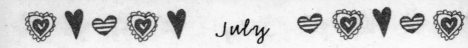
4 p.m.

Scarlet is refusing to let me stand with her and Trevor at break in the all-new goth corner (formerly maths geek corner). She says fake tan is the goth's worst nightmare. She says I can come back when I have faded to a more acceptable colour. I asked her for a rough guide and she said Waitrose toffee sauce. At this rate it will be next term before I am readmitted. To make matters worse, token Year Nine skinhead Paul Lefevre thought I was being racist and invited me to join the BNP.

Tuesday 18

Am still an alarming shade of mahogany. It is totally depressing. Bumped into Jack on the way to school. He said, 'Christ, Riley, what have you done this time? You do know you look like a wardrobe with a perm.' I said I was perfectly aware of the colour of my skin, that it was inflicted on me by a deranged madwoman and had he looked at his own hair lately because it was dangerously similar in style to Jennifer Aniston's. Then, for some reason, I started crying. Jack said, 'Shit. I didn't mean it. You look great, honest.' Which is the nicest thing Jack has said to me in a long time (even if it was only an emergency measure to staunch the flow of tears), which only made me cry even more. So Jack phoned up Scarlet on his mobile and made her come and get me. She says I can hover at the edges of goth corner at

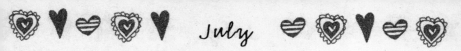

break, as long as I keep my cardigan on and pull my hair over my face a bit more.

Wednesday 19

Am now Walnut Whip on the Cuprinol scale.

Thursday 20

Still Walnutish but verging on the Antique Pine.

Friday 21

It is the last day of school. Which is always the same. Someone will set off the fire alarm, the staffroom will be festooned with silly string, and hordes of Year Elevens will hug each other dramatically and say, 'It is the end of an era' etc., etc. Which it is not. They will all be back in September for A levels and resits. Apart from the Retards and Criminals cohort, obviously, who are going straight to stack shelves at B&Q/community service. And Justin, who is going to Braintree to follow his dream. They are all having a lunchtime farewell 'rave' in the upper school canteen (i.e. Duncan Evans and his iPod dock). I will go and linger—it is my last chance to snog Justin before he falls for some arty

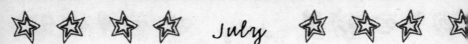

sixth form college type with piercings and ironic dungarees. If only I were more pale and tragic looking and less like a hairdresser.

3 p.m.

Oh my God. Justin is back with Sophie Microwave Muffins Jacobs. She let him feel her 34Bs behind the fire curtain in a fit of last-day-of-term adrenalin and nostalgia. I only know this because I was at the time behind said fire curtain with Sad Ed waiting for my chance to infiltrate proceedings. Sad Ed said it was the natural order of things and I should set my sights higher. There is no one higher than Justin. He is a supreme being. Also Kev Starr is now engaged to Lucy Davies and the staffroom is out of bounds due to excess funny foam. Mrs Leech is campaigning to ban Year Elevens from school after GCSEs. She says it causes nothing but heartbreak and maintenance issues. She was consoling Mr Vaughan at the time with a Cadbury's Highlight (Turkish Delight variety).

Saturday 22

This is typical. It is the first day of holidays, I have faded to an acceptable light ash on the Cuprinol chart, but it is now pouring with rain. I have a good mind to write to WHSmith and suggest they remove any mention of St Swithin from their diaries as it is confusing, weather-wise.

Am going to go round to Scarlet's—the goths welcome rain—it is further encouragement to stay inside in the gloom.

3 p.m.
Bob is right. Suzy has totally forsaken her household duties now that she is a celebrity sexpert. There were piles of dirty Jamie Oliver crockery stacked all over the indigenous Iroko wood worktops and even more sex manuals littering the carpet than usual. Plus the smell coming from the den, which I had attributed to drugs or strange incense, turned out to be one of Tony's or Gordon's poos.

Jack and Justin were eating Hula Hoops in the kitchen when I arrived (another sign of Suzy's neglect, pre-celebrity it would have been Kettle Chips or M&S mini bruschetta). Jack said was I all right because I looked a bit pale. I said his puerile jokes were beneath me. But it was actually quite amusing. In truth, Jack is a lot funnier than Justin. When I said to Justin that I was delighted that the path of true love had been restored and that he was back with Sophie (a lie, I was being poetic— or possibly ironic—I get confused), Justin said, 'Yeah, whatever.' Maybe he is regretting following his end of term urges! Or more likely he has no interest in speaking to me at all.

Watched *Raven* in the dark. Then Scarlet and Trevor said they wanted to snog so came home. I think I preferred Scarlet when she was single.

177

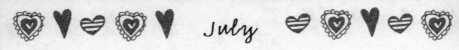

Sunday 23

Still raining. May revive my genius first novel if this inclement weather carries on. Although my kitten notebook (formerly whimsical, now menacing with eyes scratched out) is now dedicated to my journalistic career so would have to buy a new one. Which would mean going out in the rain. It is a wonder we get anything done in this country at all. It is so wet and inhospitable. Although these are ideal conditions for tortured literary works. Look at the Brontës stuck in the Peaks with endless drizzle. It is a total Catch 22.

It is Mum's driving test tomorrow. She is getting an early night (7.45—a new record) to prepare. There is no possible way she can fail. Dad tested her on her Highway Code and she got every question right. Then she tested Dad and he only got four out of ten. Mum says she is signing him up for refresher lessons with Mike. Dad says he would rather chew tinfoil than spend any time with Mr Wandering Hands, but his resistance is futile. Once Mum has made her mind up about something there is no swaying her. Like when she decided Dad had to stop wearing shorts.

Monday 24

Mum has failed her driving test. She says it is down to mini-roundabout madness in Bishop's Stortford. Apparently they have sneakily installed a badly-signposted gyratory system

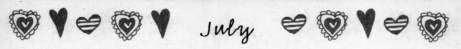
near the Hockley Road, confusing Mum, who ended up circling the sofa shop for ten minutes before the examiner took over and drove them to freedom. She is writing to the council to complain. Dad is not pleased. It means she is back behind the wheel of Mike's Fiesta and back within his Casanova-like clutches for another month. But on the plus side, his refresher lessons are off the agenda while he pays for her to actually pass in the first place.

Tuesday 25

According to Tracey Hughes (who told Mark Lambert who told Thin Kylie who told Cherie who told Mum outside Gayhomes), Stacey O'Grady tried to rob Barclays with a pump-action water pistol and is facing a six-month prison sentence. He has blamed boredom for his criminal tendencies. I know how he feels. Saffron Walden in the holidays is torturous. Mum is over the moon though—it is one O'Grady down, one to go in the housing stakes. She has totally forgotten about failing her driving test.

Wednesday 26

Asked Mum if we were going away anywhere this holiday. She said she and Dad were taking James to Granny Clegg's for a fortnight at the end of August. I said what about me, and

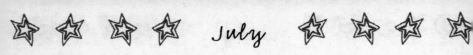

she said there was no room, that I had spent all last summer there (yes, but in enforced exile) and that anyway she needed me to supervise her cleaning schedule, given Grandpa and Treena's spillage tendencies. It is utterly unfair. Not that I want to share a Fray Bentos-smelling bed with James or spend two weeks listening to Grandpa Clegg's borderline racist rantings but even so, it shows that I am the outcast of the family. It is totally like *Cinderella* (the Hilary Duff version).

Thursday 27

Rain has stopped. So have put off novel in favour of wandering aimlessly around town with Sad Ed and Scarlet.

5 p.m.
Scarlet thinks I should have a birthday party. Fifteen is almost coming of age after all. I suggested an ironic tea and fairy cake party (totally vintage and very vogue, according to *Vogue*) but Scarlet said the irony will be lost on most of the guests and they will just think I am a prat, plus there is no way she is wearing a floaty lacy dress and a hat. Sad Ed agreed—on the hat grounds. Am going to ask Mum later. Will say I am treating it as a test of responsibility and promise to clean up all post-party stains.

6 p.m.
Mum has agreed to a party, but has imposed a fifteen-person headcount limit (following *Supernanny*'s one guest

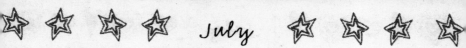

for every year rule—normally only applicable to under-eights), banned all food products, and is only allowing pale drinks i.e. water or lemonade. Did not argue as it is a wonder she has agreed to anything at all. Am going to do guest list later. With a strict no Retards or Criminals door policy.

8 p.m.

Guest list is harder than I thought.

- Me, Scarlet, and Sad Ed, obviously.
- Trevor, because Scarlet will not come unless he comes.
- A bat friend for Trevor because he will not come unless he has another goth to commune with when Scarlet is in the loo.
- Jack.
- Justin (Am not inviting Sophie, obviously. Once he has seen me and my vintage and edgy party he will realize that I am his destiny, despite me still being an A cup.) Then realized have no other actual friends. So guest list is seven, including me.
- Maybe will invite Thin Kylie. After all, she did invite me to her party.
- And I suppose I had better invite Mark Lambert to keep her occupied.
- And Fat Kylie.
- Could invite Oona Rickets—every party needs a gay person there to start the dancing—it is a well-known fact.

So just need four more people. Will ask Scarlet tomorrow.

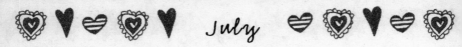

Friday 28

2 p.m.

Scarlet says I absolutely have to invite Sophie Microwave Muffins or Justin won't come. Which makes twelve. And that Sophie won't come without Pippa. So that is thirteen. But I still need two more. Why am I so utterly friendless? Maybe it is because I am a tragic loner. Like Lord Byron.

4 p.m.

Or mad Miss Crawley who has a moustache and seven cats. Oh God.

5 p.m.

Have decided to invite Ali Hassan and his maths geek friends. At least they will keep the numbers up. And are unlikely to cause any stain- or sex-related issues.

Saturday 29

10 a.m.

Have posted invites (James got all the addresses off some stalker's website). So now will wait for my RSVPs.

10.15 a.m.

Forgot to put RSVP on invite. So am reduced to hoping for the best. Only three days to go. It is quite fraught having a

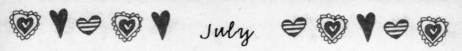
party. There are so many things to worry about. Particularly when the venue is owned by someone with borderline OCD cleaning issues.

Sunday 30

Have begged Mum and Dad to go out during the party. Dad has suggested the golf club but Mum is insisting on being within a twenty-five metre radius so they are going to Clive and Marjory's. Mum says that way she can measure decibel levels and be home in eleven seconds (tested) in a spillage emergency. It is better than nothing. James is going to Mad Harry's for a sleepover. They are going to build a robot alligator. So I will just have the dog, Grandpa, and Treena and Baby Jesus to worry about. Please God do not let Grandpa try to dance. Also am going to hide Treena's leggings. Do not want anyone witnessing her in those. And will ask her not to say 'bag of shite' or 'piffy on a rock bun' (no idea) or any other weird Northern things.

Monday 31

Only a day to go. Went round Scarlet's to get in the mood. They are getting a new cleaner now that Suzy is too busy investigating celebrity sex issues. I said that wasn't very

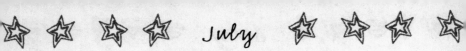

left-wing and I hope she wasn't an illegal and repressed Filipina. Scarlet said *au contraire* it is very New Labour to keep the proletariat in work and she is not a Filipina but is called Edna and is sixty-seven. So I said that was all right then.

I'm RACHEL RILEY
- welcome to my so-called life.

August

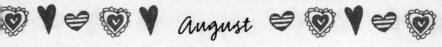

Tuesday 1

8 a.m. (9.5 hours to go to party)
Presents received:
- flip-flops (not £15 black Havaianas from Topshop as requested but £2.99 red ones from discount shop so obviously will not be wearing them).
- 'Now That's What I Call Music' something like 579 featuring utter chart pap so obviously will not be listening to it.
- Lifetime membership of Mole Hall Wildlife Park (which still has out of bounds flamingos and no man-eating animals, so obviously will not be visiting it).
- A jelly bean dispenser, beans already consumed by James, so cannot use it even if wanted to.

But will get more relevant and thoughtful presents at party later, for which now only have nine hours to prepare—i.e. choose outfit, music, experiment with mood lighting, purchase lemonade etc. Must get started immediately. Will call Sad Ed for reinforcements.

8.15 a.m.
Sad Ed not thrilled at being woken. He says he will be over at a normal hour (i.e. this afternoon) and has forbidden me to do CDs until then as he says my taste in music is questionable and I cannot be trusted not to throw in some Bee Gees. (Who are utterly retro and

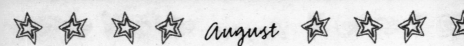
therefore cool. He just doesn't like them because they have big hair.)

8.30 a.m.
Have chosen outfit. Am going to wear leggings and stripy T-shirt in manner of continental-style supermodel. Also have blacked out most of flip-flops with marker pen. Will look utterly excellent and mature i.e. fifteen. Only nine hours to go.

1.30 p.m.
Have done playlist with Sad Ed. He has vetoed the Bee Gees (hair) and Corinne Bailey Rae (hair and annoying serenity) and instead has made me a special Ed Party Mix CD to play. He says it is guaranteed to get people in the mood. Yes but for what? Suicide?

1.45 p.m.
Have run out of things to organize. Will have a power nap to prepare me for the excesses of the evening.

5 p.m.
Oh God, have slept for five hours. Have only two and a half hours to have bath, remove excess body hair, control absurd Leo Sayer-style hairdo and usher family out of house.

7.15 p.m.
Done. Mum and Dad have been banished to Clive and Marjory's. James is experimenting with batteries and kitchen

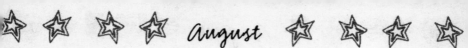

implements at Mad Harry's. The dog is in the shed with the radio (Radio 4—it likes *The Archers*). Baby Jesus is asleep. Grandpa and Treena are upstairs conjugating. Sad Ed's special party mix is on the hi-fi (currently playing something about stabbing yourself with a fork—thank God it will be over before anyone arrives) and there are fifteen paper cups laid out on the table amid an array of Perrier, Evian, and Waitrose Lemonade (cloudy, but nonstaining—Mum did a patch test). Now just need guests.

7.30 p.m.
Oooh, doorbell. This must be everyone.

7.31 p.m.
Was Cherie asking if Dad could unblock her pipes. Hope it is not euphemism. Sent her round to Clive and Marjory's.

7.45 p.m.
Where is everybody? They are now fifteen minutes late. Which is fashionable. But annoying.

7.50 p.m.
Oooh, doorbell again.

7.51 p.m.
Was Sad Ed.

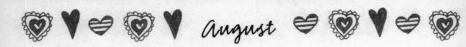

8.05 p.m.

And Scarlet and Trevor. So far not really a party. We are just watching *Holby City* and drinking fizzy water.

8.15 p.m.

Doorbell. Can see Mark Lambert, Thin Kylie, Ali Hassan, and at least twenty other people in the drive. Well, just a few more won't hurt. It will all be civilized. After all, there is no Bacardi in the house. What could possibly go wrong?

Wednesday 2

Am grounded for ever. On the following grounds:

- Headcount exceeded fifteen. (Actually thirty-eight. The Kylies rounded up everyone at Barry Island including Darryl Stamp and some other O'Gradys.)
- There is Bacardi Breezer vomit in the dining room (belonging to Ali Hassan and several maths geeks). Thin Kylie smuggled twenty bottles in inside Fat Kylie's smock top and told them it was Britvic.
- There are stiletto holes in the hallway parquet due to Fat Kylie's weight/heel ratio.
- The dog has had a 'go faster' stripe shaved down its back (Fat Kylie using Treena's Ladyshave—lucky she did not use Mum's epilator or the dog would not have been so compliant).

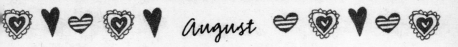

- Baby Jesus is fractious after the Kylies insisted on waking him and sticking him up their T-shirts so they could see what it felt like to be pregnant.
- All Mum's Duchy Original biscuits have gone missing (Mark Lambert claimed he had 'got the munchies' after smoking a menthol cigarette).

It is lucky Mum got back when she did (summoned by the insane revving of one of the O'Grady's Datsuns) or there would have been a serious stain-related incident with Treena's Ice Magic chocolate mint sauce. It took me and Jack until midnight to clear up the debris, no one else passed Mum's sobriety test (or dared take it—Thin Kylie disappeared taking her chav minions with her at the first sight of the Cillit Bang). Not even Sad Ed who had only drunk Shloer. It is because he is notoriously clumsy— Mum has not let him near anything breakable since he fell onto her glass-topped coffee table at the age of nine. Grandpa and Treena are in trouble as well for failing to oversee events properly. They had locked themselves in their room with the telly and four bottles of Kylie's Bacardi.

Plus did not get to snog anyone unless you count fending off Kyle with James's light sabre. Justin was too busy with his tongue in Sophie Jacobs's ear (gross) to notice me. And have indelible black flip-flop marks on feet.

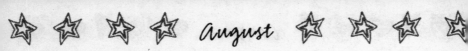

Thursday 3

Oh God, am bored. Am not even allowed round Scarlet's to mope about there. It is so unfair. It is not my fault I got gatecrashed by malign forces. Mum says I should use the time wisely to reflect on my irresponsibility. She has banished me to my bedroom with *Vanity Fair* (the book, not the glamorous magazine, chance would be a fine thing), which we are doing for GCSE English next term. She says no doubt I will relate to it in some misguided tragic way. What can she mean?

Friday 4

8 a.m.
Will read all day.

10 p.m.
Still reading.

Saturday 5

10 a.m.
Still reading.

11 p.m.
Have finished. Mum is right—I am TOTALLY Becky

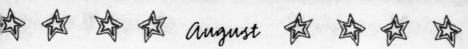

Sharp i.e. I am downtrodden and socially inferior but my superior brain skills (i.e. general literariness), wit and guile will help me rise above my lowly birth. Scarlet is clearly Amelia. Which would make Jack her brother Joseph, whom I am destined to marry then kill, but inherit his fortune, following ill-advised liaisons with all manner of random men. Interesting. I wonder who Justin is. Possibly the devastatingly handsome Captain George, who dies horribly.

Sunday 6

Mum is in an exceptionally good mood. It is thanks to the *Sunday Times*, which has informed her that the government has brought in a new law whereby rogue minibikes can be seized and crushed immediately. She says it is another vital blow against Saffron Walden's scourge of anti-social youths (aka Mark Lambert and the O'Gradys). Took advantage of her momentary joy to ask her if I could go round to Sad Ed's as I was possibly getting Vitamin D deficiency due to being locked up all day. She got me a chewable Sanatogen and sent me back upstairs.

Monday 7

Oh God, the interminable holidays stretch out before

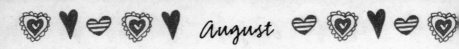

me like an interminable stretchy thing. I don't even have anything to read. I have to get ungrounded. I am fifteen and should be out getting mugged at Camden Market, not alphabetizing my *Famous Fives*. Am going to plead with Mum again.

11 a.m.
Told Mum if she didn't let me out to go to the library or WHSmith I would die from lack of literary stimulation. She gave me three Maeve Binchys. May well phone Childline. Even Nelson Mandela got the *Economist*.

Tuesday 8

Scarlet rang. She and Trevor have caught colds from lying on gravestones at St Regina's at midnight trying to commune with the netherworld. Plus Trevor has been bitten by Elspeth the church cat and has had to have a tetanus jab. God, it sounds so exciting. What I would give to lie on a gravestone or get attacked by Elspeth.

5 p.m.
Mark Lambert's minibike has been seized and crushed. *Quelle surprise*. Although, according to James, who witnessed the proceedings in Waitrose car park, it was Mr Hosepipe who was riding at the time.

Wednesday 9

Rang Scarlet to see if she has any more graveyard injuries or animal wounds (she doesn't—they have decided to give St Regina's church a wide berth since they found out that Fat Kylie and Mr Whippy have been shagging on George Henry Cummings (1898–1957)).

Thursday 10

11 a.m.
Oh my God, have to get ungrounded as a matter of emergency. Scarlet rang. Suzy's producer at Channel 5 owns a huge house near Padstow but he is in Majorca filming *Celebrity Monkey Tennis* (no idea) with Carol Vorderman and is letting the Stones have it for two weeks starting Saturday and I am invited. Everyone is going— including Trevor and Sad Ed and Justin (and Sophie Microwave Muffins, annoyingly). Scarlet says to tell my mum it will be educational and supervised by responsible adults (aka Bob and Suzy).

5 p.m.
Mum says under no circumstances is she letting me loose in North Cornwall (renowned for underage beach sex) with the Stones as my guardians. She says I can come to the Cleggs' and sleep on a lilo on the landing (Mum and Dad are in the spare room, James is on the sofa). I said no

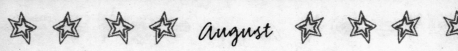
thanks I would rather stay with Grandpa and Treena and Baby Jesus but she says she is putting Marjory in charge of her cleaning utensils and I am going to St Slaughter like it or not as I have proved myself untrustworthy and incapable of basic mess prevention. It is hopeless. I am doomed.

9 p.m.

Have had an epiphany during *Neighbours*. Becky Sharp would not be lying on her M&S duvet whingeing that she was hard done by, she would be doing something sneaky and excellent to get her own way. So am going to be model child and totally transform Mum's image of me as spill-prone vandal in twenty-four hours.

Friday 11

10 a.m.

Mum and James have gone out to shop for things we will not be able to buy in St Slaughter (i.e. everything except tinned vegetables, giant sanitary towels, and pasties) so have checked all food cupboards for out of date produce (findings: some weird-looking chocolate, owner unknown, no date but have thrown out anyway due to its greasy consistency and Mum's fear of processed sugars), brushed the dog (much to its annoyance, it was trying to get inside the airing cupboard at the time), arranged the cleaning products by height and colour, and watered the mung beans, so that when she gets

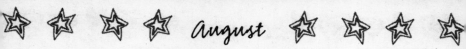

back she will say, 'Oh, but Rachel, I am utterly wrong, you are indeed a responsible young adult and of course you may go to Cornwall with Scarlet etc.' Or something like that.

11.30 a.m.

Mum is back. She did not say, 'Oh, but Rachel, I am utterly wrong, you are indeed a responsible young adult and of course you may go to Cornwall with Scarlet etc.' In fact her words were, 'Where is the Chocolax? James is all bunged up and I do not want to be stopping at Taunton Deane for a poo emergency like last year. Honestly, Rachel, I go out for five minutes [actually two hours] and when I get back the cupboards are all willy nilly, the mung beans are drowning and the Cillit Bang has been moved without permission. This is exactly why you are coming to Granny Clegg's. Now fetch the Dustbuster before we all choke on dog hair.' Then, as if on cue, the dog had an accident on the kitchen floor. It must have retrieved the Chocolax from the bin when I was watering the mung beans. It is hopeless. Even Becky Sharp would have a hard time against Mum. Am going to spend two weeks of perpetual misery with backward relatives eating Viennetta. Plus Dad is making us get up at four in the morning to miss the traffic.

Saturday 12

7 a.m.

Am miserable already. Have spent three hours in close confinement with James and the dog. (Amazingly, we are

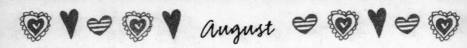

bringing it with us. Mum says she will sleep more soundly knowing it cannot in any way eat, dismantle, or vomit on any part of the house while we are gone. It is lucky we left at 4 otherwise Grandpa might have protested. As it is he is going to get a shock when he wakes up.) Plus Mum has ignored pleas (including Dad's) to stop at the drive-through McDonald's on the M5 so we are now eating Marmite sandwiches and Fruesli bars at a so-called beauty spot on Dartmoor (i.e. some gorse, a mangy sheep and several other overloaded estate cars). This is not a good start to the holiday.

10 a.m.

We are in St Slaughter after six hours and seven wee stops (three for James, four for the dog), and a near collision on the A30 at Polyphant (the dog tried to climb into the driver's seat to get a better view of a Jack Russell in the BMW in front). Granny Clegg is delighted at 'Valerie's' arrival. She is making a bed for it next to the telly. (It gets better accommodation than we do. I am outside the bathroom door under several pictures of Great-Granny Clegg, who looks like notorious serial killer Fred West. I will have nightmares.) Bruce and the dog are less pleased. The dog is trying to assert its authority by sitting on the coffee table but Bruce has topped it by perching in the serving hatch, guarding the kitchen from all who dare enter.

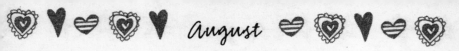

11.30 a.m.

Grandpa Riley has rung to report that the dog is mysteriously missing. He says he has done a sweep of the house in case it accidentally locked itself in a cupboard but has now resorted to calling the police. Mum said did he not see the note? Grandpa said which one? (There are notes and instructions on every available surface including one on the freezer saying 'This is the freezer'.) Mum said the one on the dog food, which he would have seen if he had bothered to try to feed the dog. Grandpa says he got distracted by *CBeebies* and forgot until half an hour ago. Then he read the note and said it is dognapping and he could sue. Mum said, 'Try me.' So Grandpa hung up. He will not try. Even he knows better than that.

1 p.m.

Lunch. Mum offered to heat up a Waitrose quiche but Grandpa Clegg said quiche is for 'poofs and foreigners' and anyway Granny Clegg had done something special. It was not special. It was Brain's faggots. Do people actually eat this stuff out of choice? The dog seemed to like it though. It had two helpings and a Mr Kipling French Fancy (how this passed the 'poofs and foreigners' test, I do not know. Or the faggots for that matter.) I may well go vegetarian. Then at least I would only have to suffer claggy Smash.

3 p.m.

A family has arrived at Seaview Cottage (aka Hester's battery chicken shed, actually eleven miles from the sea and

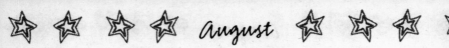

with a view of a silage bin). Sadly they are not from Fulham, nor do they have any potentially fanciable teenage children. They drive a Renault Espace (purchased from Clive Studley Premium Motors, Solihull) and have identical triplets who were fighting with flashing, winged Barbies in the back seat. James is going over tomorrow to see if they want to swap one.

5 p.m.
Tea. Spam and boiled potatoes (tinned). Ate potatoes. Will be non-Government-approved size 0 by end of summer, and not through choice.

Sunday 13

10 a.m.
James has gone to Seaview Cottage to try to procure a Barbie. I do not know what he is swapping though as his *Lord of the Rings* doll collection and sticker album are still here.

11 a.m.
James has returned without a Barbie but with a Puppy in My Pocket and the information that the triplets are ten and called Parker, Presley, and Peyton (i.e. pseudo-American and on Mum's absolute proscribed list); that Parker is allergic to fishpaste; and that Presley once got electrocuted

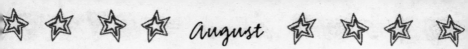

when she weed on a Flymo. He is like Granny Clegg in his ability to wheedle information out of complete strangers. James says he is in love. I said with which one. And he said he wasn't fussy, they all looked the same, so what did it matter.

12 noon
Granny Clegg has asked where her electric can opener is. I have my suspicions.

1 p.m.
Am going vegetarian. Lunch was Chilli Con Carne (tinned) with Alphabetti Spaghetti. Will tell Mum before dinner.

4 p.m.
Told Mum that I was becoming a vegetarian. She said, 'Don't be ridiculous, you will become anaemic and fail your GCSEs.' I said it was a matter of principle (i.e. I refuse to eat Granny Clegg's food as it is vile) and she should respect my wishes. She said, 'On your head be it,' but I can tell she is planning to force-feed me goulash when we get back to civilization. If I was in Padstow Suzy would be congratulating me on my forthright stance against animal cruelty. Grandpa Clegg said, 'She'll be shaving her head and piercing her backside next.' I said, *au contraire*, vegetarianism was no longer the province of the lesbian community, and that, as everyone knows, meat is murder. James said, actually it isn't murder, as defined by the *Oxford English Dictionary* online

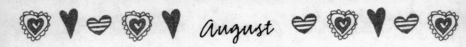

version, and anyway, it is all quite humane with an electric shock probe thingy and it only hurts if the probe slips and only gets half the brain, and then the cows stagger about mentally for a bit. Which made me feel ill and has only fortified my beliefs.

5 p.m.
Tea. Reminded Granny I was now a vegetarian and she said, 'This is tongue.' I said tongue was in fact meat. She said, 'Norman, did you know that? Tongue is meat.' He said, 'No it's not, it's tongue.' I ate carrots (tinned) and strawberries (tinned) with condensed milk (tinned and utterly banned in our house so actually a rare treat). Dad looked like he might join me in my vegetarian stance. He struggled with every mouthful.

Monday 14

Went to Museum of Mines. Looked at bits of tin and ancient pasty remnants. Came home. When we got back Parker was on the doorstep with Granny's electric can opener. She says her mum says it is not an electric wand and it has congealed stuff on it and could she have her Puppy in My Pocket back. Mum has sent James to his room to reflect on his swapping problems. James says no punishment can keep him down, he cares only about the triplets and will do anything to secure their love.

Ate mushy peas for tea. Vegetarianism isn't as nutritionally fulfilling as I thought.

Tuesday 15

Went to Spar with Granny Clegg to do her weekly shop (four Fray Bentos, a Viennetta, sixteen Andrex, a packet of Heinz potato waffles and the *St Slaughter Reporter*). Maureen tried to get Granny to buy some olives and a tin of capers (specially imported 'from up country' for the hordes of tourists St Slaughter is confidently expecting now that Hester has got the ball rolling) but Granny said she would sooner eat rabbit droppings. Maureen agreed. Then they started on what lovely hair Mr Nuamah the dentist had so I went outside. James and the triplets were on a bench. He was letting them kiss him in turn. Even my brother is more successful, snog-wise, than me and he is only nine.

Got home and informed Dad that James was groping the triplets on the High Street. Dad said, 'Lucky him, triplets, eh.' But Mum said, 'Go and fetch him, Colin, before he picks up anything.' She doesn't mean disease, she means a Birmingham accent.

Wednesday 16

9 a.m.
Finally we are going to do something interesting i.e. go to the beach, i.e. I will be able to swim and dive off rocks and will be utterly like Gwyneth Paltrow in *The Talented*

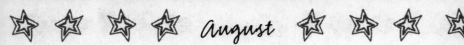
Mr Ripley. We are leaving the dog and Bruce at home. Mum has warned Granny Clegg that this is asking for trouble but Granny Clegg says they are warming to each other. I do not think so, I saw the dog wee on Bruce's bowl last night.

5 p.m.

Was not like *Talented Mr Ripley* at all. For a start Gwyneth did not have Grandpa Clegg and his 'beachwear' (i.e. a vest and suit trousers) to contend with. Plus James went AWOL and was discovered skinny dipping in a rock pool with Parker. Luckily it was me and Granny Clegg who found him. Granny shouted, 'Put your trunks on, no one here wants to see your widgie,' thus adding to my utter shame and embarrassment.

When we got back the dog and Bruce had eaten my lilo. So am now sleeping on the carpet. It is all too depressing for words.

Thursday 17

9 a.m.

Am going to the community playground (still disused but the only point in St Slaughter to receive mobile phone signals) to call Scarlet and Sad Ed. Hopefully they will be having an equally pants time and we can commiserate together about the crapness of Cornwall.

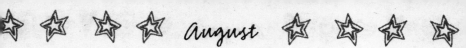
11 a.m.

Aaagh. They are not having a pants time. They are having an excellent time involving an outdoor pool, croquet, and barbecues. The only downside is that Justin is not there. He got a better offer—he is in Florida with Mr and Mrs Microwave Muffins.

This is typical. I am stuck in Hicksville, Arizona with an oversexed nine year old and not one but two mental and vomiting dogs, plus I am getting no sleep due to the itchy carpet and Grandpa Clegg's weak bladder. I cannot take it any more. Am going to have to run away to Padstow. I will become a missing person and Mum and Dad will be utterly sorry they ever grounded me and made me suffer Granny Clegg's 'cooking'.

4 p.m.

Have checked the bus timetable. There is one bus a day to Bodmin, at 7.30 a.m. It gets in at 11 (which seems quite a long time for twenty miles). Have rung Scarlet and told her my plans. She says it is totally excellent and rebellious and is getting Bob to pick me up from the bus station in the Volvo.

Friday 18

6 a.m.

Have packed my essentials (i.e. bikini, hair products, copy of *Vanity Fair*) and have written a note for Mum. It says:

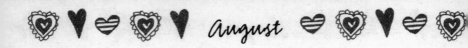
By the time you read this I will be gone. Please do not be sad or angry. I am in a better place.

I intend to stay with Suzy and Bob, who can better cater to my new vegetarian stance, plus they will not make me sleep on the landing.

PS can you pick me up on the way home? According to Scarlet it is the big white house with the statue in the front garden, a hundred yards down from the sign saying 'Trespassers will be persecuted'. Tell Mum this is not a spelling mistake.

See you there. You cannot miss it. It has huge gates and a sign saying 'Heaven'.

7.30 a.m.

Everyone was still asleep when I got up so I packed emergency rations (pink wafers) and pinned the note to the dog's collar. Am now on bus. Unfortunately so is Maureen Penrice from Spar. She is sitting next to me.

8 a.m.

Have moved seats. Cannot listen to any more stories about her trigger-happy son Damian. (He is in the army, not just a random mentalist.)

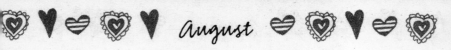

9 a.m.

Now I know why the bus takes so long. We are stopping at every village, hamlet, and pig shed on the way to pick up indigenous people and their pets. I imagine this is what it is like in Chichicastenango, but with goats instead of bull terriers.

10 a.m.

Am surprised that Mum has not rung my mobile in panic. It is clear that they absolutely do not care about me.

11.10 a.m.

Ah, civilization (well, Bodmin) at last. I can see Scarlet, who is in goth beach wear, i.e. a black lace vest and floor length skirt, and Jack, who is in normal beach wear i.e. a Meteors T-shirt and shorts. Sad Ed must still be asleep. Feel a bit sick. It must be the joy at being reunited with interesting and literary people.

5 p.m.

Have just spent glorious day by the pool rereading *Vanity Fair* and eating an exotic fruit platter. This is utterly what life should be like. Suzy says I should ring Mum and Dad but I said I had left a fully explanatory note and that they had my mobile number if they needed to call. Which they haven't so obviously they are not concerned at all at my disappearance.

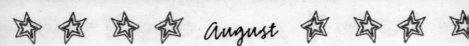

6 p.m.

Oh my God. Have just watched *West Country Today* (i.e. crap local news) and I am the top story! According to the reporter I am missing, presumed dead, and there is a countywide search going on for a body. Then they interviewed Granny Clegg (Mum and Dad clearly too distraught to speak) and she said that I had been showing worrying signs like going off my food and reading dark matter (she means *The Bell Jar*) and then she held up what she claimed was a suicide note. I do not understand. How can this have happened? Why didn't anyone ring me? Worst of all why did they use a photo of me taken last summer by Granny Clegg i.e. with an eight-year-old boy/lesbian haircut?

6.03 p.m.

Have checked mobile. The battery is dead! Aaagh. Bob is calling the police now to confirm that in fact I am alive and well and eating mangos in a luxury holiday villa. Sad Ed says at least it shows my parents care about me. I said it did not show that, it showed they are utterly mental.

6.15 p.m.

Have spoken to Dad (Mum too angry to speak). I said I had made it perfectly clear where I was and what was all the hoo-ha about the suicide note. Dad said all they had found was a chewed bit of paper (cursed dog) that said:

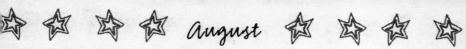

*By the time you read this I will be gone. Please
do not be sad or angry. I am in a better place
. . . See you there. You cannot miss it. It has
huge gates and a sign saying 'Heaven'.*

Which I can see might be misleading. Dad says he is
coming to get me in two hours. I pleaded with him not
to take me back to St Slaughter but he says he is under
strict instructions from Mum and he is not going to take
his chances against her. But Dad says on the plus side Mum
and Auntie Joyless are on speaking terms again, now that
they have runaway children in common. I have nothing in
common with Boaz. He reads the Bible and wears beige.

9 p.m.
Am still at the villa! Oh joy! It is all thanks to Suzy and her
persuasive ways. When Dad arrived Suzy said had he and
Mum thought what effect a return to St Slaughter might
have on me? Dad said Mum had considered it but had
decided that a ban on fake suicide should do the trick. Suzy
says this was retrogressive something or other and that if he
did drag me back to the Cleggs', it would only aggravate my
misery and drive me to run away again, or worse! I think it
was the 'worse' that got him, or perhaps the fact that Suzy
was wearing an underwired bikini top and sarong at the time,

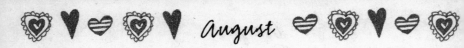

because then he agreed that conditions at the Cleggs' were not ideal (this is an understatement) and that maybe it was best that I did stay with the Stones. Thank God Mum didn't come with him. There is no way Suzy's bare midriff would have won her over. I bet Dad wishes he could stay here too.

Excellent. I have won my freedom and can enjoy an actual bed, an inside toilet, and conversations that don't revolve around Terry Wogan for the next few days.

10 p.m.
Dad rang. Mum is not best pleased but has agreed on the condition that I use the time to reflect on my behaviour. I said absolutely. They are collecting me at 10 o'clock next Saturday night, to avoid the traffic on the A30.

Saturday 19

The *Cornish Times* have rung. They want to interview me now that I am 'back from the dead'. I said I was not back from the dead, that I had been sunbathing the whole time and had only left St Slaughter to get away from my embarrassing family. Then they asked if it was true that I was staying with TV sexpert Suzy Stone. I said yes. So they asked if they could interview her instead. I put her on the line. This is typical. My possible tragic and untimely death is being eclipsed by best friend's mother and her vibrator collection.

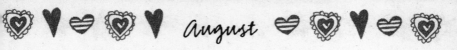

august

Jack asked if I wanted to go down to the beach to escape the media frenzy. I said yes. We will have a beach party and barbecue Linda McCartney sausages and drink and Sad Ed can play his guitar.

4 p.m.

Did not have a beach party. Scarlet and Trevor refused to come in case they accidentally got a tan and Sad Ed was helping Suzy answer fan mail and problem letters (now that he is a Year Ten sex guru he thinks he is fully qualified to dole out advice on penile dysfunction). So it was just me and Jack in the sand dunes. Which was actually OK. We talked about school and what we are going to do when we leave i.e. move to London, probably Camden, and when I looked at my watch four hours had gone. This is unprecedented. Normally Sad Ed drives me to desertion within an hour. Jack said he thought my fake suicide was 'legendary Riley' and a complete stroke of genius. I was about to tell him about the bit of the note that the dog had eaten but for some reason I didn't. It is nice being thought of as a legend.

Sunday 20

Suzy is in the *Cornish Times* women's pages talking about the dos and don'ts of holiday sex (do use condoms, don't expect an orgasm from some man you have just met in Whispers in Newquay). It is alarmingly progressive for

Cornwall. This just shows that in fact St Slaughter is in some sort of timewarp and everywhere else is normal, relatively speaking. Except for Bodmin Moor, where their idea of fun is a museum with stuffed kittens in period costume.

Monday 21

11 a.m.
There is a French girl by the pool. She has long French hair and equally long French legs. Plus she seems to know Jack very well. They are talking in French, which I do not understand, and which is worrying as my French GCSE is in less than a year. I may well write to the Prime Minister to complain about the quality of language teaching in the state education sector.

11.30 a.m.
According to Scarlet the French girl is called Marie-Claire, is 17, and is the niece of the Pitt-Watsons who are from Surrey and staying two luxury villas down from us. She and Jack went to a club in Newquay last week and Scarlet is predicting they will snog before Friday.

Feel annoyed. But no idea why. I do not care about Jack in that way any more.

5.30 p.m.
Do I?

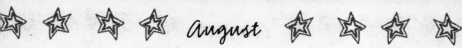

Tuesday 22

Went to beach with Sad Ed and Jack (beach still out of bounds to goths, who are spending most of holiday inside with curtains drawn). Marie-Claire turned up in a French bikini and rattled on in French with Jack. Then, worryingly, Sad Ed joined in. (I am clearly a dunce and am going to fail French and have to work with Pie Shop Pearce.) Or maybe Marie-Claire has some kind of hard-to-understand regional Parisian dialect that Sad Ed and Jack have managed to pick up through practice. That will be it. Luckily she had to go, as (according to Jack, who helpfully translated) the Pitt-Watsons were going to eat line-caught mackerel at some uber-hip beach shack in Rock. Sad Ed said he'd walk back with her, as he had forgotten his sunglasses and might damage his sensitive eyes and have to be like Stevie Wonder (but white and less talented). This is a lie. It is because it was hot and he didn't want to have to expose his upper arms to the general public.

So it was me and Jack again. I said Marie-Claire was very pretty. He said, 'I suppose so, if you like that sort of thing.' I said, 'What's not to like? She has absolutely coltish limbs [learnt from *Vogue*], hair that does not attempt to defy gravity and at least 34C breasts.' He said, 'Put it like that, yeah, she is pretty.' Then we just lay there in silence and I pretended to be engrossed in his *Mojo* magazine until Suzy came to tell us it was time for hummus.

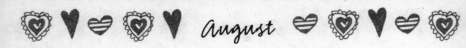
4 p.m.

That was not what he was supposed to say. He was supposed to say, 'Yes, but she has a slightly wonky tooth and says "paff" instead of "whatever".' But he didn't. Which proves he is going to snog her. Scarlet is always right about these things.

Wednesday 23

Oh my God. Tuesday is in Cornwall! Me and Scarlet were in Padstow with Suzy buying essential food items (organic muesli, marinated artichokes, and pain au chocolats) when Suzy suddenly shrieked, 'Tuesday, my dark angel, is it you?' Answer—yes. It turns out she is staying with Mr Wilmott at the Bedruthan Holiday Park (i.e. totally not literary and tragic) while Edie 'overcomes some problems' (i.e. is back in rehab). Suzy has insisted she comes over to visit tomorrow. Sad Ed is going to get a shock. Me and Scarlet have agreed not to warn him in case he panics and tries to run for freedom. Then Suzy got star spotted by a coachload of pensioners from Rhyll and had to sign autographs for an hour.

When we got back Marie-Claire was in the pool again—topless! I do not approve of all this continental breast-baring. It is very distracting, not to mention depressing when she is clearly several sizes bigger than me. Jack and Sad Ed did not seem to mind though. Nor did Bob.

Thursday 24

Jack's GCSE results arrived this morning. He has got nine As so he is definitely staying at John Major High to become a genius politician and musical legend. (Justin got four Cs and three Ds. He is doing resits at John Major High as not even Braintree want him at the moment. Maybe I can become his tutor and help him pass his exams and he will fall hopelessly in love and realize I am THE ONE after all. Excellent.)

Suzy is going to throw a party to celebrate. She is inviting the Pitt-Watsons, Marie-Claire, the man from the *Cornish Times,* and the druid of St Petroc, who is influential in these parts. She is also inviting Tuesday. Scarlet and I begged her not to invite Mr Wilmott but Suzy said that would be rude and she is sure he likes a good party as much as the next man. I am not so sure he will like one of Suzy's.

2 p.m.
Tuesday is here. Mr Wilmott dropped her off in his Skoda. (Tuesday made him park several hundred metres up the road, but I spotted him from the balcony.) Sad Ed dropped his Magnum in shock when he saw her but they have now gone for a walk to 'discuss their relationship'. What relationship?

7 p.m.
Sad Ed and Tuesday are back together! I said didn't he care about her adultery and the fact that she is actually not tragic

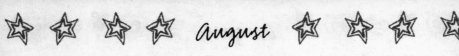

at all, but he said she has been thinking of chucking Dave for a while as he has stretch marks, and she once jumped into the fountain in Trafalgar Square in her underwear which is totally brilliant and edgy. There is no telling some people. They have sealed their love with a grope by the pool.

Friday 25

Rang Mum and Dad to check what time they are picking me up. Dad said 10. I begged him to delay until midnight but he said the roads would be perfectly clear by then and Mum says if we leave any later the dog and James are in danger of getting overtired and fighting. Asked him what everyone was up to. He said Mum was removing some unidentified sticky stuff from the bath, the Cleggs were at the Spar buying Bird's Eye things, and James was sunbathing with the triplets. He says he is looking forward to going home.

Tuesday is here again, lying on top of Sad Ed by the pool. She says there is no way Mr Wilmott is coming to the party. She is going to stay the night and he is picking her up from the top of the road tomorrow. At least we will be able to drink celebratory alcoholic punch without fears of repercussionary detentions next term.

Marie-Claire is here as well. She is listening to Jack play 'Chelsea Dagger' on his guitar. They are obviously waiting for the right moment to snog, i.e. the party

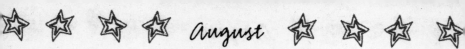

tomorrow with its atmosphere of general sexual abandon,
knowing Suzy.

10 p.m.
Why do I care whether Jack snogs Marie-Claire? Maybe I
don't care.

10.15 p.m.
Oh, I think I do care. Oh God. What am I going to do?

Saturday 26

10 a.m.
Cannot decide if I actually fancy Jack. Am hoping it is
mere annoyance at Frenchness of Marie-Claire and general
absence of Justin that is confusing my feelings.

11 a.m.
Just seen Jack in swimming trunks. Definitely do fancy him.
Oh God, this is not good.

12 noon
Maybe it is good. Maybe he really loves me too.

1 p.m.
No is not good. Will stop thinking about him and concentrate
on first celebrity party (i.e. druid man).

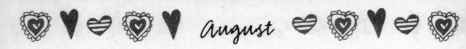

5 p.m.

Oh, but have just seen him do backwards dive into swimming pool. He is sensitive, artistic, and excellent at sport. Unlike Justin, who can only do breaststroke and bombing.

7 p.m.

No definitely must not tell him. He thinks Marie-Claire (i.e. tall with straight hair and no mental relatives) is pretty and therefore will absolutely not want to be near me. Will just ignore him and enjoy company of friends. And Tuesday.

10 p.m.

Am in the wet room hiding from *a*) Jack and *b*) dog-related chaos (Mum and Dad have arrived and dog seems to have taken a dislike to Druid Man, whose beard is now slightly chewed). Everything was fine until Scarlet, Trevor, Tuesday, and Sad Ed (who had clearly been talking to the druid) decided to go and stand on a 'ley line' next to the surf shop and Jack and I got somehow left alone on the balcony, in a sunset. Which should both be banned as they are totally romantic and make you want to do things that under normal circumstances (i.e. level ground and drizzle) you are easily able to not do. Jack said Marie-Claire had asked him out. I said that he should totally go out with her. That she had French legs and French hair etc. and was seventeen. Then he said, 'But she never faked her own death, or dyed herself

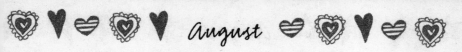

to look like a wardrobe or thought Karl Marx was one of the Marx brothers.' I said, 'No, she isn't that stupid.' Then Jack touched me on the shoulder and it was like that bit in films where all the background noise disappears and it was just me and him in extreme close up and he asked me if I was really saying he should go out with Marie-Claire. And I really wanted to say, 'No, go out with me!' but for some reason, what came out was 'Yes.' And then I was back on the balcony with the sound of the dog barking manically and Druid Man's screams ringing in one ear. Maybe it is all for the best. After all he is Scarlet's brother.

10.05 p.m.
It is not for the best. I think he is THE ONE. Oh my God. I am going to tell him immediately before Dad drags me to the car with the dog.

11.30 p.m.
Have not told him. It was too late. When I went downstairs he was by the pool with Marie-Claire's arms around him and her perfectly glossed lips whispering French nothings into his ears. Then just as he went to kiss her I said, 'Jack.' He pulled away and looked at me. But I couldn't do it. So I just said, 'Goodbye.' He rolled his eyes and said, 'See you at school, Riley.' Then Mum appeared and said, 'I've been looking everywhere for you. We are going now before the dog tries to eat the druid; Dad and James are strapped in already.' So now I am halfway up the M5

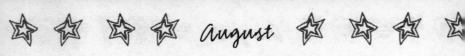

august

and Jack is probably halfway up Marie-Claire's stripy sundress. It is utterly unfair and tragic and like *Romeo and Juliet*. Maybe I will swear chastity and poison myself with herbal Nytol.

12.30 a.m.
Have gone off chastity—remembered Miss Crawley again. Am going to write him a letter declaring my love. All poetic types can only communicate their true feelings on paper, it is a well-known fact. Will post it when we get home.

4 a.m.
Have posted letter. Mum asked what was so urgent that I needed to get it in the postbox tonight. I said 'destiny'. She said Miriam Stoppard was right, the teenage years are worse than the terrible twos. Then she got inside and found that Grandpa and Treena had left the oven on and several windows open, breaking all manner of security rules.

Sunday 27

Not only had Grandpa and Treena broken security, they have also broken four plates, stained the upstairs toilet, and filled the cupboards with Wagon Wheels and Wotsits. Mum says she is going to see Mr Lemon as a matter of urgency. Otherwise, she cannot be responsible for her actions. This is worrying. She is the most responsible person I have ever met.

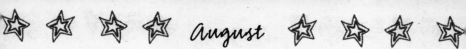
1 p.m.

Oh my God, Saffron Walden is on the lunchtime news. There has been an illegal rave on a sheep farm in Great Chesterford. This is typical. I leave for two weeks and I miss the only interesting thing to happen ever. According to the BBC, literally a dozen drug-crazed youths fled to freedom from riot police across treacherous train tracks (not likely—there is one train an hour and James can outrun it—he proved it once). Then they showed grainy footage of what looked suspiciously like Fat Kylie's enormous miniskirted behind wobbling towards Hadstock in the moonlight. Mum says this is what happens when her ceaseless campaign against anti-social behaviour decamps to the south-west.

Jack gets back tonight. Which means he will get the letter tomorrow morning. My fate is sealed. His holiday romance will be long forgotten and he will fall into my English arms.

Monday 28
Bank Holiday

Except that it is a bank holiday. So he won't get it until tomorrow. I should have posted it by hand. Curse Barclays and their need for random Mondays off.

The rave is in Grandpa's *Daily Telegraph*. There is a quote from evil Tory MP for Saffron Walden and environs Hugo Thorndyke. He says,

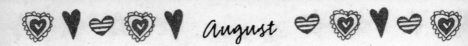

'I am outraged that local youths
have endangered not only their
lives but those of our respected

(hardly)

and hard-working

(barely)

local police officers. But it is clear
that many of those involved had
crossed into our Conservative, in all
senses of the word, constituency
from Labour-run Harlow, where
mob rule runs free. You can be sure
I will be speaking to Barry Goggins
at the first available opportunity.'

It is the farmer I feel sorry for. I bet his fields are ruined
with Fat Kylie bouncing around on them.

3 p.m.
I have been a fool for love. The unthinkable has happened.
Jack has gone to Paris with Marie-Claire until Friday! I rang
Scarlet to discuss the rave but she was round at Trevor's
painting his toenails black so I casually asked Suzy about
Jack and she said she dropped him at Dover last night with

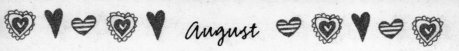

a copy of *Madame Bovary* and a packet of condoms. She is hoping he will have his sexual awakening. Hung up as the thought of Jack awakening with Marie-Claire made me feel sick.

Thank God for bank holidays. I will intercept the post tomorrow and destroy the letter before Suzy does anything stupid like forward it to Paris or read it down the phone to him. He will never know of my utter devotion. Until I die tragically (and for real this time) and my diaries are published and he will be racked with guilt and remorse and will kill himself so he can be with me in everlasting peace (or vampire-ridden netherworld, according to Scarlet and Trevor). Except that by then I will have married Justin in a barefoot ceremony and have several children called tragic Shakespearean things like Ophelia and Romeo.

4 p.m.
Oh not Romeo. That is totally Beckham i.e. chav.

7 p.m.
Have given up vegetarianism. Mum made moussaka for tea. It was organic lamb mince though, so it is almost veggie, because the sheep were happy before they died and got pulverized. Also it is pointless being vegetarian if Jack does not love me. Especially as would have to shop in lentil-smelling health food outlet Nuts In May, run by hunchback Mr Goldstein and his ailment-ridden assistant Rosamund.

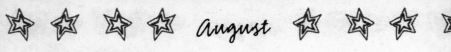
Tuesday 29

9 a.m.
Went round Scarlet's to intercept post. Their new cleaner, Edna, was there, rearranging the cutlery. She would not pass Mum's strict cleaning ability tests. For a start, she was smoking a Rothman's while she worked. The letter had not arrived. This is typical of the Royal Mail. According to James the post office is rife with criminal activity and my letter has probably been stolen by organized gangs of postmen. This is not good. Our postman is Beefy Clark who is a notorious gossip and will no doubt report the sordid details to everyone else on his post round and they will be all round the school by next week.

Wednesday 30

Still no letter. Scarlet checked with Edna but she says she put all the post where it belonged, on top of the fridge. I said I didn't know the post belonged on the fridge, but apparently Edna is imposing a strict, if slightly random, new system.

Mum has been to see Mr Lemon. He says he will call her when there are any developments and to please stop harassing him as he is finding his job increasingly stressful with all the O'Grady issues.

Thursday 31

No letter. James is right. It is probably stolen or thrown into a bin. On the plus side, this means that it will never reach its destination, i.e. Jack, and my secret will die with me.

Edna's new system is causing havoc. Scarlet says Bob was an hour late for work because all his pants had disappeared and he refuses to do pelvic surgery going commando. They were eventually located in the bedside cabinet.

The rave is in the *Walden Chronicle* with several grainy photos of perpetrators and an invitation to 'name that hoodie'.

I'm RACHEL RILEY
— welcome to my so-called life.

September

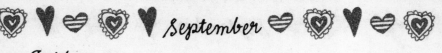

Friday 1

2 p.m.

Jack gets back in three hours. I am going to resist the temptation to go and lurk at the Stones' in order to catch a glimpse of him. It will only fuel my sorrow.

3 p.m.

Two hours to go before Jack is back. Am still being resolute. Will stay in my bedroom and read poetry.

4 p.m.

But maybe he and Marie-Claire discovered that their lives are separated by more than the English Channel and that actually they have nothing in common, and the condoms have been abandoned, unopened, on the Champs Élysées and Jack is all fired up after reading *Madame Bovary* and is rushing home to throw himself at my English mercy.

5 p.m.

Yes, that is utterly what will have happened. Am going to Scarlet's immediately.

8 p.m.

That is not what happened. Jack is still snogging Marie-Claire. He is already talking about having gap years in Paris and going to the Sorbonne. And, worse, it is all my fault. When I arrived he said, 'Riley, you were right—Marie-Claire

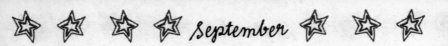

is amazing.' Then he went on for two hours about how they saw a baby deer in the Bois de Bologne on their last night and how her mother is an actress who once appeared nude in a Fellini film and her dad is a left-wing anti-government radical. This is typical. I left before I threw up.

Saturday 2

Called Sad Ed so I could feel better about my utterly non-progressive existence (his family make mine look like the Stones) but he was round at Tuesday's painting an art installation on her bedroom wall. Even Sad Ed is more tragic and interesting than me. Although I do not envy him when Mr Wilmott finds out they have defaced the Hint of Barley.

Sunday 3

School starts tomorrow. A new and crucial year. Have got a Year Eleven appropriate schoolbag i.e. black and inconspicuous instead of Milletts rucksack with an 'I've climbed Snowdon!' sew-on patch.

Monday 4
School starts.

Davey MacDonald is back and the vending machine is gone. They are both the victims of political correctness gone mad, according to Scarlet. This is not true. Davey MacDonald is the victim of his own idiocy—on top of the Thin Kylie fracas at Sadler's Wells, he kept revealing his penis to the rehearsal pianist. The vending machine is a victim of Jamie Oliver. It has been replaced with a fruit and nut dispenser.

Mr Wilmott gave all the Year Elevens a talk about how this is the most crucial year of our school career and that it is time we knuckled down to our GCSEs, which are only ten months away etc., etc. Then he announced we would be getting our mock results tomorrow. They were located in Mrs Leech's bottom drawer under her Nurofen and tampon supplies. A general feeling of fear hangs over 11 Hopwood-White. Except for the Kylies who are too busy going through Year Seven applications to their gang.

Tuesday 5

Got eight Bs and a D (rural studies). This is shameful. Even Stacey O'Grady passed rural studies. Bs are not so bad though. Loads of philosophical and literary types are mediocre at school and their talents only come to light in the nurturing intellectual atmosphere of Cambridge University. Or maybe I can claim I am dyslexic like Keanu

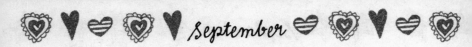

Reeves or Eddie Izzard. Or Fat Kylie. Although hers is still under review as to whether or not she is just thick.

No one is using the fruit and nut dispenser. They are going to Mr Patel's instead for kingsize Mars bars and Coke. His profits must be soaring. He already has a new people carrier and a conservatory. With the vending machine ban I predict he will be moving to a five-bed on Seven Devils Lane, formerly home to pint-size Eighties pop sensation Nik Kershaw.

5 p.m.
Mum says I am not dyslexic, as proven by my freakish ability to spell Mississippi at the age of five, but that I will be soaking up the less than intellectual atmosphere at Harlow Further Education College unless I start to take my GCSEs seriously.

Wednesday 6

The apples are rotting in the fruit and nut dispenser. Mr Wilmott has taken the drastic measure of banning anyone from leaving the school premises during breaks, including staff (they are dependent on Mr Patel for their supply of cigarettes and microwave samosas). Fat Kylie says she is suffering malnutrition and is threatening to get her mum in. Ms Hopwood-White says you cannot get scurvy from crisp withdrawal and has sent her to Mr Wilmott.

Thursday 7

Fat Kylie's mum has set up a crisp and Coke stall and is doing a roaring trade selling Fanta and Wotsits through a gap in the sheep field fence. Mr Vaughan has asked if she can start doing Benson and Hedges as well. Mr Wilmott is not so enlightened. He has ordered Mr Cheesmond (scary giant beard, lingering smell of goat) aka the head of Rural Studies aka Cowpat Cheesmond, who is in charge of sheep, to turn the electric fence on at all times.

Friday 8

The crisp and Coke stall is no more. Fat Kylie's mum got electrocuted seven times in five minutes. She is suing the school for singeing her velour jogging bottoms. Mr Wilmott has offered her a generous out-of-court settlement of £100 but she says she is going for a million. She will not get it. I know for a fact that they cost £12.99 off the market.

Saturday 9

Went round Scarlet's for lunch. Edna is causing havoc with all her rearranging. The CDs have been rehoused in the bathroom and no one has seen Gordon for a week. Bob wants to sack her but Suzy says Bob can't complain as it was his idea and they can't sack Edna on grounds of an illogical

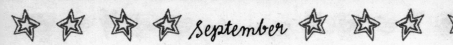

system, it is against union rules. Bob said there is no way Edna is unionized but Suzy said on the contrary she is a long-standing member of the carpet-fitters and weavers union.

Jack was on the phone to Marie-Claire when I arrived, doing loads of giggling and sighing. It was disgusting.

Scarlet says she rings him every day. I said it was lucky her parents were happy to fund her astronomical phone bills but Scarlet says Marie-Claire earned £20,000 last year from a L'Oreal mascara advert and was financially independent. Could my life possibly get any worse?

Sunday 10

Apparently it could. Baby Jesus has inserted a mini pizza into the DVD player, consigning it and my copy of utterly tragic *Romeo and Juliet* to history. He is potentially more destructive than the dog. Which is saying something.

Monday 11

The Retards and Criminals are being temporarily reintegrated into society following flooding and smoke damage on D Corridor. It is because Mark Lambert set fire to Davey MacDonald's crêpe paper collage of Man City's defence and set off the sprinklers. We are getting three—Mark Lambert, Davey MacDonald, and Caris Kelp, who eats glue.

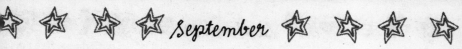

Tuesday 12

Ms Hopwood-White has been forced to lock the stationery cupboard. Two Pritt Sticks went missing during registration. All signs point to Caris.

Wednesday 13

Drama Club started today. They are doing *The Sound of Music* and have instigated a school-wide search for Maria, culminating in a live final next Friday lunchtime in the lower school canteen. I am not auditioning, despite my excellent acting ability and Julie Andrews-like air of innocence and practicality. Jack is bookie's (i.e. Ali Hassan's Maths Club gambling ring) favourite to play Captain Von Trapp and I do not think I could bear to be within his treacherous arms, not even in the name of Art.

Thursday 14

Ms Hopwood-White says she is thinking of suing the government over their ad campaigns to recruit teachers. I do not blame her. They are full of clean and clever multicultural children asking inspired questions like 'What is the difference between fluff and dust?' Or 'What is dark matter?' It is misleading. In reality most questions are 'Are

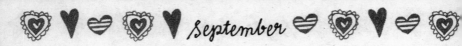
fish actually reptiles, miss?' Or 'Was Shakespeare, like, a bender, miss?'

What is the difference between fluff and dust though? I bet James will know.

Friday 15

Apparently it is down to fibre content.

Saturday 16

Mum has got her new driving test date. It is on 25th October. She is writing to the council to demand details of all proposed road amendments and additions. But, in a potentially marriage-breaking move, she is not telling Dad about the test. She says he will only panic unnecessarily about Mr Wandering Hands. James said she would live to regret her deception. Mum told him not to be so melodramatic and to go and tell the dog to stop licking the hifi.

Sunday 17

Treena is going back to work tomorrow. It is so she can save up for a pink wedding dress, as seen on Katie Price. It is a bad idea. Katie Price is thin, albeit with enormous breasts,

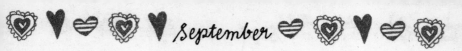

whereas Treena is still carrying three stone of baby/Golden Wonder weight. Grandpa is not happy about her going to work. He says her place is in the home looking after him, but she says he doesn't pay £7.80 an hour. She is going to take Jesus with her. Mum said wouldn't that be difficult trying to take care of him at the same time as looking after all the old people but Treena says it will be like taking drugs into a prison. The inmates (aka old ladies), will be fighting to get hold of him and all she'll have to do is dole out the nappies.

Monday 18

Mr Vaughan asked if I had given any thought to auditioning for *The Sound of Music*. I said I didn't think I would have time with all my other extra curricular activities. This is a lie. I do not do any activities. I just cannot bear to be near Jack. Scarlet says he and Marie-Claire phone each other up every day. It is lucky Suzy is a rich celebrity now so she can afford to foot his phone sex bills.

Tuesday 19

Maria madness has taken over the school. Everyone is auditioning, including Fat Kylie and Sad Ed, although he is only doing it because Tuesday says being in a musical is actually totally offbeat. He has no chance. Even Mr Vaughan,

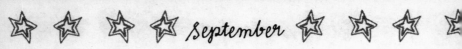

who is known for his sexing-up of school productions, would draw the line at a gay male nun. Thin Kylie says she is too busy to audition. I have seen the evidence. She now has seventy-three badges on her parka, dominated by the national potato week motto 'Eat More Chips'. They should have Fat Kylie as the face of their campaign.

Wednesday 20

Baby Jesus is missing. Treena forgot to bring him back from work. She was watching *Neighbours* when Grandpa asked her where he was so he could give him his Heinz jars. They have searched the Twilight Years Day Centre but he is not there. Grandpa is pacing uncontrollably. Mum has pointed out that he can't have gone far, as he is incapable of moving more than a few metres but Grandpa says you read about this sort of thing in the papers all the time and Des has probably kidnapped him and taken him to live in Libya. Treena said don't be daft Des doesn't even know where Libya is. They are doing a phone round the old people to see if anyone can remember seeing him.

8 p.m.
Baby Jesus has been located. And not in Libya. Although he was in a dictatorship i.e. the Pink Geranium Sheltered Housing Unit, where Grandpa used to live before he got thrown out by the fascist warden Mrs Peason for abusing

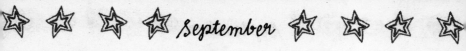

the buzzer system and Treena. Mrs Peason rang after finding him in Elsie Stain's blanket box. Elsie said she thought he had been abandoned so she decided to give him a good home. Dad asked Mrs Peason how she knew who Jesus's parents were. She says he has Grandpa's obsession with breasts and Treena's moronic stare. It is true. Grandpa has banned Treena from taking Jesus to work. He says old women and babies are a recipe for disaster.

Thursday 21

5 p.m.

Bumped into Jack in the car park after school. I tried to hide but he saw me and asked what in God's name I was doing crouching down behind Mr Vaughan's Civic. I said I had lost an earring, which was the first thing that came into my head. Even though I don't even have my ears pierced (banned until I am sixteen and then only a single hole in regulation earlobe i.e. not ten in one ear like Tuesday). Then he asked me if I was auditioning for Maria. I said I wasn't, and that I was going to concentrate on my GCSEs. He said that was a shame as it would have been a laugh if I was doing the show. Then he said he had to go and meet Justin and Sophie to rehearse their audition pieces but as he walked off he turned and smiled and said, 'You don't wear earrings, Riley.'

Aaagh! So now he knows I am trying to avoid him. Which means he knows there is a reason for me avoiding him.

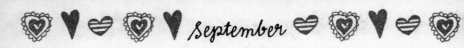
Which means I have to not avoid him. Which means I have to audition. Also Justin is auditioning. So he might get to be Captain Von Trapp. He is more classically good-looking than Jack after all. And is two centimetres taller. Although I suppose Mr Vaughan is not likely to give him or Sophie lead roles given their sexual *ménage à trois*.

11 p.m.

Have learnt 'The Hills are Alive' and 'My Favourite Things' off by heart, with the aid of James, who knows the entire score and dialogue. It is a throwback from his short-lived obsession with becoming a nun (swapped for another obsession with marrying Granny Clegg—thankfully also only temporary). So am totally prepared for Mr Vaughan's live final, with Mr Wilmott as Andrew Lloyd Webber and Ms Hopwood-White as Graham Norton.

Friday 22

The audition did not go brilliantly. I forgot what my favourite things were and had to make some of them up (bright coloured kettles and warm woollen kittens). On the plus side, I was definitely better than Fat Kylie, whose impression of a lonely goatherd will go down in John Major history. Anyway, at least I did audition. So now Jack knows I am not avoiding him i.e. I am totally over him.

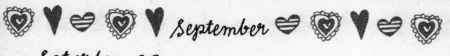

Saturday 23

James has received letters of devotion from all three triplets. Mum is not amused at his new-found status as a nine-year-old Casanova but Grandpa says he is following in Riley tradition. Mum said there was no such tradition and that Dad was a model of self-restraint in his youth. Grandpa said, 'That's what you think,' and then wandered off mysteriously. It is Mumtaz I feel sorry for. She has been thrown aside carelessly like a dirty sock.

Sunday 24

Mum's web of deceit is spinning out of control. Dad asked her if she was thinking of reapplying for another driving test. Mum said no. Strictly speaking this is not a total lie as she has applied already and applying again would be pointless and wasteful but I fear Dad will not see it like that. I don't like all this subterfuge. James is right. It will all end badly and I will end up homeless or in the evangelical care of Auntie Joyless.

Monday 25

The Sound of Music cast list goes up tomorrow. Not that I am eager with anticipation or anything. It is just an observation.

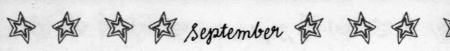

Tuesday 26

4 p.m.
Sophie Microwave Muffins is Maria. It is an outrage. She is neither practical, nor eccentric, plus she hates goats. It is obvious that Mr Vaughan is only doing it to prove he bears no grudge against her. Or else get back in her good books and/or knickers. Not that I wanted the part anyway. Especially now that Jack is definitely Captain von Trapp. On the contrary I am delighted to be eldest Von Trapp Liesl. Especially as Justin is Nazi youth Rolf, on account of his Aryan hair. So I will have to snog him.

5 p.m.
I mean get to snog him. It is good thing. I mean I have wanted to kiss him for ages and now I can, so it is excellent. Isn't it?

Wednesday 27

Had first rehearsal for *Sound of Music*. Am not entirely convinced that Mr Vaughan's casting of Dean 'the dwarf' Denley as five-year-old Gretl is entirely politically correct but I suppose he is the only person short enough to do it without resorting to shuffling about on his knees—the favoured method of portraying children

and old ladies in John Major theatrical tradition. And I don't think any audience will be able to suspend their disbelief long enough to believe Fat Kylie is Mother Superior. Everyone knows she is far from nun-like in her habits (ha ha). Also Sad Ed is regretting auditioning now that he is Chief Nazi. He is not so sure it is offbeat to have to feign a cod German accent and bleach his hair. Scarlet is doing set design. She says her goth beliefs forbid her from religious entertainment. This is not true. It is because she does not want to have to be a man again.

Thursday 28

New CCTV cameras have been installed at 'crime hotspots' according to the *Walden Chronicle*. Mum is delighted. She says it will drive troublemakers out of the town centre and back where they belong—i.e. Harlow. Sad Ed and Tuesday do not agree. They say it is the first step to a police state and that we will all be taking orders from Big Brother within a year. I think they mean in the Orwell book, not the man with the Newcastle accent. The cameras are pointed at Barry Island, the bins outside Abrakebabra, and the entire Whiteshot Estate. I bet the Kylies are outraged. That is all their potential shagging spots ruled out. Unless they have ambitions to become porn stars or be on *You've Been Framed*.

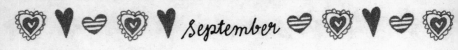
Friday 29

Tracey Hughes says the police are thinking of suing the *Walden Chronicle* for publishing the locations of their highly secret CCTV cameras. I said they weren't that secret, given that they are six metres high and bright blue. She said that is what the *Walden Chronicle* said. Anyway, the mental capacity of criminals like the O'Gradys is such that they will forget by next week and still get caught.

Saturday 30

It is Sad Ed's birthday tomorrow. He will be sixteen i.e. allowed to have sex and smoke but, weirdly, not join a library without his parent's permission. Although I doubt Mrs Thomas will let him do any of the above. He is having a party tonight and some of Tuesday's friends are going to be there. This is a major risk, given the unwritten John Major rules that you are not allowed to fraternize with anyone from the Quaker school due to their *a*) crap school uniform and *b*) weird religion where you don't say anything in church, you sit there all silent. I mean how boring is that? But he says he is trying to bridge a social divide and this will be like when they got rid of apartheid in South Africa and we will all be able to drink latte together instead of us having to go to the Mocha while the Quakers dominate the Coffee Stop. He is right. It is time to break down the barriers of repression.

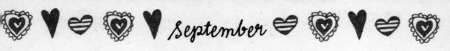

11 p.m.

The barriers of repression are still standing. It is because one of Trevor's bat friends tried to snog Daisy Truelove, who is apparently strictly property of the Quaker boys, and then a goths v. Quakers fight broke out, and Mrs Thomas ended the party before anyone damaged her Aled Jones figurines.

I'm RACHEL RILEY
— welcome to my so-called life.

October

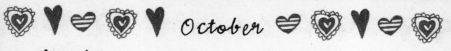

Sunday 1

Called Sad Ed to check if he had indulged in any coming of age activities. He said chance would be a fine thing. His mum sent Tuesday home with the Quakers and him to bed at nine with a hot chocolate and a *Beano* annual. He says he will be lucky to lose his virginity by the age of thirty at this rate.

Monday 2

7.30 a.m.
Granny Clegg rang in a new-found religious fervour. She has seen the face of Jesus (the bearded Messiah, not my uncle) in a slice of Nimble toast. Auntie Joyless is on her way over to confirm if it is the good Lord himself. James answered. He is excited. He says she is sitting on a potential gold mine. Apparently a girl in Portugal found God in an aubergine and is now a millionaire. He has told Granny Clegg not to do anything daft like expose it to damp or spread it with Nutella.

4 p.m.
It is definitely Jesus, according to Auntie Joyless and Father Abraham (seriously), her ecclesiastical consultant. And they should know. Grandpa Clegg is stocking up on refreshments for all the pilgrims they are eagerly expecting and Granny has called the *St Slaughter Reporter*. James said she was underselling herself and she should call Jeremy

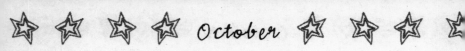

Paxman but then Mum grabbed the phone and told her under no circumstances to call the BBC. She said they will try to sabotage the story. This is not true. It is because she is worried that Paxo will wheedle all sorts of idiotic things out of her and expose her for the yokel she is.

Tuesday 3

Bruce has eaten Jesus. Granny Clegg is devastated but Grandpa says it serves her right for putting the toast on a plinth on the windowsill so that passers by could catch a glimpse. Granny says she has toasted the rest of the loaf in case it is all divine but all she has got so far is Maureen from the Spar and a wonky Gary Lineker.

Wednesday 4

3 p.m.
Had my first rehearsal with Nazi youth Rolf i.e. Justin. Mr Vaughan said he was concerned at the lack of chemistry between us, despite my excellent innocent smouldering. Justin said he was finding it hard convincing himself he was in love with me. Mr Vaughan said, 'You will never be Robert de Niro with that kind of attitude. If this is stretching your talents then I suggest you go back to dodgeball.' Justin said, 'Oh, bog off, Vaughany, you perv,' so Mr Vaughan threw

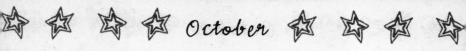

October

him out. But Mr Wilmott threw him back in and took Mr Vaughan outside for a quiet chat (overheard by Fat Kylie who was having a fag break) and told him that he had to stop personal feelings interfering with his teaching or he would be back doing supply at Newport Boys.

Thursday 5

Suzy is doing the Year Nine sex lecture tomorrow. I hope Mr Wilmott knows what he is letting himself in for. There are bound to be graphic details and free condoms.

Friday 6

Suzy has been banned from any future sex education classes. Things got out of hand when she simulated the missionary position with Kyle O'Grady. Plus she suggested the age of consent should be fourteen. So the Year Nines are back with Miss Beadle and her plastic penis model.

Saturday 7

James is one triplet down. Presley has dumped him for an eleven year old called Biffer who has a BMX. He got a letter this morning on Hello Kitty notepaper. He says he is not

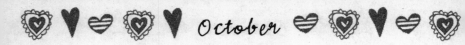
hurt as he still has Parker and Peyton under his spell but I know he is just putting on a brave face. He asked Mum if he could get a BMX but she said no, on the grounds that my old Raleigh is still perfectly functioning, so he has gone round Mad Harry's to sulk.

Sunday 8

Am officially bridesmaid to Grandpa and Treena. They have confirmed the wedding date with the White Horse. James pointed out that Treena still hadn't had her Decree Absolute in the divorce proceedings but she says it is a technicality. I do not think the police will see it like that. The good news is that Treena's job means that she now has a bridesmaid's dress budget so I will not have to wear one of Mum's horrendous cast-offs. The bad news is that she says she is not shopping in Steinberg and Tolkien (i.e. utterly famous vintage shop in London favoured by Kylie (the real goddess-like one, not the Primark Pretenders)) and I can go to Berkertex in Cambridge with her next Saturday. She is still going for voluminous pink, unadvisedly.

Monday 9

The CCTV cameras have caught Mr Whippy doing 'It' on Barry Island. Tracey Hughes says she watched the video

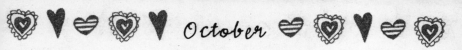

with her mum last night and the female recipient of Mr Whippy's attentions is definitely NOT Fat Kylie—the thighs are too small. I said she had better not tell Fat Kylie but Tracey said it was too late as she had lent the video to Thin Kylie at break.

Tuesday 10

Mr Whippy is in hospital with a broken nose and fractured ribs. I asked Fat Kylie if her brothers had come to her aid to protect her honour. She said, 'My honour don't need protecting, I done it myself.' So I asked her if she had found out who the girl was. She said her minions were searching Saffron Walden for a 'slag with a fat arse and white cowboy boots'. That could be any number of people.

Wednesday 11

Davey MacDonald has a Nazi dance solo. I said I didn't recall this being in the original version but Mr Vaughan says he is not going to let good talent go to waste, even with the potential for genital exposure.

The Mr Whippy sex DVD is selling well in the sixth form common room. Justin says it is like Paris Hilton but with wobbling.

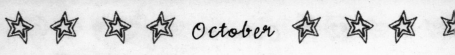

Thursday 12

Mr Whippy has been sacked by the ice cream company for bringing them into disrepute. This is a bit far-fetched as they are already facing a legal suit following last summer's mass 99 poisoning. On the plus side, he is moving back in with his mum above Dorrington's for a bit until the hoo-ha calms down (and until Fat Kylie calms down), which means the other O'Grady can move into his three-bed semi, which means Grandpa and Treena are now at the top of the housing list! Mum is delighted. She is scouring the obituaries in the *Walden Chronicle* for any potential council house deaths.

Friday 13

Spent the entire day avoiding ladders, magpies, black cats, and other superstitious Friday 13th portents of doom. Then got home and found that the dog had unravelled one sleeve of my enormous fluffy jumper. This is typical.

Saturday 14

9 a.m.
Have got my bridesmaid's dress fitting later. Am determined to persuade Treena to go for demure off-white silk with absolutely no lace, bustles, or bows.

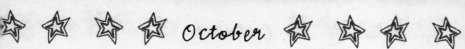
2 p.m.

Have got bridesmaid's dress. It is not demure off-white silk but is a vile pink net thing with puff sleeves and a fairy wand. Begged Treena not to choose it but she is going for a pink theme. I suppose I should be glad I am not James or Jesus. Or the dog. They have pink sailor suits, complete with ribboned hats. Dad says we will look like a gay burlesque show. He is right. Even Grandpa is wearing a pink waistcoat.

Sunday 15

'Shiraz' was registered five times as a baby name last year according to *The Times*. Mum is outraged but Treena said there was nothing wrong with it and if the next one was a girl she was going to call it Shiraz, or Elvis for a boy. Mum went white and said, 'Please God do not tell me you are pregnant again,' and Treena said, 'Not yet, but if Ern keeps at it the way he is I'll be walking down the aisle at the White Horse two months up the duff.' Mum is not happy. I do not blame her. Having one baby in the house is bad enough. He has joined the dog in being a perpetual source of noise, sick, and destruction.

Monday 16

Mr Whippy's paramour has been identified. According to several Year Twelves and Mr Camden (history and metalwork)

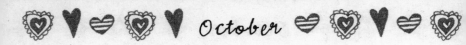
it is Leanne Jones. Fat Kylie is going round her house after school with several other O'Gradys. It is Kyle I feel sorry for. This could compromise his star-crossed relationship with Leanne's little sister Primark Donna. Where will his loyalties lie?

Tuesday 17

With Primark Donna, apparently. He has a black eye after trying to fight Fat Kylie at the Joneses' household last night. The police were called and, according to Tracey Hughes, one of the O'Gradys is now in custody. She cannot remember which one, as there are so many. Mum is hoping it is the one on the housing list, then Grandpa and Treena can move straight into Mr Whippy's. Fat Kylie is no help either. She is off school with alleged whiplash.

Wednesday 18

It was not the right O'Grady. It was one I had never heard of called Dane. So Mum is back to waiting for a convenient death on Harvey Road.

Rehearsals went well, apart from the absence of Mother Superior, due to her ongoing whiplash, and a minor fight between the nuns and the Nazis (aka the Retards and Criminals). Mr Vaughan and his assistant director Oona

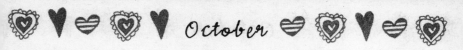

Rickets say they are still concerned at the lack of seething sexual desire between me and Rolf. I said, well it wasn't my fault, I was positively oozing with it. Which is true. Especially, and weirdly, in his uniform. But Mr Vaughan says we need to sort it out soon or he will have to rethink his casting.

Thursday 19

The *Walden Chronicle* have started their annual search for Saffron Walden's 'bonniest' baby, sponsored by crap hardware shop, the unironically titled Gayhomes. The prize is £200 and a year's supply of squeegees. Grandpa is entering Jesus. He will fit in well in the yearly parade of Jades and Darryls.

Friday 20

It is half term next week. To mark this auspicious occasion, Mark Lambert and Davey MacDonald (now working as one formidable super-Retard-like force) blew up a science lab by trying to gas a frog. They are suspended for a week. Sad Ed says it is down to poor parenting. He is right in the case of Mr Hosepipe. He strips to Britney Spears songs.

Also Mum had a driving lesson today. Dad got back from work early and asked where she was. I said she had gone for emergency Cif following a particularly nasty dog incident. When she got back Dad asked her where the Cif was. She

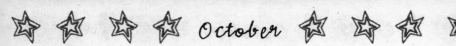

said in the cupboard between the Bold 3 in 1 and the Cillit Bang, where it always is. So I diverted attention by dropping a glass of lemon barley. Thank God her test is next week. I cannot keep this charade up any longer.

Saturday 21

Baby Jesus has had his photo taken for the bonny baby competition. Grandpa borrowed James's camera and a selection of fancy dress outfits. I like the one of him as a policeman best, but Treena thinks Bob the Builder will nail it. They are desperate for the £200 to pay for their wedding reception entertainer—Pelvis Presley (aka Paul Presley from the garage on London Road).

Also, James is down to one triplet. Parker has decided to focus on her pony Sizzles as she has a crucial gymkhana season coming up. James is panicking and has demanded that Dad drives him to Solihull at half term for the sake of his love life. Dad has refused. This is because the last time he drove to Birmingham he got lost and ended up circling Spaghetti Junction for two hours with Mum shouting, 'Left, Colin, for God's sake, left.'

Sunday 22

Bumped into Cherie who was struggling to lug her Debenhams bags out of her jeep. I asked her how life

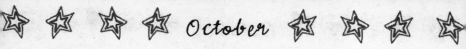

was treating her. She said, 'Like a bastard. Don't ever get involved with a plasterer. Women flock to them like moths to a flame and then they betray you and leave you with nothing but a dodgy satellite dish and half a bottle of Tia Maria.' Strictly speaking Terry did not leave, she threw him out. And her drinks cabinet is vast. But I did not say this as Cherie did not look like she would be concerned with that sort of technicality.

Love is fraught with dangers. In fact I am lucky not to be gripped by its charms.

Monday 23
Half term.

Went round Scarlet's to celebrate the first day of the holidays by lying around watching telly. Jack has gone on an emergency trip to Paris to see Marie-Claire. According to Scarlet their long-distance relationship is fraught with petty jealousies and he has gone to check that she is not secretly fluttering her l'Oreal eyelashes at some boy called Henri-Claude. What is with the French and all their double-barrelled names?

Tuesday 24

Mum's driving test is in twenty-four hours. She is having an intensive half-day revision session with Mr Wandering

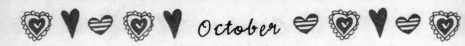

Hands. Thank God the web of deception will be torn down tomorrow. Dad has already rung twice. Once to ask her to cancel his subscription to *Golf World* as he can get it for nothing off Malcolm in IT and once to ask whether Alan Whicker was dead (office bet). I said Mum was busy trying to get a piece of Lego out of the dog's windpipe and put James on instead. He knows things like that.

Went round Sad Ed's. He was busy making a CD of songs to tell Tuesday how he feels about her. I said I didn't think 'Girlfriend in a Coma' necessarily conveyed feelings of love and devotion. He said, 'That is why you are single, and I am a love god. Now go away, you are disturbing my creative juices.' I left before any of Sad Ed's juices could get near me.

Wednesday 25

8 a.m.
Mum is nervous. She has actually spilled a cup of Nescafé, which is unprecedented. Dad said she should call a doctor immediately. He thinks it may be the onset of Parkinson's or Mad Cow disease. James asked what her other symptoms were and had she experienced any loss of bowel control, so Dad said he was late for a meeting to discuss new chairs and disappeared before James could go into any more detail. I knew this was all a mistake. It will end in tears. And divorce.

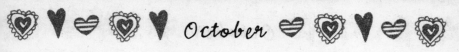

6 p.m.

Mum has passed. Thank God. Now the horrible deception can end. She has cooked Dad's favourite meal (vile liver), and is going to break the news to him after *Lovejoy*, when he will be in a good mood.

8.30 p.m.

Dad has taken the whole test thing remarkably well and has forgiven her for her evil tissue of lies. It is because Mum let him drink two glasses of Waitrose brandy, which is usually only allowed out on special occasions. He says at least now there is no risk of her and Mr Wandering Hands brushing fingertips over the Fiesta gearstick, plus she can ferry James and Mad Harry around at the weekends while he watches sport.

Thursday 26

Mum is on a winning streak. There has been a potential council house death. According to the *Walden Chronicle*, ninety-three-year-old Dennis Waters is in hospital after electrocuting himself with a hairdryer in the shower and is only clinging on by a thread. Treena says she knows him from the Twilight Years Day Centre. He is Elsie Stain's 'fancy man'. She is going to ring the hospital later to check on his condition.

3 p.m.

Treena has rung Addenbrookes. Dennis is still at death's door. I said I didn't think they were allowed to impart this

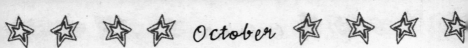

sort of information unless you were a family member but Treena said she told them she was his girlfriend.

7 p.m.
Dennis has sat up and asked for a slice of Battenberg.

Mum is livid. But Treena has assured her that it was a brief moment of clarity and that he is still in intensive care and, where there's a life support machine, there's hope.

Friday 27

9 a.m.
Dennis has died. Apparently his last words were, 'Where's the marzipan, you thief.' Mum is ringing Mr Lemon now.

9.15 a.m.
Mr Lemon said that he was slightly shocked at Mum's swift and emotionless reaction to death, but that, technically, Grandpa and Treena could be in within the next fortnight. Mum is jubilant.

Went round Sad Ed's to tell him the good news that the house will soon be a Jesus-free zone but he and Tuesday were busy taking advantage of the fact that Mrs Thomas was in Braintree verifying the signature on an Aled Jones boxed set. He answered the door in his pants looking sweaty. I asked him if he had 'come of age' yet. He said not technically, but on a points basis, he was

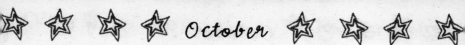

almost there. I left before I could work out what that meant.

Saturday 28

Mum and Dad have gone to Cambridge. They are going to take it in turns to drive. I am not sure this is going to be the bonding experience they are hoping for.

2 p.m.
I was right. Mum and Dad are back and are in a mood. Dad says it is because Mum drives like Marjory, i.e. refuses to overtake anything and hums incessantly. Mum says it is because Dad broke the speed limit five times and only checked his mirror to see if he had missed a bit shaving. She is booking him in for his refresher course as a Christmas present. Dad said, 'Why don't you just give me socks, Janet, and really spoil me.' Mum is not happy. They are going to look at new cars tomorrow before they start fighting over custody of the Passat.

Sunday 29

Mum and Dad have gone to Motor World in Bishop's Stortford. They have taken James with them as he is encyclopaedic when it comes to engine efficiency and boot

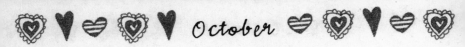

volume. He says his extensive internet searches have already whittled it down to the Renault Clio (1.4 litre engine, 35 miles per gallon and convenient cup-holder), an Audi A2 (1.4 litre engine, 38 miles per gallon but questionable MW radio reception), or a BMW 3 series (3 litre engine, no miles to the gallon but has heated seats and a ten-stack CD changer). I do not see Dad agreeing to the last one. Or Mum.

3 p.m.
Mum has got a Fiesta. She says she feels comfortable behind the wheel in a Ford. Dad says I bet you do, maybe I should get a giant cut-out of Mike to sit beside you. She said, 'Well I'd rather that than you telling me to speed up every five minutes.' Dad has gone to the golf club. Grandpa says this is what happens when you let women get behind the wheel, the way of the world gets off kilter. If he had his way, we would all still be milking cows and weaving bonnets.

Monday 30
Back to school.

Bumped into Jack at the fruit and nut dispenser. I asked him if he and Marie-Claire had overcome their sexual jealousies and he said yes, because it turned out that Henri-Claude is experimenting with being gay. I said that was excellent news. Then he said that Marie-Claire was worried about

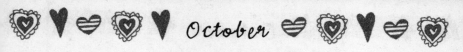

me. I thought at first he meant that she had some kind of sixth sense and could sniff terminal illness on me or something (I saw a dog do this on *This Morning* once) but he said that she could feel something between us. I said, 'As if.' Jack said, 'That's what I said.' And then the machine dispensed his yoghurt-coated blueberries so he went back to the sixth form common room. No doubt to drink black coffee and discuss Sartre, which is, according to Scarlet, what sixth form is all about. Unlike Year Eleven, which is about drinking Fanta and discussing reality TV.

Also Mr Lemon called. Dennis's funeral is on Wednesday and the will is being read on Thursday so he says Grandpa can move in Friday. I think he is seeing the advantages of Mum's obituary system. He said he would have waited months before anyone in the rents department even noticed that payments had stopped. So not only has Mum secured Grandpa and Treena a home, she is saving taxpayers at least £254.

Tuesday 31
Hallowe'en

Scarlet is off school. It is because it is Hallowe'en, a traditional goth holiday. I texted her and asked how she had managed to persuade Bob and Suzy. She said she didn't, Bob is busy aborting and Suzy is signing sex manuals at Bluewater. And Edna doesn't know which day of the week

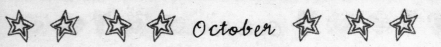

it is so is not likely to comment. Trevor is going round later to try to raise the dead. Have volunteered to take James trick or treating. It will be excellent. He is bringing Mad Harry, who is widely considered an expert at extortion, so I am confidently expecting a huge haul. James is going as Catwoman (in Mum's old yoga leotard and a pair of tights) and Mad Harry is Pinhead. I am going as me, in my huge fluffy jumper (one-sleeved but it is a statement) and black leggings, i.e. very this season.

8 p.m.

Trick or treating was not an entire success. Mad Harry was more keen on implementing the trick element of proceedings and egged four houses, including Marjory's. Although, frankly, what do you expect if all you offer is a Blue Riband. Thank God they didn't try Mum though. She is positively puritanical when it comes to treats and has been known to dole out satsumas. Got £2.80 (a fifth share, due to lack of costume, according to Mad Harry) and four mini Milky Ways. Which is a poor haul for having to run for my life with a catboy and a menace in a wetsuit hood with nails in it. Plus several people commented on my costume. Who do they think I was?

I'm RACHEL RILEY
– welcome to my so-called life.

november

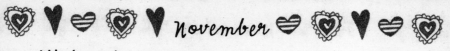

Wednesday 1

Jack did 'Edelweiss' in rehearsals today, reducing several impressionable Year Eights to tears. I did not weep. I am hardened to Jack's (admittedly many) talents now. Mr Vaughan has asked to see Scarlet's set design. She said she had been plagued by women's problems and had not been able to finish the blueprints for fear of leaking on the drawings (this is a lie—it is because she has been mentally preparing for Hallowe'en). Mr Vaughan went a bit pale and said she could have an extra week.

Treena went to Dennis's funeral to check that he doesn't have any relatives who might try to move in. She said there were only three people there—her, the vicar, and Elsie Stain. They played 'The Only Way is Up'. Treena said she nearly cried. Not because of Dennis but because the song reminds her of losing her virginity in a Capri on the Bolton to Ramsbottom road. When I die I am going to have inspiring Mozart played at the funeral. Plus I will get Scarlet and Sad Ed to read appropriate bits of *The Bell Jar* and *Jane Eyre*.

Treena is going to the will reading tomorrow as well. I said wasn't this unnecessary but she said it will give her an idea of whether or not she needs to get a new sofa, or if they can keep Dennis's. Gross.

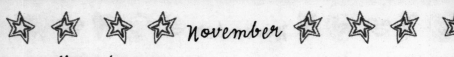

Thursday 2

Dennis left everything to Elsie Stain. But as she is ninety-five and lives at Pink Geranium Housing Shelter, where non-regulation furniture is strictly outlawed, she has agreed to let Treena have everything in return for a bottle of gin. Treena says it is an excellent deal but I am not so sure. She has not seen the state of the mattress yet. They are moving in tomorrow. Mum is driving them over in the Fiesta. So it is Baby Jesus's last night in the clean and law-abiding atmosphere of Summerdale Road, before he is destined for a life of crime at 19 Harvey Road (the address is strangely familiar but cannot work out why). The dog is staying. Mum is worried that if it goes it will cause trouble and get them evicted within a week.

Friday 3

8.30 a.m.
It is moving day. Grandpa is all upset and says he is having second thoughts but Mum has already loaded the Fiesta. We are going round for tea later to inspect the new house.

5 p.m.
Oh my God. Now I know why the address was so familiar. It is from last year's contraceptive pill/Smint mix-up!

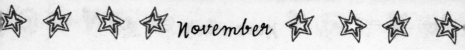
Grandpa and Treena are now semi-attached to Fat Kylie and her horde of feral siblings. Thank God the dog hasn't gone. He wouldn't stand a chance against Kylie's poodle Tupac. I asked Grandpa if he had met his new neighbours yet. He said no but that a small child had already weed on the driveway. It is Keanu, the youngest and deadliest O'Grady boy.

Am not very impressed with the new house. It smells of old man, the carpets make a funny noise when you walk on them, and there is a 1972 topless calendar still on the kitchen wall. Mum has volunteered to forensically clean. She is determined that they are not coming back to Summerdale Road under any circumstances. The dog thinks otherwise. It is now plodding miserably around Grandpa's old room, occasionally whining. Mum says it will not last. It will be back to its usual vomiting and idiotic self after half a tin of Pal and a bourbon.

Saturday 4

Mum has packed her entire cleaning cupboard plus two dozen bin liners and the Vax. She says it will be her toughest task to date. She is relishing the thought. I have not seen her so excited since Granny Clegg let her rearrange the larder. I have volunteered to take Baby Jesus out while she fills the house with potentially deadly chemicals.

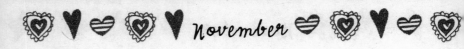

2 p.m.

Have just spent depressing two hours walking round town with Fat Kylie and Whitney, her brown half-sister. I bumped into her at the bottom of the road. She said, 'I didn't know you had a kid. Was it, like, in *Chat* where you didn't know you was up the duff then he fell out on the loo?' I said he was my uncle, and that I had never been, nor had I any intention of being, up the duff. She said she couldn't wait for the responsibility. Then we walked to the Parade (i.e. Smeg Launderette and Mr Patel's 2, run by Mrs Patel) where she bought herself twenty Marlboro and Whitney an E-number saturated packet of Skittles. Cherie's estranged husband Terry was sitting outside Smeg looking miserable. I asked him how he was and he said, 'Crap.' I said Cherie was much the same except that also her satellite dish is broken so she has been without *Extreme Makeover* for a week. Terry said, 'Christ, she must be desperate.' I said she was.

In contrast, Mum had the time of her life cleaning. She has used a record three bottles of Dettol, two Mr Muscles, and an entire six-pack of double-sided scouring sponges. The carpet has changed from a sludgy khaki to lime green and the walls are now yellow instead of nicotine-swirled brown.

6 p.m.

Dad has gone down the football field for this year's Round Table Firework Spectacular. He is official rocket lighter.

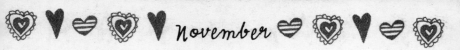

Mum asked if his will was up to date before he left. I do not know why she is worrying, it is not the lighters who are at risk, it is the gawping masses. Last year Mrs Leech got singed by a rogue Catherine wheel. I am not going. According to Scarlet, fireworks are unenvironmentally friendly and a drain on taxpayer's money. The dog is already cowering in the shed. He can smell the tang of gunpowder in the air.

10 p.m.
Dad is back, without predicted third degree burns. All went well, apart from a mild panic when they realized someone had put Dean 'the dwarf' Denley on top of the bonfire.

Sunday 5

11 a.m.
Terry is up a ladder at the side of the Britchers' house. Mum has catalogued him in her anti-social behaviour book for potential burgling conduct and called the police to be on the safe side.

11.28 a.m.
Police have arrived. Terry is shouting something at them.

11.30 a.m.
Terry has fallen off the ladder and is writhing in agony on the blue gravel.

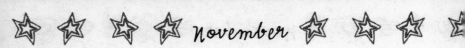
11.40 a.m.

Terry's screams have roused Cherie and Thin Kylie, presumably from the *Hollyoaks* omnibus. Clive and Marjory are outside as well with their matching coffee mugs and disapproving expressions. Am going outside to investigate. So is James. Mum is content with watching from the landing. She has James's binoculars for close-up action.

1 p.m.

It turns out Terry wasn't burgling at all. He was trying to fix the satellite dish in a bid to win back Cherie. He has been taken to Addenbrookes. On the plus side, Cherie and Thin Kylie have gone with him. So there is hope for a reconciliation yet.

3 p.m.

Cherie is back. And so is Terry, with his leg in plaster. He actually punched the air when he got out of the car, but then fell over because he had let go of a crutch and knocked Thin Kylie into the hedge. I wonder if he is back for good.

Monday 6

Walked to school with Thin Kylie. I said it was brilliant that Terry was back and they were a real family again. She said Cherie says he may be a twat but anyone who would risk their life to make sure she could see *Extreme Makeover* and

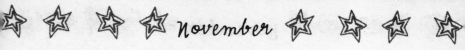

november

Plastic Surgery Gone Wrong is a twat worth keeping. Will not tell Mum it was my good deed that has smoothed the path of true chav love. She still thinks Terry is a threat to civilization (i.e. Summerdale Road).

Tuesday 7

Caris Kelp is off school. According to Mrs Leech, who knows these things, she had moved on from glue and ate a tube of expandable gap filler. She is like the dog. It has no ability to differentiate between what is or isn't edible. This morning it ate four pieces of Marmite on toast and a holepuncher.

Wednesday 8

Scarlet has unveiled her *Sound of Music* set design. It involves a lot of creaky staircases and a crypt. She says it is based on *Nosferatu* (i.e. old film involving badly made-up vampire— in other words, essential goth viewing). Mr Vaughan said she might have been better off basing it on the film *Sound of Music* and where were the nuns supposed to go but Scarlet got all militant about artistic licence so Mr Vaughan just sighed and went outside for a cigarette. He is losing patience with the drama club. It is because it is a constant reminder of his forbidden love with Sophie Microwave Muffins. Plus the Nazis keep looking up the nuns' habits.

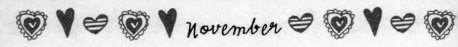
Thursday 9

Oh my God. Jesus has won the baby competition. He is on the front page of the *Walden Chronicle* under the headline 'Jesus knocks out Whitney in battle of the babies'. The article says:

Adorable

(in no sense of the word)

> Jesus Harvey Nichols Riley has been crowned this year's Gayhomes Bonny Baby. Proud mum Treena said, 'Jesus is the light of my life. He brings joy to all he touches.'

(More like jamprints)

> His fame comes at a price though – and that price is heartbreak for exotic Whitney Chanel Martini O'Grady, who was disqualified at the last minute for being seventeen months over the age limit.

This is excellent news, prize-wise, but I predict it is not going to be good for neighbourly relations with the notoriously vengeful O'Gradys.

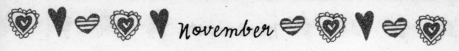
8 p.m.

Grandpa rang. He has asked for Mr Lemon's number to complain about excessive noise from next door. Apparently Mrs O'Grady is playing Status Quo at full volume.

Friday 10

It is Scarlet's birthday party tomorrow. She is sixteen on Sunday. I asked her if she was going to use this momentous occasion to allow Trevor further than her black and purple lace bra. She said not likely. They are waiting for the winter equinox. Plus she is worried he will tell all his bat friends who will then discuss Scarlet's nether regions in alarming detail. Sad Ed is still a virgin too. Though he is planning to use this momentous occasion (i.e. the fact that we are all staying over and Suzy's free and easy attitude to teenage sex) to amend his status. Obviously, I will not be doing anything of the sort being *a*) boyfriendless; *b*) crap at snogging (allegedly); and *c*) not French or Sophie Microwave Muffins. Instead I will sip Waitrose organic cider, discuss twentieth century literature and watch Suzy try to stage dive off the sofa.

Also Grandpa has been told to keep a noise diary. He has to write down all his noise complaints for a month and then, and only then, will Mr Lemon take any action. Mum is going to supervise. She is good at cataloguing that sort of thing.

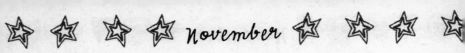

november

Saturday 11

8 a.m.

Have woken up with two spots on face. This is typical. Am now grotesque gargoyle, as well as having crap hair.

Mum and Dad are having a romantic night in. They have rented *Love Actually* from BJ Video and have a selection of M&S nibbles. James is being despatched to Mad Harry's and the dog is going on an overnight visit with Grandpa. I think they are trying to rekindle their passion following the Cherie/Mr Wandering Hands arguments. Although the thought of them rekindling anything is utterly revolting.

11 a.m.

Have been to WHSmith to buy Scarlet a bat-related birthday card and browse the glossy magazines. According to *Cosmo*, I am going about the whole boyfriend thing in the wrong way, i.e. not paying enough attention to what my clothes say about me. Apparently I need to exude unobtainability, at the same time as being totally 'up for it'. Annoyingly I got caught by Mrs Noakes before I could find out what outfit exactly captures this look. Now have three spots. How are they multiplying so quickly? Am going to drink a litre of orange juice in a bid to poison them with Vitamin C.

2 p.m.

Have tried on entire wardrobe but nothing seems to quite capture a sense of 'look but don't touch, and then I might let

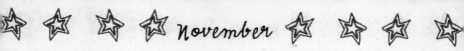
you touch later when I've had a bottle of Smirnoff Ice'. Am going to have to wear ironic Brownie T-shirt and leggings. Which say, 'My mum won't let me actually go to Topshop and I used to be a Leprechaun.' Spot count now five.

3 p.m.
Eight spots and rising. Oh God, have caught acne overnight. Am going to have to make emergency trip to Boots for Clearasil and industrial concealer.

6 p.m.
Now have spots on chest and stomach and am itching uncontrollably. Maybe have caught leprosy or SARS. Am going to show Mum in case it is one of those things where you die within twenty-four hours.

6.30 p.m.
Oh my God. It is worse. I have been struck down with chickenpox—a disease for five year olds! Mum has checked in her Hypochondriac's Bible (aka Dr Le Fanu's *Book of Family Health*) and confirmed the worst. I said I thought I had had it when I was little but Mum said no, just ringworm and nits. Cannot go to Scarlet's party as am now salmon pink and crusty due to Calamine lotion daubed liberally all over body and pair of mittens to stop scratching. A look which only says 'stay away I am contagious or mental, or possibly both'. Mum is not happy. Not because I am at death's door but because I have thrown a spanner in her M&S nibbles and romcom fest.

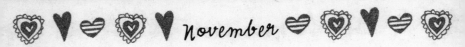

7 p.m.

James is back and is also covered in chickenpox. Mrs Mad Harry caught him and Mad Harry scratching each other under the table. Mum and Dad have abandoned their romantic evening. Dad says it is hard to be overcome with desire with two children scratching themselves and eating HobNobs in the same room. We are going to watch *Casualty* instead. Have texted Scarlet to tell her of my horrifying news. She says she will phone with a full report tomorrow, including details of any sexual activity.

8 p.m.

The dog is back. It does not have pox, but it has eaten two square feet of carpet and is looking green. The source of the infection has been isolated though. It is Jesus. Apparently he has been scratching for days but Treena thought it was fleas.

Sunday 12
Remembrance Sunday

Scarlet rang. Sexual activity as follows:
- Scarlet and Trevor—mutual viewing of goth underwear but no touching.
- Justin and Sophie—no activity due to row about size of Mr Vaughan's nipples and whether small ones (Justin) were better than big ones (Mr Vaughan). I

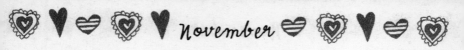

do not see what the problem is, they are pointless anyway so size does not come into it. Unless they are on man boobs. Which are wrong. Sophie is mad to even think about rejecting Justin's undersize nipples anyway. I have seen his sweaty chest on stage. It is a thing of beauty.

- Sad Ed and Tuesday—some activity reported, but interrupted by Tuesday being sick due to a claimed overdose on Waitrose cocktail blinis, or more probably the mini bottle of Jack Daniels she had stolen from Edie's 'cupboard of shame'.

- Jack—two phone calls to France. Both ending in shouting. Then Jack came on the line to see how my spots were. I asked him what the shouting was about. Apparently Henri-Claude thinks he might not be gay and has asked Marie-Claire to test the theory. Jack has forbidden her to do it but Marie-Claire thinks he is being repressed. So does Suzy. On reflection, Suzy is very French. They are totally at one with sexual experimentation. Apparently it is practically compulsory to be adulterous there.

Monday 13

Went to see Dr Braithwaite to have Mum's home diagnosis confirmed. He gave us lollipops and told us not to go back to school until the weeping had stopped. What weeping? I have not cried since I thought I had leprosy.

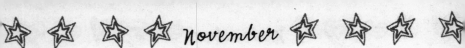
11 a.m.

Oh. That sort of weeping. The spots are oozing liquid. It is vile. Will never be able to go out in public again. Will have to stay on sofa watching daytime TV and drinking Lucozade. James says he is enjoying it. This is because he has called seven different daytime TV quiz competitions so far and is confidently expecting to win the top prizes. Mum does not know about this or she would ban it for sure. It is £1 a call.

5.15 p.m.

James has been banned from phoning TV quizzes. He got through to one of the live shows but Mum had picked up the other phone to disinfect it with her special wipes and heard all the incriminating evidence. James said she overreacted as he could have paid off the £29 phone bill he has clocked up, as well as bought several mobiles, with his prize money. Mum said there is no guarantee of winning. James said she is wrong, and he would have got at least £6,000 as the questions are aimed at idiots.

Tuesday 14

Grandpa came round to show us his O'Grady noise diary. It lists, among other things:

- Unidentifiable child shouting, 'I done it in me pants.'
- Music about 'lady lumps' being played repeatedly, disturbing *Countdown*.

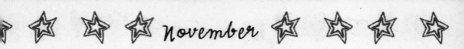

- Sound of child headbutting wall. (This is Keanu, who has a death wish and possible mental issues.)
- Thunderous stamping to *Dirty Dancing* soundtrack. (This is Fat Kylie, who is trying to lose weight with the help of now-dead Eighties legend Patrick Swayze. It is a shame there isn't a bit on the DVD of Patrick shouting, 'Put down the doughnut,' in an inspiring but slightly sexy manner.)

Wednesday 15

Scarlet and Sad Ed came round after school. Apparently there is an almighty row going on between Miss Vicar and Cowpat Cheesmond over who gets priority over the sheep field—the sheep or the hockey team. At the moment they are sharing it, which is less than ideal as the sheep huddle in one of the goals, and end up getting injured. But, more interestingly, Justin and Sophie have broken up! It is because of Saturday night's nipplegate. Sophie broke down in rehearsals and Mr Vaughan had to comfort her, no doubt with his supersize nipples.

Thursday 16

My spots are definitely less red but still alarmingly visible. I hope the weeping stops soon. Cannot face another week of

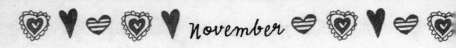

playing Monopoly with James. He takes it far too seriously and has made himself a rent book for all his hotels.

4 p.m.
Thank God. The dog has eaten Park Lane and several Community Chests. Monopoly has been abandoned in favour of *Mary Poppins*—James's favourite musical film. He knows all the words and can do the chimney sweep dance routine thing. Dad says he cannot bear to watch—it sends shivers down his spine.

Friday 17

Weeping subsiding but still look like possible leper. Oh God, I hope I am not permanently disfigured. Scarlet says Mr Vaughan is already thinking of recasting Oona as Liesl if I am still spotty by next week. This is a huge mistake. She may not be spotty but her underarms are repellent. And there is no chance of chemistry between her and Justin, even with her new-found possibly heterosexual ways.

Saturday 18

Ventured into town with James. Mum says it is part of our rehabilitation into society. It did not go well. Mrs Noakes had to ask us to leave WHSmith as our spots were putting

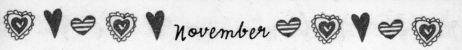

customers off their copies of *Horse and Hound*. Went to Goddard's to watch Justin making sausages for a bit. I said I was sorry to hear about him and Sophie. He said, 'I hope those have gone by Wednesday.' Then Mr Goddard asked us to leave as we were putting people off their mince.

Sunday 19

Granny Clegg rang. I told her we had chickenpox. She said I should rub lemon juice into the spots to make them disappear. It is an old Cornish remedy. Am going to get the Jif Lemon out later to try it.

2 p.m.
The Jif Lemon stings. But that is probably because it is working.

2.15 p.m.
Rang Granny Clegg to ask her if it should hurt this much. She said it never hurt her and Hester but that was in the 1950s and maybe modern lemons were more powerful. Will persevere.

2.30 p.m.
Am in agony. Cannot move as entire body is screaming in pain.

2.35 p.m.
Mum has called Granny Clegg to shout at her. Apparently the lemon juice is for freckles, not spots, and she has

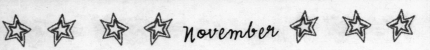

potentially set me back weeks. Have been sent to have shower before the citric acid eats away any more flesh.

3 p.m.
Look like burn victim. Am never going to school again and it is all Granny Clegg's fault with her backward Cornish cures. It is like the time she told James beetroot would cure his squint and he ate four jars in a day and his poo went red and everyone thought he was dying.

Monday 20

9 a.m.
Mum says I have to go to school as she cannot afford to keep me and James at home any longer. We are getting through too many packets of Duchy Originals and the phone bill is immense. Plus it interferes with her strict cleaning schedule. So am preparing for a day of utter misery. Now I know how the elephant man felt. We are both super sentient beings trapped in our hideous earthly bodies.

4 p.m.
Mark Lambert is in detention. It is for claiming I slept with Herpes McGill (aka Mr McGill, woodwork teacher who has psoriasis). Mr Wilmott called me to his office to demand to know my version of events. He is perverts-in-schools paranoid now that Sophie is single again. I said I had not

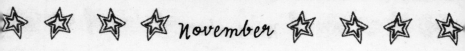

slept with any teachers, and that, in any case, Mr McGill was not contagious. He said, 'Yes, well I wouldn't take my chances if I were you.' It is pitiful. What hope do we stand if even the teachers do not grasp basic biology.

Tuesday 21

Oh my God! The John Major High Drama Club production of *Sound of Music* is facing closure! It is because of frog-like impresario Andrew Lloyd Webber. Mrs Leech got a letter from his office today threatening to sue Mr Wilmott if he ploughed ahead with the production, as it poses a potential threat to his own West End version. Scarlet is beside herself with potential rally excitement and wants to go to London to picket the Palladium. Mr Vaughan says that is not an option, due to the various bans on Viceroy buses, school trips, and political activity of any sort. I do not know why Mr Lloyd Webber is worried. I do not think potential audiences will be confused and detour to Saffron Walden instead of the glittering West End. For a start we do not have any exotic nightlife. Unless you count Barry the Blade moon-walking outside Abrakebabra.

Wednesday 22

Mr Vaughan has come up with a genius idea. We are going to rewrite the entire musical. It is still going to have nuns and Nazis but is going to be called *Over the Hills and Far Away* and will be a rock version! Jack and Justin are mental

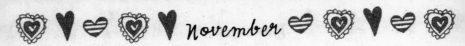

november

with excitement. It is because Captain Von Trapp and Rolf are going to be members of rival rock bands and the school orchestra is being replaced with electric guitars and a set of decks. Maria is going to be a former prostitute who is only pretending to be a nun to escape her pimp and Mrs Von Trapp is not dead at all but is fighting for custody of all the smaller Von Trapps, despite being an alcoholic and adulteress. She gets to sing Amy Winehouse's song about rehab! Mrs Matthias in costumes is not so happy though. She is having to totally rethink her lederhosen and run up hotpants and catsuits instead. It means we are having loads of extra rehearsals and Mr Vaughan has secured Mr Wilmott's permission to use the lower school canteen on Sunday!

Thursday 23

Grandpa has abandoned his noise diary. It is because Mrs O'Grady threatened to start one of her own due to the constant sounds of sex and *CBeebies* coming from number 19. They are having a noise truce. It will not last. There is no way the O'Gradys can watch *QVC* at anything less than ear-damaging decibels.

Friday 24

James has joined the St Regina's school orchestra. He is on triangle. They are giving a recital of various popular TV theme tunes. Mum has been ordered to go.

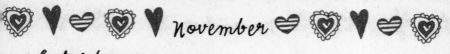
Saturday 25

Have learnt my new duet for *Over the Hills*. It is 'Dead Ringer for Love' with me as Cher and Justin as Meat Loaf, and is all about how he cannot live by rock 'n' roll and 'brew' alone. I think he means beer. Which does not seem appropriate for a sixteen-year-old Nazi youth.

Sunday 26

It is weird going to school on a Sunday. Maybe this time it really will be like in *The Breakfast Club* and we will all forget our social cliques and the Retards and Criminals will mingle happily with the maths geeks, and the goths will be at one with the beautiful people.

4 p.m.
It was not like *The Breakfast Club*. No one mingled anywhere, the goths got all up in arms because they don't like having to sing a Beyoncé song, and then Davey MacDonald let the school sheep into the language labs via the B Corridor fire exit and they chewed the headphones and peed in several booths.

Monday 27

Mr Wilmott has banned use of the school premises at weekends and says he is minded to abolish the Drama

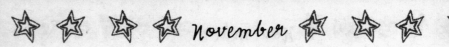

Club as well as it seems to overexcite the Retards and Criminals. This has not deterred Mr Vaughan. He is only more determined to make *Over the Hills* a success, now that we are fighting for our very existence. To be fair though, Mr Wilmott does have a point. Maybe Mrs Duddy should take over—she has a zen-like influence over her charges. It is all the *Angelina Ballerina* DVDs she lets them watch.

Tuesday 28

Yet again the Drama Club has been struck with misfortune. Two of the smaller Von Trapps are moving to Newmarket. Scarlet says it is Andrew Lloyd Webber trying to sabotage us from afar. I do not think so. He did not offer their dad a job at Spillers Pet Food. Mr Vaughan says he cannot face another gruelling audition schedule and is rewriting again with fewer Von Trapps. He says at least our dance routine to Sham 69's 'Kids Are United' will not be so overcrowded now.

5 p.m.
Oh my God. Maybe Scarlet is right. James googled Andrew Lloyd Webber and he owns a company in Bury St Edmunds, which is in close proximity to Newmarket.

Wednesday 29

There has been another *Over the Hills* catastrophe. Sophie Microwave Muffins has resigned as Maria. It is because Mr

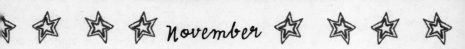

Vaughan is resisting her charms and has his eyes set on a higher prize i.e. biology teacher Miss Lexington (aka Sexy Lexy) who is not a potential sex offenders risk.

Thursday 30

Sophie is back. It is because Mr Vaughan threatened to cast Pippa as Maria and Sophie says Pippa has had her eye on him for months now and there is no way she is letting her get near his giant nipples. Why does anyone want to get near his nipples, big or otherwise?

I'm RACHEL RILEY
— welcome to my so-called life.

December

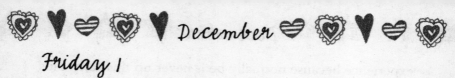
Friday 1

The dog has eaten the entire contents of James's nondenominational Barbie advent calendar and it is only Day One. Sad Ed has also eaten his Buzz Lightyear one. Christmas is not what it used to be. St Regina's nativity this year features a Jedi Knight and several Incredibles.

Saturday 2

Went round Treena's to help her finalize the wedding guest list. She is inviting all the residents at the Twilight Years Day Centre and her cousin Donna, who is, according to Treena, 'double mental'. Apparently this is a good thing. I asked her if her mum and dad would be making the arduous journey from Torremolinos to see their only daughter wed, again, but she says they aren't allowed back in the country. There is going to be a pink-themed buffet, featuring strawberry Angel Delight, Iced Gems and taramasalata, and the wedding list is at Argos. I am going to get them a cruet set. It is on special offer at £2.99.

Sunday 3

Sad Ed has done 'It'! He phoned at 8 o'clock this morning to tell me the good news. It is obviously a life-changing

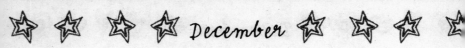
experience because normally he is never up this early. Plus it turns out that Tuesday was not the slut she made out to be (i.e. still a total virgin) so according to Sad Ed it is a totally poetic experience and he is going to write a song about it later and that maybe she is THE ONE after all. So it is between me and Scarlet now. It is bound to be Scarlet first. She has Suzy and years of sex manual browsing behind her. Although Trevor asked her to touch him and she said no. I asked where and she said in the metalwork rooms at lunch on Friday.

Monday 4

Scarlet and Jack came to school wearing non-regulation yellow shirts. Apparently Edna had been storing her dusters in the washing machine and they have dyed everything. Bob is not happy. His white coat was in the wash as well. He has demanded that Suzy takes immediate action. But Suzy says if he wants to sack Edna he will have to do it himself as she is too busy delving into the many sexual secrets of Trevor McDonald this week.

Tuesday 5

Bob has not sacked Edna. It turns out her (dead) husband Stan was a miner (for three weeks before his claustrophobia

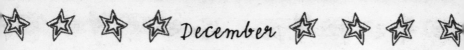
got the better of him) and they are like talismans for New Labour and can do no evil so she has a job for life. She has agreed to store her dusters in a more appropriate place though. And to stop watching *Loose Women* when she is supposed to be hoovering the den.

Wednesday 6

Rehearsals went excellently today. The nuns do a brilliant version of 'Losing My Religion' where they discard their habits to reveal catsuits—Chicago style. Justin and Jack's battle of the axes (i.e. guitars) went well too. It is hard to choose between them.

4 p.m.
Not that I want to pick Jack.

4.30 p.m.
And he wouldn't want to be picked anyway.

Thursday 7

London has been ravaged by freak weather! A tornado has swept through Kensal Rise ripping the roofs off several BMWs. Why does nothing like that ever happen in Saffron Walden? The best we get is when it rains really

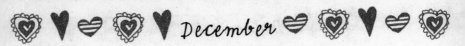
hard the shopping-trolley-clogged Slade floods, putting the roundabout and seesaw out of action for literally hours.

Friday 8

It is James's recital today. He is very excited and has asked if he can have a violin for Christmas if it goes well. Mum says she will think about it.

4 p.m.
Mum has thought about it and the answer is no. Apparently James (triangle) and Mad Harry (fake police siren) got carried away during the theme to *Casualty* and scared a lot of the Year Threes on chime bars and maracas. Two of them wet themselves and James and Mad Harry have been banned from the orchestra.

Saturday 9

Granny Clegg rang to see if there was anything special me and James wanted for Christmas. I said an iPad (totally what Hunter S. Thompson would be using today if he hadn't spent all his money on drugs). James has asked for a pony (he is hoping to win back Parker with his equestrian skills). This is pointless. They don't sell livestock in Trago Mills. Or electrical equipment. We will get out-of-date selection boxes like we do every year.

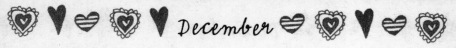
Sunday 10

Grandpa came round to visit the dog. Mum was right. It is showing a remarkable lack of distress at Grandpa's departure. It gets more sofa room now and does not have Jesus sticking crackers on its fur. It barely looked up from *Countryfile* when Grandpa came into the room. Dad asked Grandpa where he was taking Treena on honeymoon. Grandpa said he is considering his options. Dad asked what they were and Grandpa said, 'Limited.' It is because he keeps spending his pension on internet poker.

Monday 11

8 a.m.
It is show week! Everyone is overexcited at our ground-breaking and possible school-rule-breaking production. Me and Justin are having our snog rehearsal later. Have eaten two packets of tic tacs and read several back issues of *Cosmo* to ensure I am neither repulsive nor lacking technique. It is a seminal moment to get to finally snog Justin Statham—legendary guitar player and meat-mincing genius.

4 p.m.
Have snogged Justin. I am clearly making acting progress because I managed to stay completely detached i.e. did not feel all hot and bothered like I did when I had to kiss Jack. In fact, kissing Sad Ed was marginally more stimulating.

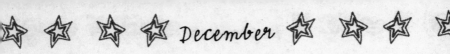

Maybe I do have Oscar-winning potential after all. Will practise stage crying next. That is the next step. Am currently having to resort to putting Vick inhaler under eyes at crucial crying moments.

Justin went red though and bit breathless. Maybe he is an acting genius too.

Tuesday 12

Mr Vaughan has axed my and Justin's stage snog! He says it is still lacking passion plus the height difference makes it look slightly freakish. Jack agreed. He suggested we just gaze at each other instead. Justin said they were making a huge mistake and hadn't yesterday proved the seething sexual chemistry etc. But Mr Vaughan said no. That is what comes from my excellent detachment.

5 p.m.
Or maybe I don't fancy Justin after all.

7 p.m.
No, that cannot be true. He is a living god. It is impossible not to fancy him.

8 p.m.
But kissing Jack was definitely more like it is supposed to be, according to *Cosmopolitan* and Tuesday, i.e. make you

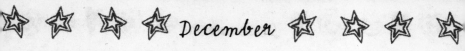
breathless and feel a bit sick. Oh God. Am utterly confused. In fact it is lucky whole snogging thing is cancelled. I am better off never getting involved in it again.

Wednesday 13

Today is the dress rehearsal. Mrs Matthias and her needlework A-level group are on standby for any wardrobe emergencies. I predict several. Fat Kylie has burst out of her hotpants four times already.

4 p.m.

Mr Vaughan has given everyone a director's debriefing. He says he has woven his magic and now it is down to us whether we are stars or the Drama Club gets banned. It is a lot of pressure. Sophie Jacobs was hyperventilating by the end of the talk. Although it might have been because Mr Vaughan's shirt was slightly undone and she was trying to glimpse his fat nipples. I predict it will all be a success. As long as the Retards and Criminals don't try to reverse their cardboard Nazi patrol cars off the front of the stage again.

Thursday 14

It is opening night. Mum and Dad are coming with James and Mad Harry. Grandpa is going to babysit the dog after

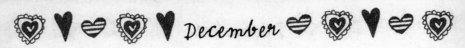

last year's fiasco. I said didn't Grandpa want to come and see the show but he says he had enough of Nazis as a child and it might awaken repressed and dangerous memories. Mum pointed out that he was at Primary School during the Second World War and that, as far as she knew, there was no Nazi invasion in North Essex, but Grandpa is adamant. Also his telly is on the blink and there is a *Hollyoaks* double bill on E4 tonight.

10 p.m.
Mr Vaughan is livid. It is because *Over the Hills* was beset with technical difficulties including Scarlet's vampiric staircase partially collapsing sending a Von Trapp spiralling into the front row. He says our stage careers are doomed. I do not know why he is so upset. The audience loved it.

Mum and Dad said they thought it was 'interesting'. I asked Mum what she thought of my duet with Justin and then she had to admit that she was in the toilets with James and Mad Harry for most of the second half because Mad Harry had got a Chupa Chup stuck in his hair. She has no sense of parental responsibility. I bet Kate Winslet's mum did not spend half of *Titanic* in the toilets with an idiotic nine year old.

When we got home Grandpa and the dog had eaten an entire tin of festive shortbread and eight slices of ham. Mum said wasn't Treena feeding him and Grandpa said no, that her cooking skills were limited to heating things up in the microwave, and as they didn't own a microwave, they had been living on toast for a month. Mum packed him

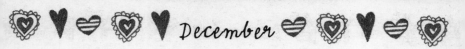

some sandwiches and a flask of Bovril before he could try to infiltrate the spare room.

Friday 15

6 p.m.
Mr Vaughan says we have one last chance to rescue our reputations and ensure quality drama has a place at John Major High. Mr Wilmott is in the audience (with Tuesday) and he is going to make the crucial decision right after the show.

9 p.m.
We are saved! *Over the Hills* was an entire success. Jack is being besieged by love-drunk Year Eights backstage right now. Plus Mr Wilmott got called out to a sheepfield emergency (sheep entangled in goal nets) and had to rely on the testimony of Tuesday as to the quality of the show. She said it was 'a landmark in British theatre'. She is right. I expect Andrew Lloyd Webber is wishing he had never started the whole hoo-ha now. His traditional nun-based production must look tame and uninspired compared to ours. We are all going to the backstage party now!

12 midnight
Something weird and enormous has happened. I was in goth corner mark two with Scarlet and Trevor, who were trying to snort Coca Cola up straws (according to Tuesday the bubbles

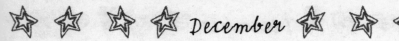

make you high), and Justin came over and asked if he could have a word behind the fire curtain. Then he said that he was sorry our snogging scene was cut but that now the play was over, Mr Vaughan couldn't stop him doing 'this'. And then he sort of loomed in my face, but just as his lips got within snogging distance, Mark Lambert set off the fire alarm by trying to burn Dean 'the dwarf' Denley's shoe and by the time everyone was allowed back in, Bob showed up in the vomit Volvo to take us all home. So our love is totally unconsummated. And am now utterly in dilemma. It is not the nipples—small ones are not a barrier to true love in my book—it is Jack. I know he is with evil French Marie-Claire and does not love me but I think I might still like him. And maybe it is better to be single and true to yourself than go out with someone just because they are beautiful and talented and can make sausages. Worst of all cannot ask Scarlet for advice as she is *a*) anti Justin because he wears Gap and *b*) Jack's sister and totally pro Marie-Claire, despite the annoying French hair and legs, because she wants to go to Paris at Easter. Am racked with indecision. Will sleep on it and find someone to ask in morning.

Saturday 16

9 a.m.
Love dilemma still unresolved. James says I should be glad anyone wants to snog me as vital statistically I am a medical marvel and do not fit into any accepted concept of beauty. Am going Christmas shopping to take my mind off the matter.

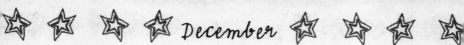
3 p.m.

Have done entire Christmas shopping in WHSmith. Not because it had a comprehensive range of excellent present ideas but because Goddard's is opposite and I could clearly see Justin lurking by the chop display and I had to wait for two hours until he went on a break round the back before I could leave the shop. Have bought a laundry marker (Mum—the only cleaning related item), a light-up calculator pen (Dad—so he can do accounts in the case of a power cut), *Wear This, Look Amazing* book (James—he is currently obsessed with TV makeover shows), a Fimble (the dog—it likes Florrie for some reason and gets all calm when she comes on the telly), a Peter Andre calendar (Grandpa and Treena—it was cheap), and a *Baby Einstein* DVD (Baby Moron Jesus—someone has to take charge of his education and it clearly isn't going to be Treena). Have not got anything for the Cleggs as Mum is giving them a dog-training book from all of us. She is hoping they will have Bruce under control by the time we visit again. She will be sorely disappointed. Granny Clegg lets Bruce get in the bath with her. She does not believe in tough love.

Sunday 17

10 a.m.

Yet another politician has fallen prey to the charms of the flesh (or of his secretary, who is less than charming). This

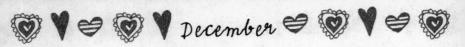

time it is a Lib Dem one though. Mum is going to join the Greens instead. Dad says at least they are all so busy knitting yoghurt they do not have time for sexual scandal.

Monday 18

8 a.m.
Oh God, have got to go to school and Justin will be there. Have tried to feign illness (chickenpox relapse) but Mum checked in Dr Le Fanu and it is medically impossible. Feel sick with nerves. And not sure if it is because I do love him or because I don't.

4 p.m.
Thank God. Justin has gone to Lanzarote for Christmas with his parents and lesbian Aunt Renee (Leslie is not going as she is in panto in Rotherham). So I do not have to make any decisions until the New Year.

Tuesday 19

It is the last day of school and the Retards and Criminals' final taste of integrated freedom. They are going home to D Corridor next term. They have got a fully refurbished unit complete with therapeutic colour lounge and their very own fruit and nut dispenser. Fat Kylie has requested to join them but Ms

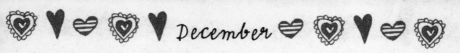
Hopwood-White says she is not stupid or criminal enough. This is not true. She is notoriously idiotic and dangerous.

Wednesday 20

2 p.m.
Am feeling utterly festive. Have decorated the tree (fake—i.e. environmentally friendly and non-messy) using ten-year-old tinsel and some biscuit decorations James made at school (apparently shaped like Baby Jesus but actually looking more like a jellyfish). Have also eaten four mince pies whilst watching *Home Alone* (James's favourite film—it is his ambition to be abandoned for forty-eight hours and have to battle the O'Gradys single-handedly with a variety of cunning inventions). It is definitely the season to be jolly etc. and am possibly thinking of snogging Justin. After all, even if he is not THE ONE, the practice will come in handy.

4 p.m.
Tree has been devastated by dog madness. It has eaten all the edible Jesus-shaped biscuit decorations and the non-edible tinsel plus it tried to swallow a fairy light and got an electric shock, which has melted the plastic needles so tree has caused molten green spillage, which is far worse than dropped needles. Mum has gone to B&Q in the Fiesta for a new, real one.

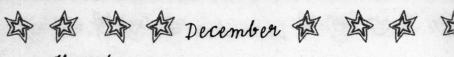
Thursday 21

Grandpa rang in a panic. There has been a wedding setback. Apparently the White Horse is turning into a Starbucks and is being bulldozed a week today, ending his dreams of walking Treena down the aisle (i.e. between the vast array of fruit machines). He said Treena is devastated and is lying on the sofa in shock eating a jumbo bag of Skips. I told him not to panic and that it could be like when Ross and Emily got married in *Friends* in the derelict church—we could festoon the rubble and discarded dartboard with fairy lights and play Il Divo (Treena's current favourite band) and it would be totally romantic. But then Treena got up from her Skip stupor and said she wasn't getting married in a building site, gay Italian singers or not, and that the wedding was off unless alternative arrangements can be found. She has no imagination. It is because her mum and dad only had the *TV Times* in the house when she was little and she had to learn to read by checking the *Coronation Street* schedule. Also she is from Bolton.

Friday 22

The wedding is back on. In a stroke of either genius or idiocy, Grandpa has secured permission to use the Twilight Years Day Centre for the whole thing. One of the dominoes team is going to perform the ceremony in the TV room. I said I wasn't sure this was entirely legal, particularly given the fact

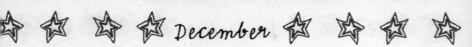

that Treena still hadn't got her Decree Absolute through. Grandpa said he had rung the court in Harlow to chase it up but they were all drunk after their Christmas lunch at TGI Fridays and so he is going to try again next week.

Saturday 23

Oh my God. Dad knows Tuesday's mum Edie! We were in Waitrose delicatessen section when a voice from the other side of the olive cart said, 'Sex Beast Riley?' and Dad said, 'Weirdy Edie,' and then their eyes met over the marinated anchovies and it was all a bit freaky so I went to calm down in the pet food aisle and watched Gary Fletcher rearranging KiteKat. When I met Dad at the checkout he looked a bit panicked and said they knew each other at school and he would prefer it if I did not mention it to Mum, in case she had one of her funny turns (i.e. scrubbing the bath with a passion verging on the maniacal). Am going to phone Suzy immediately for more information. She was a year below Dad at school and knows everything.

3 p.m.
According to Suzy they do not just know each other, they have done 'It'. Suzy says they were like the Danny and Sandy of John Major High (then the Clement Attlee Comprehensive), but that their love was thwarted when Edie ran off to London to marry a gay lawyer. I said I

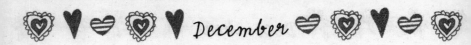
found this hard to believe but Suzy insists that Dad was a sexual legend in Saffron Walden before he met Mum at Accountancy College.

First Cherie and now Edie. Mum is going to have to get makeovered fast if she does not want to lose him now he is fast regaining 'sex beast' status. Have swapped her present with James and am giving her *Wear This, Look Amazing* which means James will have to settle for the laundry marker. He won't mind. I will say it is an indelible spy pen.

Sunday 24
Christmas Eve

Less than a day to Christmas and I do not see any packages under the tree resembling my requested presents, i.e.:
- iPad—a must-have for aspiring journalists etc., etc.
- Giant furry boots from Topshop.
- Subscription to *Vogue* and the *Times Literary Supplement* (so I can look excellent whilst reading about Salman Rushdie).

James keeps checking the shed for any signs of pony activity. He is going to be disappointed. There is no room in there anyway what with the quarantined mini trampoline, the lawnmower, and Dad's ill-advised mountain bike purchase—disused after he failed to make it up Hill Street let alone a mountain.

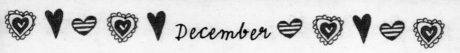
Am going to midnight mass later with Scarlet, Trevor, Sad Ed, and Tuesday. According to Scarlet it is essential Christmas activity—even for vampire-worshipping goths. Everyone goes and stands at the back and sings 'Hark the Herald' whilst drinking cider. Jack isn't coming. He is going to Stansted Airport to pick Marie-Claire up.

Monday 25
Christmas Day (and first birthday of Baby Jesus, nonreligious variety)

Have been banned from St Regina's Church. Apparently Marjory saw me and Tuesday doing the conga to 'We Three Kings'. Plus Trevor was sick in the font.

Presents received:

- Laptop computer (Mum and Dad)—it is not at all an iPad, it is Dad's old laptop from work and weighs about a tonne but at least will mean my journalism will not be hampered by James's endless googling.
- Dictaphone (James). It is an essential piece of equipment for any journalist and creative type so I can record my amazing ideas at all times. Although I fear for its provenance. The tape in it has someone sounding suspiciously like Mrs Mad Harry talking about custard recipes.
- Rosemary Conley DVD (Grandpa and Treena—assume it came from Ducatti Mick and his limited pirate DVD

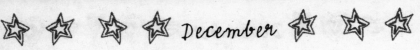
service. Unusable until we get a new non-pizza-filled DVD.)

- Seven-pack of Playboy Bunny pants (Granny and Grandpa Clegg—now confiscated by Mum as unsuitable). They have a Trago Mills price tag but at least they do not have a sell-by date.
- A CD called *Recorder Magic* (Auntie Joyless). It features three beardy men playing assorted-sized recorders. James has got it. He says he can swap it at St Regina's, where recorders are de rigueur.
- An iTunes voucher (Scarlet and Sad Ed). Which would be excellent if I had an iPod. Which I don't. Will swap it with Sad Ed later for a giant Toblerone. He always gets one.

James did not get a pony. He got a fish tank (empty). Mum is taking him to PetWorld tomorrow to fill it. She says at least fish are clean and can be flushed down the toilet when they die, unlike rabbits or other larger pets i.e. the dog.

3 p.m.

Laptop is broken. It is because James tried to use it to google fish facts and it is obviously only used to adding up paperclip budgets because it made a strange whiny noise and then went black. Dad is going to get Malcolm to fix it.

4 p.m.

James has just pointed out it is Baby Jesus's birthday, which got forgotten in the laptop computer hoo-ha and general over-consumption of sherry (Grandpa), stout (Treena), and

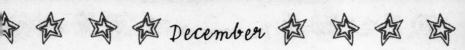
liqueur chocolates (everyone, including dog). Have given him Rosemary Conley DVD as emergency present. He will watch anything. He gets that from Treena.

Rang Scarlet. She got: black skull-decorated Converse, Urban Decay make-up set, tickets to the Whitby Goth Convention, and a pair of skinny-fit Levis. Apparently she is thinking of branching out from gothwear, as it is limiting, fashionwise, and going more EMO. I said Trevor wouldn't be too pleased but she says he will do anything she tells him as she is wielding the most powerful tool known to teenagers around the world—access to her underwear. It will be weird to see her not swamped in layers of voluminous black and purple. It will be like on *She's All That* when the badly dressed studious type is revealed to be drop-dead gorgeous.

Also, I asked how Marie-Claire had enjoyed her nut roast and apparently she never arrived! It is down to striking French baggage handlers, which has caused a row because Jack is pro-striking (i.e. it is totally Labour) and Marie-Claire is anti it. So they are not soul-mates after all. Maybe this is the beginning of the end for their Anglo-French concorde. He will realize he prefers nice English granary to a baguette after all.

Tuesday 26
Boxing Day

Have been using my Dictaphone. It is excellent—like having a constant voiceover. Life would be so much

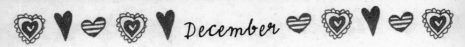
better if everyone had voiceovers. It makes everything sound dramatic and like you are about to get murdered or something.

James has filled his fish tank with African frogs. Mum is not happy but James says the frogs are more intelligent and will eat meat from your fingers. The dog does not like them and is eyeing them suspiciously. Particularly because they are getting bits of chuck steak and he is on dried biscuits after eating an entire bowl of brandy butter yesterday.

Granny Clegg rang. Mum asked her what she was thinking of with my Playboy pants but she said, 'What's wrong with rabbits? There's nothing dirty about them, they are a very clean animal.' Then James said they eat their own babies and poo and he got sent to his room.

Wednesday 27

Grandpa called the court again. The divorce is in the post. James says they might as well have just thrown it in the bin as it will never arrive. He is right—my confession to Jack is clearly festering under a mound of landfill—thank God. Grandpa says nothing is going to stop him marrying Treena. Not even potential bigamy.

The frogs have been moved to James's room. It is because the dog keeps sticking his face in the tank trying to eat the floating meat bits and it is upsetting the frogs.

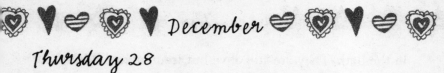
Thursday 28

James is single again. He got a card from Peyton. It said, 'Happy Christmas. I don't want to go out with you any more because I am in love with Harry.' For a minute there was concern that his best friend had betrayed him but it turns out she means Potter. James says he does not care and that he and Mad Harry have more important matters at hand anyway (they are trying to invent gold) but I know that secretly he is devastated because I heard him talking Elvish to the frogs earlier. Will ask Mum to lend him the makeover book. He will be able to revamp his wardrobe and win back Mumtaz.

4 p.m.
James has been dealt a double blow. Not only has Peyton heartlessly left him for a fictional wizard but his frogs have mysteriously disappeared too. There is a soggy trail across the landing carpet. Mum says she told him to keep the lid on but James says he cannot think about amphibian security at a time like this. My suspicions are on the dog. It has never liked the frogs—they are rivals to its position as number one pet. Although I think it is worrying unnecessarily. Frogs actually make the dog look lovable.

6 p.m.
Mystery solved. And not due to usual incriminating dog vomit. Frogs tried to flush themselves down toilet in bid for freedom and have blocked u-bend causing a back-up

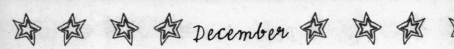

in the bath. They are still alive but traumatized. Mum says they are going to have to go back to PetWorld. They are clearly unhappy on Summerdale Road. James says he does not care. He is at his lowest ebb and nothing can make him feel better. Not even pink milk.

Friday 29

The wedding is tomorrow. Still no sign of divorce but they are ploughing ahead anyway. Grandpa is staying the night so that he does not see the bride before she walks down the aisle. He is bringing Jesus too because Treena has got her cousin Donna over and they are notoriously irresponsible.

Saturday 30

Look like mental person in hideous pink fairy costume. Thank God no one I know is going to the wedding. Although, unless the divorce arrives in this morning's post, no one will be going to the wedding at all.

9 a.m.
Postman (aka Beefy Clarke) has been. No divorce. Luckily Mum is busy trying to pin on James's and Jesus's sailor hats so she does not know the wedding is potential Jeremy Kyle material.

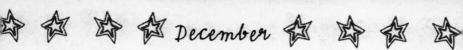

10 a.m.

Crisis averted. Des has just been round. Apparently the divorce had been posted to him by mistake and he took it round to Treena's. He says it was lucky he did because apparently she and Donna were comatose on the floor in a sea of dry roasted peanuts. I think it is excellent that Des is being so forward thinking about Treena remarrying Grandpa. It is very modern and shows that even men with tattoos and criminal records can be in touch with their feelings.

10 p.m.

Des has tried to sabotage the wedding. Events unfold as follows:

3.00 p.m.

Guests assemble at Twilight Years Day Centre awaiting arrival of bride.

3.30 p.m.

Bride's cousin rings to say bride has had to stop bridal carriage (i.e. Donna's Nissan Bluebird) to be sick outside the train station.

3.45 p.m.

Bride arrives in enormous pink and slightly vomit-stained dress, accompanied by cousin Donna (all seventy-six kilos of her) in a Tinkerbell outfit.

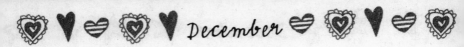

4 p.m.
Octogenarian dominoes player and one time Irish priest Finlay O'Grady (yes—of the O'Grady O'Gradys) asks if anyone present knows of any reason why the happy couple should not get married.

4.01 p.m.
Des Nichols (formerly of HMP Harlow) appears, as if by magic, by the tea trolley and declares undying love for Treena, threatening to kill himself if she goes ahead with ceremony.

4.15 p.m.
Ceremony goes ahead.

4.30 p.m.
Ambulance called to take Des to Addenbrookes with cake-slice-related injuries.

4.45 p.m.
Guests take seats at communal trestle tables for wedding feast of pink food. Dog eats entire bowl of taramasalata and is sick on the whist table.

5.00 p.m.
Phyllis Dubbs falls asleep in strawberry mousse.

6.30 p.m.
Phyllis Dubbs still asleep in mousse, holding up clearing of

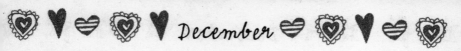

trestle tables for evening entertainment.

6.45 p.m.
James reports that Phyllis Dubbs not asleep but actually dead. Second ambulance called.

7.00 p.m.
Pelvis Presley rings to say he is stuck at the garage because his trusty assistant Darryl Stamp (former joyrider extraordinaire) has phoned in sick with a broken elbow (is that possible?) and he will not be able to make it until possibly tomorrow.

7.15 p.m.
Grandpa does Elvis impression. No one applauds. Treena puts Take That on the portable CD player. Old ladies get overexcited and start conga.

9.00 p.m.
Mrs Peason, fascist warden from Pink Geranium Sheltered Housing arrives in minibus and demands party is closed immediately as several of her residents have broken their curfews and are in danger of compromising their hip replacements with ill-advised conga dancing.

9.01 p.m.
Old ladies and ageing religious O'Grady loaded onto minibus and despatched to living hell with Mrs Peason.

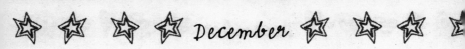
9.10 p.m.
Minibus returns to repatriate Baby Jesus. Mum and Dad take him home, along with dog and James, both of whom are showing signs of sugar overload and mental exhaustion.

9.15 p.m.
Rest of party departs for karaoke at Axe and Compasses. Rachel Riley forced to walk home through town in absurd fairy outfit, attracting attention from Mr Whippy, several Retards and Criminals (on the plus side they did stop fighting in shock when I went past), and Barry the Blade.

10.30 p.m.
Rachel Riley goes to bed in hope sleep will obliterate memories of Barry the Blade trying to get her to turn him into Wayne Rooney with her fairy wand.

Sunday 31
New Year's Eve

It is New Year's Eve. A time for reflection on what has been achieved in the last year:

1. Attempt to discontinue friendship with Thin Kylie. (Achieved—although she does still walk home with me occasionally when she is not menacing Year Sevens or winning badges off Mark Lambert behind the mobile science lab.)

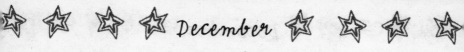
2. Repatriate Suzy's glow-in-the-dark rabbit vibrator (achieved—though not without consequences).

3. Concentrate on GCSEs (partially achieved, though with blossoming journalistic career will not need to know about maths or rural studies).

4. Experiment with drugs, alcohol, and sex. (Momentarily achieved—vis á vis the Kyle O'Grady fiasco. But the year is not over yet and it is Bob and Suzy's party tonight, which is bound to be full of all of the above.

5. Find THE ONE. Utterly not achieved and am still in confusion as to who exactly this might be. Though have definitely ruled out Sad Ed. And Kyle, obviously. So just leaves Jack and Justin. Except that am not sure I fancy one of them and not sure the other fancies me.

Mum and Dad are coming to the party. Dad thinks he is going to get to meet Jeremy Clarkson, who is Suzy's latest sex celebrity. James and the dog are staying at home. Marjory is babysitting. She is bringing Giant Jenga with her. I am taking my new Dictaphone with me to record important events in journalistic fashion. And do voiceover thing. It is weirdly addictive. She said, in her sultry but intelligent voice. See.

8 p.m.
Oh God. Weirdy Edie is here with Tuesday. She has spotted Dad. Have steered Mum to the buffet before there is any sex-beast-related hoo-ha.

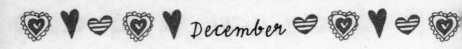

8.15 p.m.
Oh God. Mr Wandering Hands is here too. Apparently he is one of Suzy's clients. Probably for sex addiction. Or maybe he is one of those people who get turned on by the smell of leather. Or vinyl, in the case of Ford Fiestas.

8.30 p.m.
Mum has spotted Dad talking to Edie. She has gone over to investigate.

8.45 p.m.
Mum has stormed off and is being comforted by Mr Wandering Hands and a bottle of sherry.

9.00 p.m.
Marjory has rung to say that James has been on the phone to Birmingham for two hours and she can't prise him off and the dog has eaten a Giant Jenga piece and is now whining hysterically. Mum is in a panic. She was supposed to be driving but is too drunk on sherry, and Dad has been on Suzy's life-threatening punch all night and is still pacing the house looking for Jeremy Clarkson, so Mr Wandering Hands has offered to take her home! Worse, she has accepted! Oh God, am going to be in children's home by next year; i.e. tomorrow. Am hiding in Scarlet's wardrobe with a bottle of Britvic and a bowl of Twiglets for emergency sustenance while I plan ways to reconcile parents. Oh, someone is coming.

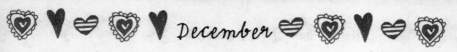

9.45 p.m.

It was Edna looking for Jack. She says she has got something for him. I hope it is not one of her vol au vents. (She is in charge of canapés, another mistake on Suzy's part—she should have left it to Marks & Spencer like she usually does). I said he was on his mobile in the den, arguing with Marie-Claire.

10 p.m.

Am still in wardrobe. But think have thought of plan. Am going out. Oh no am not. Someone is coming.

10.30 p.m.

Oh God. It was Jack. He said he needed some peace as he was waiting for another call from Paris. I asked him why he needed to use the wardrobe and he said everywhere else was taken—Sad Ed and Tuesday were doing 'It' in the walk-in closet in Bob and Suzy's room, the den was full of Labour Party members playing political 'Who'd You Rather' (i.e. who'd you rather—the Prime Minister or the Chancellor—answer: 'I'd rather stick needles in my thighs'), Marlon from *Emmerdale* was signing autographs in the toilet and my dad was asleep on Jack's bed. (Which is a good thing—at least he can't engage in any marriage-nullifying activity with Edie if he is comatose.) But then Edna appeared in the doorway smoking a pink cocktail cigarette, and waving a horrifyingly familiar envelope, which she said was for Jack. It was my confession letter from August! (Not stolen by organized criminal postmen, or festering in landfill, but

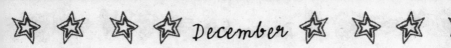

filed mistakenly by Edna on the freezer, not the fridge.) Jack said, 'Oh, look, Riley, that is just like your handwriting,' and was just about to open it when his mobile went off again so he had to go into the corridor to get better reception for shouting. Now what do I do? Am going to have to stay inside wardrobe for ever with only Twiglets to survive on. Oh God, now someone else is coming. Is there no peace?

11.30 p.m.
It was Jack again. He demanded to know if what I said in the letter was true. I said, 'Do you want it to be true?' He said, 'Maybe.' I said, 'What about Marie Claire?' And he said she lived in Paris, which is not really an answer. I said I needed to think about it because I am at a crossroads and am very tormented and Sylvia Plath, which I know he will totally understand, as he is literary and tragic. He said I have until midnight.

So now, not only are my parents about to get divorced, but I have to decide between Jack—who is lovely but is my friend's brother and possibly actually in love with someone else, who is French, or Justin—who is lovely, and knows all the words to every Rolling Stone song including possibly racist 'Brown Sugar', but is potentially actually not the love of my life, except that I don't know that because I only kissed him on stage, which is not actual real kissing. Will have to make list. It is the only way to deal with these matters, according to James, who makes lists for everything, including a daily wardrobe rota.

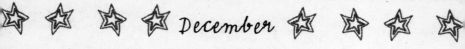

OK. So Jack has good hair, laughs at my jokes, is intellectual (i.e. has read Jack Kerouac and not just Dan Brown, who is good, but not self-improving) and does not have nipple issues. BUT he is Scarlet's brother i.e. vast potential for awkwardness etc. and has done it with a French girl so may be disappointed with my general non-Frenchness.

Justin on the other hand is excellent at guitar, has muscly arms from all the meat mincing, and has a lesbian aunt, i.e. is totally progressive. BUT he is not very good at getting my cleverly ironic comments. And has done it with Sophie Microwave Muffins, who is normal height, has 34B breasts (i.e. two sizes bigger than me) and does not have weird hair.

11.59 p.m.

Have made decision. Am definitely going to . . . Oh God. Can hear someone coming. Am turning off torch. Pants. Where is Dictaphone button? Oh God, who is that? Can only hear heavy breathing. OK, am going to stop talking now because whoever it is will think I am mental talking to myself. Shut up, Rachel. Oh . . . Mmm . . . Jack?

Hang on.

Justin . . . ?

Joanna Nadin grew up in the small and tragically normal town of Saffron Walden in Essex. In a bid to make her life more like it is in books, she went to university to study drama and become a famous actress. Instead, she somehow ended up as a Special Adviser to the Prime Minister. The Rachel Riley books are based entirely on these failed formative years, and her own peculiar family (she sends apologies to James for not even bothering to change his name).

As well as this bestselling series, Joanna has written numerous award-winning books for younger readers, has been shortlisted for the Roald Dahl Funny Prize, and thrice shortlisted for Queen of Teen. She now lives in Bath with her daughter Millie.